MARISSA BURT

STORY'S END

HARPER

An Imprint of HarperCollins*Publishers*

Bur *J*

Library of Congress Cataloging-in-Publication Data
Burt, Marissa.
    Story's end / Marissa Burt. —1st ed.
        p. cm.
    Summary: A deadly Enemy has threatened the future of Story—
and twelve-year-old Una Fairchild is the only one who can stop his
plans and save the character world from destruction.
    ISBN 978-0-06-202054-3
    [1. Fantasy. 2. Books and reading—Fiction. 3. Characters in
literature—Fiction. 4. Adventure and adventurers—Fiction.]
    I. Title.
PZ7.B94558Sue 2013   2012011519
[Fic]—dc23   CIP
                                                              AC

Typography by Alison Klapthor
13 14 15 16 17   CG/RRDH   10 9 8 7 6 5 4 3 2 1
❖
First Edition

For Kate, Rachel, Sasiwimol, Thomas, India, Jones, Ben, Daniel, Elizabeth Austin, DuBose Jr., Virginia Grace, Megan, and all the fatherless

PROLOGUE

⊠ ⊠ ⊠

CALLING ALL CHARACTERS OF STORY

⊠

All we have believed about
THE INFAMOUS UNBINDING is a lie!
We were told *THE MUSES* broke their oaths and
turned against us.
A lie.
We were told that *THE MUSES* made our loved ones
disappear.
A lie.
We were told *THE MUSES* killed the *WIs*.
A lie.
We were told to lock up the Old Tales because *THE
MUSES* were tainted with evil.
A lie.

We were told Tale Master Archimago defeated
THE MUSES and saved Story.
A lie.
We were told that
THERE IS NO KING.
*A*ll of it. Lies.

There once was a King in Story,
and he appointed his Muses to write our Tales.
We have recently discovered Archimago's
confession, wherein he
reveals
THE TRUE BACKSTORY.
ARCHIMAGO and
THE RED ENCHANTRESS DUESSA
plotted with *THE MUSE FIDELUS*
to rebel against *THE KING*.
It was *THE MUSE FIDELUS* who was responsible for
the many deaths of the Unbinding.
The other innocent Muses have been
wrongfully accused.

WE MUST UNITE.

The Enemy being once again at our very doors,
it behooves every character to come forward
and join the Resistance:

SPREAD THE TRUE BACKSTORY.
STOP THE RED ENCHANTRESS DUESSA.
LOOK FOR THE KING'S RETURN.

Together we can save Story and find
a happy ending for us all.

⊠

Remember that only love conquers fear.

⊠ ⊠ ⊠

Chapter 1

Una Fairchild rolled the freshly printed broadside into a tight scroll, tied a piece of twine around the center, and added it to the growing stack of parchment that was the result of an afternoon's hard work. One batch of notices had already been posted at Perrault Academy, though Una didn't know how long Tale Master Elton would tolerate that. Another bundle was set to be hand-delivered around Fairy Village and Heart's Place that afternoon. The Resistance members seemed confident that characters would know that the line "only love conquers fear" referred to Heart's Place, where Resistance informants stood ready to direct recruits back to Bramble Cottage. Una hoped they were right. They needed to grow the Resistance. Fast.

Una and Peter were preparing the broadsides for

delivery, while the grown-ups worked a giant old-fashioned printing press on the other side of the Merriweathers' barn. Una had amassed quite a stack of notices. Peter, on the other hand, had barely touched the pile of parchment in front of him. He was busy recounting yet again his battle with the beasts Gog and Magog. Una was sick of hearing how brave Peter had been, but she didn't tell him to stop, mostly because if Peter's brothers were busy listening to him, they wouldn't pester her with unwanted questions.

The previous days had been filled with many heated conversations. The Sacred Order of the Servants of the King thought that the broadside should be all about the long-lost King, whereas the Resistance members were sure that they should focus on overthrowing the Talekeeper regime. They might have argued about it forever, but the imminence of the Enemy's return forced the two groups into a prickly truce, and the one conclusion the now-united Resistance had agreed upon was that they needed to share the true Backstory with the rest of Story's characters and motivate them to fight against Fidelus.

Una laid another stack of papers flat on the bale of hay next to her and winced at Peter's unpleasantly authentic description of the way his blade cut through the dying beast.

"You're a hero," Bastian said breathlessly. "My own brother, the hero."

Peter shook his head. "Sam's the hero," he said, without any of the bluster of his storytelling. "You should have seen him."

Una looked down at the cat, asleep in her lap. *Poor, brave Sam.* Una had tried to hide her shock when she had first seen him at the Healer's. One silken ear was now torn, and his beautiful coat was spotted with holes where chunks of fur had been ripped out. Una cuddled him closer. *He did this to save me.*

Sam's whiskers twitched, and Una scratched the spot under his chin, coaxing forth a deep, throaty purr. Everything had seemed like the continuation of some awful nightmare since she and Indy had returned. Their breathless escape out of the examination. The chaos in the Tale station. The man who stood on a bench and kept saying, over and over, "Crisis Code. Please proceed to the exits in an orderly fashion," until the masses surged around him, and his warning was drowned by the flow of people.

Una and Indy had lost Horace right away. Indy

had taken his belt and bound Horace's wrists with it before they left the exam, but in the mass of characters, Horace had easily slipped out of Indy's grasp and disappeared into the crowd. It had been a stroke of luck that Indy's father and Peter had found them at all in the midst of the panic. Together they had traveled to Bramble Cottage, but after that had come the endless rounds of questions. The Resistance wanted to know every detail about the Red Enchantress and what she had said to Alethia. The Sacred Order of the Servants of the King kept making Una retell the bit where the Enemy gulped down the ink. And the kids wanted to know about the fight with Tale Master Elton. Una was tired of trying to keep her story straight. She had the distinct impression that if anyone questioned her too much, she might crack like an egg, spilling her secret all over the place.

What would they all say if they knew that the Enemy was Una's father? And Duessa her mother? *No one can know.* Whenever she told the story of what had happened in Alethia's garden, she edited out the part about someone of Fidelus's blood releasing him. Her listeners assumed that the Enemy was free simply because Duessa had finally found and captured the Muse Alethia.

"Were the beasts *this* big?" Rufus was on his feet, his arms spread wide.

"How tall?" Bastian sounded skeptical. "As tall as me?"

"*Twice* the size of you," Peter said as he jumped up to reenact Sam's heroic leap onto the beast Magog's back. "He came flying through the air just like this." Peter grabbed a sheaf of broadsides and ruffled them in front of the boys' wide-eyed faces.

Una shifted into a more comfortable position and cut several lengths of twine. Her body ached. Her neck was spotted with ugly purple bruises where Elton had held her, and her jaw still hurt from the gag. She had thought she would feel safe again once she was at Bramble Cottage. But she was wrong. No matter how many friendly faces she saw, no matter how clean she scrubbed her skin, no matter how much tasty food filled her belly, the thought of what she had done gnawed at her. *I released the Enemy. Me. His daughter.*

She tied a tight little knot around the next scroll. One of the reasons she couldn't fool herself into completely forgetting about the truth sat across from her, leaning against the barn wall. Indy was doing a better job on his assignment than Peter. He was to sort through all the ink and then separate the spoiled from the good. Indy reached into his carton and pulled out a glass jar, carefully unstopped it, and dipped a quill into the bluish liquid. He made a mark on a discarded sheet of old paper and rubbed his finger over it. As if he could feel Una watching him, he glanced up.

Una quickly looked away. *How much does he know?* Ever since they had returned, he had been giving her complicated looks that she did her best to ignore. It could be that Indy was being his usual quiet self. Despite the Resistance members' persistence, Indy had very little to say, and the details remained unchanged: he had been in an enchanted sleep, waking only in time to free Una from Elton. Indy claimed that everything after that was hazy and that his thinking didn't clear completely until they were back in the Tale station, but it still made Una uneasy.

Una reached for the roll of twine and dropped it again just as quickly when Wilfred Truepenny, Indy's dad, burst into the barn.

"Heart's Place"—his usually intense voice made a broken little sound—"it's gone."

"Gone?" Griselda said. "What do you mean, *gone*?" The dryad looked up from the tiny wood letters she was sorting into neat piles.

Ordinarily, Indy's dad was intimidating, with his authoritative way of talking and his criticism of Talekeeper rule. In the days since Una's return, he had become a whirlwind of activity, relaying reports from the other members of the Sacred Order of the Servants of the King and going out on endless rounds of meetings in the different districts. But now he stood very still, leaning against the edge of the old printing press. "Demolished," he said. "There's nothing there. The buildings that haven't been burned are empty. No one seems to know where the characters have gone. The few Romantics I found cowering in the back of a shop say they were beset by a shadow army." He crumpled up one of the freshly printed notices. "I think we can guess what happened."

Una's stomach turned to ice. The broadsides with the coded message telling interested characters to go to Heart's Place had only been posted that morning.

"Elton's not taking any chances," Peter's father said from his spot on the other side of the barn. "He means to squash any opposition before we've even begun."

"No trace of those missing?" Peter's mother's forehead was creased with worry. "A whole district can't just up and disappear."

"It's happened before," Trix said as she twisted the old cloth she had been using to wipe down the press in her gnarled hands. "During the Unbinding."

The silence that followed sat heavy on Una's shoulders. The Unbinding was the darkest period in Story's history. Characters had gone missing, never to be heard from again. Families had starved in the wilderness once they were driven from their towns. When she first learned about the Unbinding, she hadn't thought to wonder why it was that characters had left their homes. Now she didn't have to wonder. She knew. Her father's book had let her glimpse the past, and she had seen him kill all those characters with one wave of his hand. She had seen how ruthless her mother had been. And now they were together again, and the thought of what they might do next sent prickles of fear up her spine.

"And so it has begun." Wilfred finally said what they all surely had been thinking. "The Enemy has returned."

His words seemed to snap the little group to attention.

"We need to stay focused," Mr. Merriweather said as he ran his hands over the steel screw that supported the whole printing press. "Have there been any Sacred Order messages from Heart's Place, Wilfred?"

"No word from any of our informants." Indy's dad shook his head sadly. "Any survivors would have known to gather at the Swan Clock—Adelaide Thornhill was clever enough to institute emergency plans in all the districts—but the clock is gone, just like Adelaide."

Hearing Professor Thornhill's name made Una think of Snow. Where was she? What had happened to her? Hot tears stung the backs of Una's eyes. Was she responsible for that as well? All the horrible things that were happening had something to do with her parents, and her secret made her feel like she was all alone, despite the cluster of people around her. For the first time ever, Una wished she didn't have to stay at Bramble Cottage. *I don't belong here anymore.* She couldn't bear to know that because of what she had done, a whole district was missing. Or worse. She blinked back the tears that were threatening to escape and willed them to stop.

"I brought the Romantics here," Indy's dad was saying. "Nine, maybe ten. They had nowhere else to go."

"Where are they?" Peter's mother gave a little cry of alarm. "Poor dears, after all they've been through, and with no one to welcome them."

"Foolish man," Trix said as she brushed by Indy's dad. "Never has a visitor gone ignored at Bramble Cottage. You should have come to me straightaway." Trix and Mrs. Merriweather were already out the door to greet the refugees from Heart's Place when the others began discussing what to do next.

"Our informants at the Ranch might be better equipped to handle Elton's counterattacks." Mr. Merriweather squatted next to Griselda and began pawing through the letters. "If we put 'the free find courage in the face of fear' as our code on the new broadsides, characters will go to the Ranch, and those who prove trustworthy will be sent here," Mr. Merriweather said. "But the Westerns must know that it will be dangerous. Once we post the notices, the Ranch might face the same fate that befell Heart's Place." He began loading parchment into the press. "Whatever this shadow army is, I have no doubt we're seeing a repeat of what happened at the Unbinding. Elton is eliminating any sizable gathering that could stop him, and, while he's at it, setting the whole countryside ablaze with fear."

Griselda rolled the little lettered tiles around in her

long fingers as she spoke. "Story will look to the Tale Master to rescue them. They'll believe anything Elton says."

A sour taste rose in the back of Una's throat as she thought of Elton's sweaty hands around her neck. "And Elton will say exactly what Duessa and Fidelus tell him to say," Una said.

The remaining grown-ups looked at Una like they had forgotten she and the other children were even there.

"Una's right," Mr. Merriweather said. "Last time the Tale Master tricked Story into believing lies. But they're forgetting one thing." He waved half a printed broadsheet. "This time we know the truth."

Chapter 2

Snow Wotton tore another strip from the mud-spattered lace front of her petticoat. She wadded it into a ball and ladled a stream of water over it. Her mother lay in a limp heap on the stone floor. Snow squeezed the rag, and foul liquid puddled next to the tray of suspicious-looking food that had been wordlessly delivered through the bars by a cloaked guard. The air smelled of mildew, like a pile of wet clothes that needed airing. Snow pressed the cloth gently onto her mother's forehead. Nothing happened.

Snow had been alone in the cell at first. Then, two of the hooded guards had shuffled in, her mother's form sagging between their unnatural clawed hands. Without a word, they dumped her on the floor, and their booted footsteps echoed out in the corridor long after the door clanged shut. Since then, Snow had tried to rouse her mother with little success. A few moans, a leg twitch, and the rise and fall of her chest were the only reasons Snow knew she was still alive.

Half her petticoat had gone to her mother's feet. Snow had cried out when she first saw them. Raw and blistered, they looked like meat freshly skinned for the cook pot. The splotches of dirt and small stones embedded in the exposed flesh couldn't be good. For the better part of the afternoon, Snow had tended these wounds. Gently digging the pebbles out of the open sores. Trickling the precious water over the worst of the soiled parts. Binding her mother's feet as best she could.

Snow arched her lower back to stretch the cramping muscles. Her mother stirred. She groaned and lifted one hand to her forehead. A moment later, Professor Adelaide Thornhill opened her eyes and looked straight up at Snow.

Snow leaned forward. "How are you feeling?"

Her mother squeezed her eyes shut and then opened them again. "Snow?" she said in a hoarse voice.

Snow took a dipperful of water in one hand and moved close enough to cradle her mother's head in her lap. Her mother drank at the water as Snow tipped the ladle forward. A trail of wetness ran down the corner of her mouth, leaving a muddy path in its wake. Snow wiped it away with the rag. Her mother reached up and laid her hand over Snow's. Snow didn't push her away. Her usual antagonism toward her mother had been dampened by the awfulness of their predicament. Tale Master Elton had betrayed them to the Red Lady, and no one else in the world knew where they were.

"How long has it been?" her mother asked. Despite the water, her voice was raspy.

"Two days. Maybe three?" Snow looked up at the tiny window at the top of their wretched cell. Twilight was fading to dark, and she could see the edge of a silver moon. "It will be night soon."

"They took you away." Snow's mother braced herself on a trembling wrist and then pushed up into a seated position. She looked at Snow, her eyes pleading for the right answer. "They did take you away." It was more of a statement than a question, and Snow knew what she meant.

"Yes," she said. "I had already left the clearing when you began to scream." Snow couldn't read her mother's expression. Was she embarrassed that she had screamed?

Or was it that she had something to hide? "What were they looking for?"

The green eyes were steady, her mother's composure returning with her strength. "The less you know, Snow, the better off you are."

Snow dropped the dipper into the bucket with a thump. "Really? After all that happened, you're still not going to tell me what's going on?" Snow shouldn't have been surprised. Her mother was the queen of secrets. "I'm in this awful place *because of you*, and you aren't even going to tell me why?" Snow wouldn't let herself cry. Not in front of her mother. She stood up and paced over to the wall with the window.

Her mother shifted behind her. "It's for your own good—" She didn't finish the sentence, because she cried out in pain.

Snow turned around. Her mother had one foot under her hips as if she was going to stand. She froze in that position, pressing hard into the ground and breathing deeply.

"They ripped open your feet," Snow said in a hard voice. "And you won't even tell me why."

Her mother set her lips into a thin line and shook her head, and Snow felt like shaking her until she told her the truth. *My feet could be next!* Shouldn't she know what was going on before the guards came for her?

Her mother's fingers trembled as she unwrapped the makeshift bandages. She stared in silence at the angry wounded flesh, her hand hovering over the stripes along one sole. Then, she took the damp cloths and matter-of-factly rewrapped her feet. She looked up at the window, her gaze marking the corners where the walls met the ceiling, and finally took in the entirety of the cell's interior in a swift searching glance.

"Ten paces square," Snow said. "I've checked. Several times." She helped her mother take a few steps over to the far wall. "It gets better. Look at this." The words on the wall were layered, etched in the endless hours belonging to the prisoners who had once shared this cell. In the midst of all the nonsensical words, one simple phrase was carved over and over: *Let this be but a dream.* Her mother reached out to touch her, and Snow flinched. In one smooth movement, her mother withdrew her hand, instead running her fingers along one of the deepest, most desperate-looking etchings.

The silence was broken by the sound of a faint scuffling in the opposite corner, the one spot in the small space Snow had tried to avoid. The smell alone told her about the chamber pot's contents.

"It could be rats," her mother said. The noises grew louder.

"Big rats," Snow said.

Her mother limped to the corner and with some effort pushed aside the filthy pot. Its contents sloshed onto the floor.

"Gross!" Snow stepped back.

"Get over here and help." Her mother's fingers scrabbled against the stones. Dirt from the mortar fell with the pressure from the opposite side. "Someone's coming through."

Snow snatched up the water dipper as she crossed the room. She took the handle and began prying at the loose stone. "What if it's the guards?"

"Coming in to surprise us?" her mother said with a small smile. "I'm guessing they'd use the door."

Snow wedged the handle of the ladle in a crack and pushed down hard. Was someone about to rescue them? She dropped her tool and tore at the chunks of breaking stone. Soon, the muffled rhythm from the other side of the wall was accompanied by singing, although she couldn't make out the words.

"Hello?" Snow tried to keep her tone low. *Please don't let the guards come back now.* She licked her lips and called again, louder. The stone in front of them wiggled.

"Hallo?" a man's voice answered back.

"Can you push on the stone?" Snow's mother asked. "We're right on the other side."

"Move away," the man called. Crumbling dirt cascaded down one edge. The biggest part of the stone inched forward. Then with one last jolt, it plopped out onto the floor and promptly split in two. A head of matted black hair followed it, and a man pulled his thin form into their cell.

"What, ho! That's not right," he said. "This isn't outside. This is my old cell." He peered into the hole, then back at their cell, and he seemed to notice them for the first time. He bowed and swept one hand out to the side. "My apologies, lovely ladies. I am at your service."

Snow didn't buy it. She scooped up the dipper and gripped it tightly. It was the closest thing they had to a weapon, and she knew she could definitely hold her own if it came to a fight. The man looked like he hadn't eaten well in a long time. Snow couldn't tell if the stomach-turning smell came entirely from the privy contents that now lay pooled next to the wall, or if he was giving off that sour odor.

"Who are you?" her mother asked.

"Who am I?" the man repeated, gathering his tattered cloak around him as though it were a robe. "What an interesting question. Who are any of us?" He eyed the plate of untouched food and began to tap his fingers together.

"How did you get here?" Snow's mother moved between the man and Snow.

The man pointed to the hole behind him. "In all work there is profit. The tunnels are vast and far-reaching."

"*Where* are we?"

"We are in a cell." The man's tongue darted out and licked his cracked lips. Dirt had gathered in the folds of his skin, and his eyes were lined with shadows.

Snow sighed. Every minute spent volleying questions with this idiot meant the guards might come back. "Will this tunnel get us out?" she asked him.

"Of course," the man said. "But why would you leave such a place? It is better to stay, my fair ladies."

Snow stooped down and peered into the dark tunnel. "Here? I don't think so." She couldn't see more than a few feet in the darkness, but anywhere had to be better than rotting in prison. She turned back around. "Where does this tunnel go?"

The stranger picked at a grubby fingernail. "Somewhere else."

"What do you mean?" her mother asked. "If there's a way out, we need to find it. When the guards return, we must be far from here." Her tone made the man look up, but his gaze was cold.

"Far, far away from here won't get you anywhere." He stared at Snow's mother with a calculating look, and it seemed to Snow that he had come to a decision. He sighed. "If you must go"—he attempted a smile after he said this, but it didn't reach his eyes, so for a moment he looked like a cunning old fox—"I will take you through the tunnel."

Chapter 3

Peter Merriweather's parents had hosted a lot of guests over the years at Bramble Cottage, but never so many at once. After Wilfred had announced the arrival of survivors from Heart's Place, things had gotten really busy. The children were sent from the barn with a long list of household chores. Peter had known the grown-ups would take over now that the Resistance was gathering, but he had at least expected to be part of the planning. Instead, he and Una were cleaning the attic.

Peter hid a groan as he lifted a large crate and carried it to an empty corner. He dropped it with a thump that made his forearms ache. Along with just about every other part of his body. The places where the beast's claws had dug into his back had scabbed over and were starting to itch. Heroes who fought wild beasts shouldn't be mucking about in dusty attics.

Una helped him move a huge oval mirror in its stand, three more heavy cartons, and a wardrobe full of old clothes. Once they had cleared enough space, Una began smoothing blankets into four neat pallets. Peter wasn't sure what was worse: having to sleep next to Rufus and Bastian, or hearing more of Indy blathering about what it meant to be a Servant of the King.

"My family's been protecting important secrets for ages," Indy had said, much to Rufus and Bastian's admiration. Una, too, had been keenly interested as Indy prattled on about his year with a caravan learning the oral histories of the Muses. Then there was the bit about meeting with the Sacred Order members scattered throughout Story. Indy had stayed at the Ranch and spent a week in Sleuth Alley, districts Peter never even got to visit. Once Indy had started telling about all the places he had been, everyone lost interest in what Peter had done.

"Your brothers are going to think this is the best sleepover ever," Una said as she unfolded a blanket. "I bet they'll be up all night."

Peter shoved back an old steamer trunk and stacked two smaller chests next to it. This was as good a time as any to try and get her to talk. "Did anything else happen? Back in the exam?"

Una fidgeted with the corners of the pillow she was holding.

"You can trust me. I promise."

Una plumped up the pillow and tossed it on the floor. Tiny feathers floated through the air. "I told you what happened."

Peter shook his head. "I know there's more."

Una brushed the down off her skirt. "Look, Peter. It wasn't exactly a . . . nice . . . experience. I'm going to have to tell it all over again to every character who comes here today, so can you just give it a rest?"

Peter didn't want to. He wanted to keep asking questions until he could figure out why she looked so sad. Maybe after they'd finished here and rustled up some food, she'd feel more like talking. "Are the other kids still in the kitchen?"

"Mmm-hmmm." Una was dragging a dressmaker's dummy out of the way, the unsewn fabric still pinned to the form. "Except for Indy," she said. "He's with the grown-ups."

"Figures." Peter crossed his arms over his chest and slouched against a wardrobe. "The rest of us have to clean, but *perfect Indy* can join their meetings."

"It makes sense, Peter." Una's voice came from the far corner, near the growing pile of junk. "Indy's done loads of things for the Resistance already. He knows what to look for and how to keep his mouth shut." She dusted off her hands. "Besides, it's better to have him there than here."

"Have who where?" Indy said as he walked into the room.

Una's face flushed red, and she looked at the rocking chair next to her as if it were the most interesting thing in the world.

"Um . . . my brothers," Peter blurted. "It's good they're helping Trix with the food. Give me a hand with this, Indy?" Maybe if Indy was moving furniture, he wouldn't talk about his marvelous adventures. Peter tugged on the end of a sofa that hadn't seen the light of day in years. What did his parents want with all this stuff anyway?

Indy came over and hoisted up the other side. "They're not so bad, your family. It must be nice to have lots of kids around."

Peter snorted. "Yeah. Nice for getting pummeled in the night or ambushed with stupid jokes or sitting through dinners where you can't get a word in edgewise. Very nice."

Indy grunted as he let the sofa fall with a thunk. "I guess that's what I mean," he said. "It was always just me and my dad."

Here we go again. Peter sighed and sat down on the nearest trunk. The only warning Peter had was a creak; then he fell through the lid, his feet poking up in front of his face.

Una's laugh sounded more like her old self at least. And then Indy was laughing, too.

Great. Peter tried to heave himself up, but his bottom half was stuck solid, and his feet kicked fruitlessly. Indy gave Peter's hand a brisk pull, and Peter tried to ignore his smile.

"Thanks," he said, and brushed himself off.

But Indy wasn't listening to him. "Hey, guys," he said. "Come look at this."

There, in the ruins of the ancient chest, was a mass of gray feathers.

"At least you had a soft landing, Peter." Una pulled out a handful of feathers. "What would your parents want with a boxful of these?" She spun one between her fingers, so it made a gray blur in the air.

Peter picked a sliver of splintered wood out of his pants and leaned over to get a closer look at the box.

"Quills," Indy said as he lifted one perfectly shaped feather. "From before the Unbinding."

"So these would have been used to write the old Tales?" Una ran the quills over her palm.

Peter peered over her shoulder. Usually Peter forgot that Una wasn't from Story, but times like this reminded him she had been Written In. Only an outsider wouldn't know about the Elements. "Quill, ink, and paper," he said as though he were Rufus reciting his lessons, "are the core Elements of Story."

"These quills have never been used," Indy said. "Quills, ink, bound papers—all of it was outlawed after the Unbinding. This box must have been up here for a long time." Indy ran the feather through two fingers. "I wonder why."

Peter thought he heard a note of challenge in Indy's tone, but he ignored it. "This is Trix's stuff." Peter pointed to the name lettered on the side of the chest. "Let's ask her about it."

Chapter 4

When Una entered the kitchen, Bastian and Rufus were just on their way out. Each boy was proudly balancing a platter of freshly buttered toast.

"Excuse us, Una," Bastian said. "The guests are waiting."

Una watched them go and then turned to Trix, who was stacking cups on another tray.

"All done, dear?" Trix asked.

Before Una could do more than nod, Trix had poured her a cup of steaming hot tea and marched her over to the squatty chair by the hearth. "Have a rest. You must be tired out."

Una accepted the drink gratefully. "Thank you," she sighed. She almost wished that she could stay in the cozy kitchen forever, but there were questions to ask.

She had volunteered to be the one to get answers out
of Trix. Partly because she couldn't take the blustering
that was going on between Peter and Indy. And partly
because she thought that what had happened during
the Unbinding might give her clues as to what her parents were planning now. The kitchen was quiet, the
crackling of the fire only interrupted by the clinking
sound Trix made as she arranged the china.

"I've sat by that very fire many a day after I'm plumb
tuckered out from cleaning work," Trix said as she
measured out tea leaves into a large pot.

Trix couldn't have given Una a better opening if she
had wrapped it up and tied it with a bow. "Have you
always lived at Bramble Cottage?"

"Aye. I had no home of my own, and the Merriweathers needed a housekeeper." Trix brushed by Una
to get the copper kettle hanging over the fire.

"What about the rest of your family?"

"My parents disappeared in the Unbinding. Same
as those poor souls in Heart's Place." Trix rested the
kettle on her worktable and stared off in the direction
Bastian and Rufus had gone. "I was very young, but
I remember the noise. The horrible sounds of battle.
Screaming. And the bright lights. My sister and I hid

under the bed until it was over. And then we were all alone. Everyone else was taken by the Muses."

Una licked her lips. "You mean they were taken by the Enemy," she said in a quiet voice.

"I suppose I do," Trix said as her hands rested on the kettle's handle. "Funny to think of it that way. I always had a hard time believing the Muses went bad, anyway. My parents believed in them through and through." Trix poured the water, and the hot steam enveloped her face.

Una didn't wait for another golden opportunity. "We found a chest in the attic. It was full of illegal quills." She played with the teacup's handle. "The chest had your name on it."

Trix didn't say anything right away. She carefully put the lid on the teapot. "My father was very trust-worthy," she said. "He crafted quills for the Muses. Once he took me with him, and we spent a whole day tromping through the woods, hunting for just the right feathers." She laughed. "He always made a game of it, saying we might find the Silver Quill if we looked hard enough." Trix put the teapot next to the cups and lifted the tray with both hands, but then she set the entire thing down and studied the worn tabletop. "You tell

Peter I meant his parents no harm hiding that crate in their attic. Archimago's command outlawing quills would have broken my father's heart. It was all I had left of him." She looked straight at Una. "Now, is there anything else you wanted to know?"

Una squirmed under the old lady's gaze. Una's father was the reason Trix had grown up alone, without a family. "No," she mumbled. "We were just, um, curious, I guess."

"All right, then," Trix said with a brusque nod. "Finish your tea, and then back to work with you, child." Before Una could say anything else, Trix had disappeared through the swinging kitchen door. A few moments later Una was out of the kitchen and down the front path to where Indy and Peter were waiting.

"Well?" Peter jumped up from his seat on the fence post.

"Trix's father made the quills," Una said evenly. "Before he was taken by the Enemy."

"And?" Indy said.

"And nothing. Trix only kept the quills because they belonged to her father." Una pushed the pain she had seen in Trix's eyes out of her mind. "She did say something else interesting, though. Do you know anything about a Silver Quill?"

"It's from the Tale of Beginnings." Indy pulled the blade of grass he was chewing out of his mouth. "The reason we use ink, quill, and paper to write the Tales is because the land of Story was written into being with magical Elements: ink made from a dragon's blood, a silver quill, and paper made all of flames. It's a child's Tale, really."

Una snorted. "Just last week all of Story believed that the King and the Enemy were children's Tales, too, and look where that got us." Una thought of what she had seen in Fidelus's book, how in the last moments before his imprisonment her father had braided the river of ink and swallowed it down. "The Enemy drank ink that day in the forest," she said. "But why?"

Peter shrugged. "No one even uses ink to write Tales anymore."

"That's the point," Una said. "While the Enemy was bound, it didn't matter. He was imprisoned in his Muse book before he had a chance to do whatever it was he was planning to do with the ink. But now that he's back, what if the ink is important?" She paused as one of the Romantic refugees passed by, a borrowed apron of Trix's tied on over her ruffled lace gown.

"You're right," Indy said. "We need to know more about the Tale of Beginnings. While the grown-ups are busy with the broadsides, we can investigate." He made a face as though he had smelled something rotten. "And, unfortunately, I know who can help us."

It didn't take Una long to figure out where Indy was taking them. She recognized the ratty tents full of merchants hawking their wares, but the bustling energy she remembered from when she and Peter had followed Snow and Professor Thornhill here was gone. Now, instead of slinking along the back routes, they climbed the broad road that led straight toward the towering cathedral. Una slipped one of the Resistance's broadsides onto the nearest merchant's table. Indy had brought a stack with them to pass out along the way, which made Una feel slightly less guilty for leaving all the others busily working at Bramble Cottage.

A woman dressed in a gray flowing robe began thumping her staff loudly once they reached the ancient stone steps that led up to the cathedral's iron doors. "It is *The End*," she called in a loud voice. "All of Story is ending!"

"I hate this place," Indy said with a groan. "Riddled with Dystopians."

The woman was waving a paper at Una as she shouted her dire warnings, and Una had to shove hard to get past her and catch up with the boys. She joined them just as they reached the landing outside the doors, where a whole cluster of people stood waving signs. *The End Is Nigh* flashed in front of Una's face, and then she was inside, her eyes adjusting to the dimly lit interior. The spicy smell of incense floated toward them, and the heavy door thumped shut behind them. Robed figures sat slumped against the anteroom's walls, staring into the distance and humming softly to themselves.

Indy whispered something to a young-looking Dystopian, who eyed them all with an unsettling gleam in his eye and then disappeared down a corridor.

While they waited, Peter unfolded a piece of paper. Apparently, he hadn't successfully avoided the pushy woman with the staff. Una peeked over his shoulder. *Join the Chosen* was written across the top in bold letters. *Before it's too late.*

Una snorted. The Dystopians mustn't have heard the latest news from Heart's Place. It already was too late. The Enemy was back.

Peter began reading the paper out loud. "Let's see. 'Did you know that Very Dark Days are coming. . . . We should abandon all hope,' blah, blah, blah. . . ." He held the paper closer to the candles mounted on the wall nearest them so he could read it. "'The final pages of Story are turning even as we speak. Bad news for everybody but the Chosen'—lucky for them."

"You should talk more quietly, Peter," Indy said as he grabbed the paper from Peter and crumpled it into a ball. "At least in this place."

"Don't tell me you believe them, Indy," Peter said. "Everyone knows the Dystopians are cheats. All this nonsense about Story's End is a way for them to fill their pockets with gold marks."

Indy didn't have a chance to respond, because a hidden door near them opened, and a gaunt-looking man appeared, bowing his head for an uncomfortable moment.

"Welcome," the man said in a smooth voice.

Una didn't like the crawly feeling his fevered gaze gave her. His face was scrubbed clean, and his eyes were unnaturally shiny. "Dark days are coming, friends," he said as he led them past a stained glass window that framed a fiery scene.

Una nodded solemnly and fought down an absurd desire to giggle. He didn't know how right he was. "Okay," she said.

"Brother"—he was talking to Peter now—"we must prepare for The End. Those who do not choose the right path now will not survive the coming trial. For five marks I will read you today's prophecy. It's very—"

"Yeah, yeah," Peter cut the man off. "I've heard your prophecies before. What is it today? Aliens coming to take us out of Story? Or maybe that you've found the bridge to the Readers' World?"

"I see you are familiar with our noble calling," the man said, and his yellow teeth glistened as he smiled at them. "Some question our intentions, but I assure you"—he reached out and touched Peter on the shoulder—"that we mean to help Story. For only a month's wages, you can join the Chosen, and you need not fear the dark days that are coming." He guided them to a grouping of hard wooden benches.

"Nobody needs you to tell us that Story's a mess." Peter shrugged the man's hand off.

Indy cleared his throat and stomped his boot squarely on Peter's foot. "Ah, yes. These are bitter times. And we are mere"—he shot a dark look at Peter—"questers."

Indy pressed his palms together for a moment. "We heard the rumors. The chaos at the Tale station. The ruin of Heart's Place. The hints of the Muses' return. Some say the Lost Elements have been found."

The Dystopian nodded sagely. "It is as the prophets have foretold. The End of Story has come. All the evils of the Unbinding will return upon us tenfold." His lips quivered. "The terror of the Unbinding was nothing compared to what is to come. The prophecies have been right so far. Increasing unrest. More and more sightings of the Taleless. Why, the very land of Story is failing!" He gave them a thin laugh. "This"—a pale fingertip emerged from the edge of his sleeve and pointed toward the front of the cathedral—"unrest is just the beginning, and then—"

"*The End* will come, right?" Peter gave him a polite little clap.

Indy clenched his jaw. "We mean no insult, Brother." It seemed to Una that he was forcing the words out.

The man nodded. "No offense taken. I know it is not me he insults, but my mission."

Una hoped Peter wouldn't say anything else. She could tell Indy didn't like the slimy Dystopians any more than Peter did, but how was she supposed to find anything out if Peter kept insulting them?

Indy's voice was smooth, but Una could hear a note of impatience in it. "Right. Your mission. Doesn't it have something to do with the Tale of Beginnings?"

"Oh, yes, the Lost Elements. Many go on pilgrimage to seek them, and Brother Geryon has even claimed to have found the Silver Quill." He made a funny little gesture with his fingers as he said the name. "When the three Elements used in creation are found once again, all of Story will be undone. It's very clear in the sacred legends."

"So the Elements are real," Una said. "We can actually find them somewhere in Story." Her thumbs were pricking with the kind of knowing that made her sure they were on the right trail. But there was no time for mistakes. They couldn't wander around Story looking for Elements that were just some moneymaking riddle for the Dystopians.

The Dystopian's feverish gaze turned on her. "Come, I will show you." He went a few paces and then paused. "Two gold marks," he said, palm held out, and, when Indy had found the required amount, added, "Each. Six total." She could hear Peter mumbling under his breath as Indy dropped the money into the man's open palm. When the Dystopian had counted it, he led Una and the boys out of the chapel and up a twisting stair to a landing. Before them, a giant round window filtered in light through its colored panels.

The Dystopian cleared his throat. "Once upon a time, before the first Tale was written, there was a character who had no name. The character felt all the stories in the world flowing inside of him, but there was nothing for him to write them down with. He looked out over the wide world, and what did he see but the mighty griffin hunting his breakfast. He spoke to the griffin, and the griffin flew to him. The man slew the beast and took the best of his feathers." He pointed up to the first panel of the window, where a half-lion, half-bird bent before a man with a bow and arrow. "The character again looked out over the wide world, and what did he see but the fiercest of dragons crouched upon the highest mountain. He spoke to the dragon, and the dragon flew to him. The man slew the beast and collected his lifeblood, black as ink."

Whoever had fashioned the window had made the dragon out of opaque glass, and its blood looked like a dark river rushing through the green forest. "The character again looked out over the wide world"—the

Dystopian pointed at the final pane—"and what did he see but a fiery phoenix rising from the ashes. He spoke to the phoenix, and the phoenix flew to him. The man slew the beast and collected her skin." The Dystopian's pale fingers hovered over the stained glass. "From the lives of these three magical beasts, willingly offered at the character's word, came the legendary Elements of Story. The character took the Silver Quill from the griffin, dipped it in the Dragon's Ink, and began to write on the Scroll of Fire. And so the land of Story was born." He clasped his hands in front of his waist. "When the three Elements are once again used, The End will be written and the old Story will be complete. Our scholars disagree on what the new Story will be like, but on this everyone is clear." He narrowed his eyes at her. "We hasten The End by hunting for the Lost Elements. Brother Geryon taught us this, and many pilgrims obey his instructions to seek out the Elements."

Una gave him a jerky little nod. "And if *we* wanted to go on—um—a pilgrimage?" she asked in what she hoped was a devout voice.

The man reached a pale hand out to clasp her on the shoulder. "Such a sensitive girl. Converted already by the signs of the times."

"Ah . . . yes," Una said. "Um. Your words have per-
suaded me."

The man flashed his yellow teeth at her. "We have
maps for zealous pilgrims. They outline paths trod by
weary feet longing for the peace of Story's End. Shops
where the finest quills were once made. Possible locations of the river of ink. Sightings of the last living
phoenix." In one swift movement he reached behind
him and pulled out a folded piece of parchment. He
pressed it into Una's hand. "For just five gold marks."

Peter snorted, but Indy fished the coins out of his
pocket.

The Dystopian pressed his palms together and gave
them a deep bow. "Happy endings to all of you."

Chapter 5

The moon was high when Snow, her mother, and their guide finally squeezed out of the hole. Snow ran her fingers through her hair, but the fine granules of dirt stayed stubbornly put. She wanted to shake off the filth of the tunnels so she wouldn't have to remember the tickly sensation of insect legs racing across her hands or the plop of unknown creatures falling on her as she burrowed after the man. But nothing she did made her feel cleaner. *No wonder this guy looks gross.*

The strange man had moved surprisingly quickly for his emaciated form, scraping along the earthen floor on his hands and knees. At one point, the ceiling had been so low, Snow had to scrunch forward on her belly. She worried for her mother and wondered how her wounded feet were faring. But one glance at her mother's face showed that sympathy wouldn't be appreciated. She wore a determined look, and the only signs that anything was out of the ordinary were her dirty skin and the gray circles under her eyes.

"Well, we're out," their odd guide said. "Which is what you wanted. Hope you're happy."

They stood in the shadow of the prison wall. In front of them, pale hills of sand lay quiet in the moonlight. The air was still, but very cold.

"It's a desert," Snow said.

"Very good! Very clever!" The man nodded and gave a polite little clap. "A desert that is impossible to cross."

Snow gave him a withering smile. *Great.* She wanted to grab the man and hold him in one place until he told them something useful. The complete silence made Snow feel like the guards were going to pop out at any moment and snatch them.

"Do the tunnels go anywhere else?" her mother asked.

"Aye," he said. "There are many cells."

"Other prisoners?"

"But of course." The man swept his head from side

to side. "There's my own person. Me. And I, of course."
He looked very pleased with himself. "They meant to
kill me, you know, but I'm alive. Tricky, tricky me.
And I."

Snow ignored him. "There has to be a way through
the desert or something at the end of this wall," she
said, slapping her hand against it.

Her mother turned to the man. "How far have you
gone into the desert?"

"Three days' journey in every direction," he said
without expression, and walked forward into the emp-
tiness. "It's a wasteland. No living things."

"And how is it that the guards let you roam free?"
Snow's mother came up behind him.

"Free?" he said bitterly. "Oh, I am not free. They
are always with me, always punishing me." The whites
of his eyes seemed to shine in the moonlight. "It never
ends. I live to serve." His face took on a crafty look, and
he began to move back toward the wall. "Well, here is
the parting of our ways. Fair travels for fair ladies."

"Wait!" Snow called, but the man dropped down
on all fours, and, faster than Snow thought possible, he
disappeared back into the tunnel. They went after him,

but by the time they reached the spot, the entrance was gone and they could only feel rocky wall where it had been.

"How is that even possible?" Snow asked as she thumped the surface.

"Illusion," her mother said, as though she were savoring the words. "All is not as it appears to be."

Snow sank to the ground next to the wall. The sand felt even colder than the stone. "That dirty rat! Do you think he's going to get the guards?"

"Doubtful. I don't think he's lying about being a prisoner." Her mother eased down next to her. "Even if he is mad. His captors might not even know about his tunnels. Or perhaps they've forgotten about him altogether." She gingerly patted the bandages on her feet. "I can't walk far," she said. "And I believe him that wasteland surrounds this place. I think we will find nothing but deadness here."

"Then what do we do? Stay put until *we* die?" Snow asked.

"No," her mother said. "Not at all. Let me think." The silence around them grew.

Snow wasn't sure when she'd last felt such absolute quiet. It hemmed her in and pounded at her ears.

She looked up into the inky sky. "There are no stars," Snow said. There wasn't even a wisp of a cloud, just the bright moon and a very empty horizon.

"None at all," her mother said.

"But that's impossible," Snow said as realization dawned. "No stars means that . . ."

"This is all a fake. A deception. You *were* paying attention last term, weren't you?" Her mother smiled at her. "If someone has woven an illusion around this place, it makes sense that the tunnel entrance would also be unreliable. If I hadn't been puzzling out the mystery of that fool, I might have noticed that the only sound is that of our own voices. And the only smell comes from our own persons." She frowned at the desert around them. "There are no other living things here. How that man traveled three days in this mirage is a riddle, but one for another day. We must find a hole in the illusion. Think, Snow. Every detail is important. What can you remember of your arrival?"

Snow thought out loud. "When they took me out of the wagon, they dropped me on my back. I felt something soft beneath me. It could have been leaves, I suppose. The wetness of it seeped through my cloak. I had the sack over my head, so I couldn't see anything."

She hated the memory of that sour darkness, the stifling already-breathed air pressing into her face. "Someone carried me. I heard the sound of footfalls, so he must have come to a road or a bridge or something like that. Then a clanging sound."

"Describe it," her mother said.

Snow tried to remember. "It sounded like something heavy scraping on stone." Her certainty grew. "Like in Weaponry, when the mistress tells you to drop your weapon, and thirty swords clatter to the stone floor. Only louder."

Her mother nodded. "What else?"

"After the noise, he told someone to open the door. I guess we must have gone inside the prison, because we went down stairs. Lots of them. And then he put me in our cell."

"It sounds like they put us in a castle dungeon," her mother said. "How appropriate. No doubt somewhere in the depths of the Red Enchantress's fortress."

"The Red Enchantress?" Snow asked. "You mean the woman from the clearing? The one who—?" She glanced down at her mother's feet.

"Yes," her mother said shortly. "We are her prisoners." She stood. "I wish our guide hadn't left us. I have more questions for him. Come, Snow. We'd best be on our way."

Snow wasn't sure she wanted to follow her mother, despite the lack of alternatives. If this was some sort of fortress populated by clawed guards and a Red Enchantress and prisoners like the madman, what good would it do for them to find a way into the real castle? But her worries were for nothing. The wall stretched in endless monotony as far as the eye could see. Each step forward brought the same scenery. Rough stone to their left. An ocean of silvery sand to their right.

Snow's stomach rumbled. Neither of them had thought to take the food, however questionable, from the tray in the cell. She tried not to think of the Woodland Room back at Perrault Academy. Were her classmates there now, enjoying a mug of chocolate by the fire and bragging over exploits in the exam? When would someone notice she was gone? She wasn't on the best of terms with Una, but surely Una would notice her roommate was missing. Eventually.

Her mother's steps were getting slower, and Snow could tell walking was painful.

Snow gazed out over the rolling sand dunes and

laughed bitterly. "It doesn't matter that we've escaped. There's nowhere to go."

"Don't tell me you've adopted that man's sour words after one day in this place." Her mother frowned at her. "At least have the good grace to give it three days of wandering before you give up."

Snow felt her jaw drop open. Her mother had never openly scolded her before. Oh, Snow had read disapproval across those icy features of hers, but that wasn't the same thing as being corrected outright. Her mother didn't take it back.

"Don't look so shocked," she snapped at Snow. "This isn't Perrault. We don't have the luxury of dancing on eggshells here. We're in trouble, Snow. In danger. I need you to keep your wits about you."

Snow opened her mouth to argue, but her mother cut her off.

"I'd think twice about wasting your breath, Snow," she said, but emotion—anger even—had replaced the icy stillness that usually invaded her mother's tone. "The things that are unspoken between us. Why it is that you hate me. It can wait. We have to work together. We have to trust each other." She reached over and grabbed Snow firmly under the chin, drawing her face up so she could look directly into her eyes.

"For better or worse, I'm all you've got now."

They had just started walking again when a speck appeared on the horizon. Or what passed for the horizon in this awful, endless night. It grew to a shadowy form, and Snow ducked into the wall's scant protection.

"Not to worry, my ladies." The madman was back, and his voice sounded thin in the enchanted air. "Not to worry. It is I, your friend and guide." He held one of the moldy rolls that had been on their tray in the cell and gnawed on the end.

"Great," Snow muttered under her breath. "Just what we need."

Her mother stepped around her. "Where does this wall go?"

"Nowhere else."

"Nowhere else," Snow echoed. "Oh, that's just perfect. The tunnel goes somewhere else and the wall goes nowhere else. Add that to the list of crazy. A pretend desert that has no end. Torturers who slash up feet for fun. Guards who hide their faces and have silver claws instead of hands. A Tale Master who delivers us to the Red Enchantress with no explanation." She looked at the man, who had stopped chewing. "And a madman is the only other living soul we've seen in ages."

"What about the Tale Master?" A mushy piece of bread was dangling from the edge of the man's mouth as he spoke.

Snow wrinkled up her nose. "Um, you've got something right here." She pointed at her face.

"Tale Master Elton," her mother said in a quiet voice. "Do you know him?"

There was a spark of interest in the man's eyes, but, just as quickly, they clouded over. He swallowed hard to force the bread down. "I feel like I should know the name. Or the face. I'm much better with faces." He licked his lips. "Except the Red Lady's sleepers. Not their faces. Awake faces are best." He snickered. "Her Taleless are hard, too. Haven't got any faces. And they never sleep. Not like the dreamers at the Ivory Gate. Dreamers never wake." The madman was shaking with silent laughter, and he looked even more insane than before. His jaw was open wide, and his tattered garments jiggled as he bent double.

"What do you mean by *the Ivory Gate*?" Her mother's voice was sharp.

The man stopped and became almost perfectly still, an empty grin stretching the skin taut across his skull.

He looked in every other direction but toward Snow's mother. "Didn't say anything about an Ivory Gate."

"Yes, you did," Snow said. "In your stupid joke."

The man looked straight at her. "There's no joke. For us or any of the others." He leaned in close so that his face was right in front of Snow's.

Snow moved back. "Get away from me!"

Snow's mother uttered a short command that Snow couldn't make out. Her hand stretched out, flesh pale in the moonlight, and then the madman crumpled to the ground. The air smelled of burned hair.

Snow's eyes felt like they would pop out of her head. "You *killed* him?"

Her mother waved away her concern. "A freezing charm. That is all." She limped over to what now looked like a pile of rags and nudged him with her toe. "I don't want him to hear us." She looked up at Snow. "He knows something of Elton, but his mind has been spoiled by magic. He has been too long under the Red Enchantress's spell." She stepped back from the man's body. "Be watchful around him. I don't want him to find you alone." Her mother squeezed Snow's arm. "Stay close to me. With luck, the farther we get from this evil place, the more his memories may return, and we will see what he knows about the Red Enchantress."

Snow peered down at the man's crumpled form. Was that what would happen to her the longer she stayed in this wasteland? She'd go mad?

Her mother raised her arms as if she were lifting the madman, even though he still lay two feet in front of her. "If nothing else, he will be of some use to us if he can lead us away from here." Slowly, surely, the bent form straightened into the air until it was standing, arms hanging limply as if he were a scrawny puppet. Snow's mother moved over to him and placed a hand against his forehead, murmuring softly.

Snow stared. She had always known her mother was a Villain. After all, she taught the subject at Perrault. Snow had even guessed that she might be a Witch. But Snow had never actually seen her mother act like one.

The old man jolted to life, and it was as though time had gone backward. He bent at the waist, his frame shaking with laughter. Then he stopped and said once again, "Her Taleless are hard, too. Haven't got any faces. And they never sleep. Not like the dreamers at the Ivory Gate. Dreamers never wake."

This time her mother approached and said in a silky voice, "How clever of you to have discovered the dreamers. Shall we follow you to them?"

The old man grinned at Snow's mother with a besot-
ted look and scampered ahead, glancing back over his
shoulder like a dog waiting for his master.

Snow forced one foot in front of the other as she
moved to catch up with him. Her mother wasn't just a
Villain. Or a Witch. Snow took a deep breath. She was
an Enchantress.

Chapter 6

Peter walked briskly to keep pace with Indy. At least the other boy had enough sense to keep a Lady safe in a place like Horror Hollow, and he and Indy flanked Una on either side. The harbor road was full of people, and the water next to them was nearly as busy. A towering ship had its gangplank down, and groups of loudmouthed sailors made their way to the deck, bulging sacks slung over their shoulders. Crowds of characters clamored to join them. News of what had happened at Heart's Place had traveled quickly, and people were leaving the main districts in droves. Peter watched a merchant thrust more sacks of coins than he had seen in his life into the arms of a shifty-looking pirate. Maybe it would be enough to get the merchant and his family far, far away, out of the Enemy's reach.

"Let me see the map again," he said. Una handed over the paper the Dystopian had sold them, and Peter ducked out of the main thoroughfare to study it. They should be getting close to the quill shrine, but Peter didn't see any likely Dystopian sites around them.

"I still think this whole pilgrimage thing is a hoax," Peter said as he scanned the map.

"The Lost Elements aren't a hoax," Indy said. He took the map from Peter, and, after a moment of consultation, ushered them toward a run-down side street. "The Dystopians may prey on peoples' fears, but they are learned oral storytellers. The Sacred Order thinks they might have access to the oldest backstories."

Peter snorted. "And does the Sacred Order also know why the Enemy would want the Lost Elements?" He took the map back from Indy and began folding it up. "Oh, sorry, I forgot, the Sacred Order didn't know anything about the Enemy to begin with."

"Stop arguing, you two. It's annoying. Who cares where the information comes from?" Una snatched the map back out of Peter's hands and slapped it across the palm of her hands. "All of the possible locations of the Dragon's Ink are in forests. Even the stained glass window showed the dragon dying in a forest. That's not just a coincidence. I think Fidelus really did find the Dragon's Ink, and that's what he gulped down before he was imprisoned." She started for the side street. "We've got to know more about the Elements, and then maybe we can figure out why he wants them so much."

Indy said nothing and easily caught up with Una.

Peter didn't need more convincing. If Indy was going, he was going too. He hurried after them. With a loud squish, Peter's boot sank into a pile of rotting fish guts. *Perfect.* He stomped through the rancid pile and shook his foot. Una had stopped in front of a crumbling brick building. A wooden sign swung out from the street-side wall. There were no words, just a faded painting of a gull, wings spread as if in flight.

"This is it, huh?" Peter said as he scraped the side of his boot on the cobblestones. Somehow he had thought a holy pilgrimage site would appear more sacred, or scary . . . or at least occupied. This place just looked like an abandoned dump. After one more consultation, Una folded the parchment and made her way up the stairs, Indy close on her heels. Peter had to duck under hanging bundles of dried herbs to follow them through the crooked front door.

"Who in their right mind—" he began, but Una

shushed him at the same moment a reedy voice called out, "Who's there? Show yourselves."

The door swung inward on its groaning hinges. Una looked at Indy. Indy looked at Peter. Peter plunged forward into the shadows.

"Children on pilgrimage, eh? Come to see my shop?"

It took a moment for Peter's eyes to adjust to the dim interior, and then he saw the hunched figure in the corner. An old woman stooped over a barely smoldering fire, stirring something in a cook pot.

"We want to know about the Lost Elements." Una's voice sounded so sure. Peter glanced sideways at her. She looked fierce, arms crossed over her chest, with her chin thrust out stubbornly. Indy stood on the other side of her; from the black expression on his face, he was as uneasy as Peter about the shop owner.

When the woman didn't answer, Una crouched next to the fire. "Please," she said. The steam embraced Una's face, and just then Una seemed exactly like a witch brooding over her bubbling cauldron.

"Many come here looking for the legendary Quill," the woman said with a toothless smile. "And then they leave, and go back to their normal lives. Only old

Jaga lives the pilgrim way." Jaga turned to a shelf and fumbled around with some sacks on it. "Would you children like some candy?"

"Una." In that moment, it struck Peter as exceptionally stupid that they had left Bramble Cottage without telling a soul where they were going. He reached down and tugged on Una's sleeve. "This was a bad idea."

The old woman looked hungrily up at Peter. "And what do you know of bad ideas? Speak up!" Peter felt icy cold start up at the base of his spine. Something about Jaga wasn't quite right. Her skin wobbled loosely around her eye sockets as though she wore it like a garment.

The liquid in the pot hissed, and the heat burned Peter's face. He stepped back.

"If it's true that you've been on pilgrimage longer than anyone," Una said, "tell us what you know about the Dragon's Ink."

The woman stared at Una for a long time. Peter glanced over at Indy, who hovered between Una and Jaga like a coiled cat ready to pounce.

"You know better than I what happened to the Dragon's Ink." Jaga stood up, more nimble than she appeared, and, edging Peter out of the way, knelt before Una. "Now you come to test my loyalty." The old woman grabbed Una's hand and kissed it. "Milady, you do me great honor to visit here. I have not forgotten your commission. Watch and wait. That's what I've done."

Peter's mouth dropped open. Una looked equally astonished, but Peter saw her expression change from disbelief to something like determination. *Who does this old lady think Una is? And why is Una playing along with it?*

"That's very good," Una said awkwardly. "Do you . . ." She hesitated, and Peter could tell she was trying to find the right words. "Have . . . um . . . have you seen anything like the Silver Quill?"

However second-rate Una's dialogue was, the old woman didn't seem to mind. A toothless smile creased her wrinkled face. "I knew it! I knew it was you, milady. You have made yourself young. An illusion many would kill for."

"Quite right," Una said, sounding surer this time. "But the Quill?"

"Wait and watch. Watch and wait. That's all I've done this past year at least, and I've found another quill for you. Perhaps it's the one you seek," the old woman

said, while hobbling over to what Peter thought must
be her bed. The misshapen pile was lost in shadow, and
as she rummaged in the darkness, two cats, a rat, and
something else much bigger scampered out and took
refuge in the other dim corners of the room. "Fools
have come and worshipped at this made-up shrine,
and I've listened to every one of them. The scholars
from the cathedral were the worst, though they were
the ones who'd had word of the Silver Quill. Brother
Geryon, they said. His family served the one who took
it from the griffin."

"Take care, Una," Indy hissed.

For once, Peter agreed with him. It didn't take a
genius to see that the old lady thought Una was someone else, someone who was hunting the Lost Elements.
There was no way this would end well. Jaga could
have anything hidden in there: a weapon, a charm of
some sort. A witch who offered children candy wasn't
doing it because she was nice. He gripped the hilt of
his sword.

Jaga scooted back toward Una, clutching something
to her chest and bobbing her head up and down. "I
keep it safe, right here with me. I have it with me while
I sleep." She hugged the soiled cloth close and reached

out her other hand. She held one long feather tightly in her filthy fist.

Peter had seen quills before, but nothing the size of the one before him. This one was the length of a man's arm, and its silver color glowed dully in the dark room.

"This was hard to come by, milady. Had to barter with the scholars myself." She handed it to Una with a little curtsy. "It could be the one. It's older than the Unbinding, or so they claimed. It's definitely older than the others I've brought you. Those fools from the cathedral say much that's nonsense, but they do know their legends. I *would* have brought it to you, milady, only there hasn't been a new moon yet." Her voice faltered. "You know I've never failed to obey before," she said as Una looked carefully at the quill. The longer Una kept quiet, the more the old woman bowed and scraped before her.

"I would've come to you, milady, I swear it. At midnight, just as you require."

Una frowned at the point of the quill.

Peter couldn't tell what she was thinking, but now they knew for sure a woman was hunting the Silver Quill from the legends, and maybe it was even Duessa. This, however, was most definitely not the Silver Quill.

Even from where he stood, Peter could see bits of gray paint flaking off it. If Peter knew anything about the Dystopians, he knew they probably had a workshop where they made fake Silver Quills and charged way too much money for them. It was time to go. *Before this old witch figures out we're also frauds.*

"Milady." The old woman held one hand out beseechingly. "Are you pleased?"

"Where?" Una's voice sounded distant, and it wavered a bit as she continued. "Where would you meet me?"

Peter glared at Una as if the force of his thoughts could make her look at him. The real woman would know exactly where they met. What was Una doing? Indy must be wondering the same thing. It was only the slightest of movements, but Peter saw Indy stealthily withdraw a dagger from the belt at his waist.

Jaga kept her head bowed but peered up at Una. "But . . . you know . . . milady?"

"Of course I know," Una said sharply. "The question is whether you are still on my side."

The old woman's head waggled again. "Oh, yes, milady. Yes. Jaga lives to serve." The flickering firelight made her eyes look like holes. "At blackest midnight. All alone. Just as you asked."

Una licked her lips. "But you are very old. Perhaps you have forgotten the way."

"Oh no, milady!" The crone bent low before Una. "I could go to your castle in my sleep."

Una slid the quill into a pocket inside her cloak. "So you say." She sounded ruthless. "But your eyesight fails you. How can I know your wits won't as well?" She waved her hand around the little room. "What route do you take? Or perhaps you have forgotten?"

The old woman whimpered. "Why do you try and confuse Jaga? You chose it yourself. Why do you distrust me, milady? Have I not served you well?"

Una gave a little cough. "You are very clever, Jaga. Of course I mean to test you." There was a long pause, and Peter could feel her scrambling for words. This was a bad idea. Jaga would have to be a fool to think her lady would keep quizzing her like this.

Peter stepped forward. "These are dark days," he said. The old woman swiveled her head slowly toward him as though she had forgotten he was in the room. "Her . . . um . . . ladyship must confirm the loyalties of all her . . . companions."

The old woman sucked in her breath. "Companions? Milady, do you consider me a companion?"

Peter almost felt bad for Jaga. This old crone was done for, however loyal she was, if it came out she was spilling some secret meeting place to anyone.

Una flashed Peter a relieved smile. She turned to the old woman. "Of course I do. But to be safe, I have one last question for you."

Peter stifled a groan. The last question could be the one that got them caught.

"You could be an enemy in disguise," Una continued. "How do I know you aren't someone else who has the appearance of my faithful Jaga?"

The woman gasped in horror and began shaking her head from side to side even before Una was finished.

"Tell me something only you would know. Something secret." Una's voice was firm. "Tell me how you get to my castle."

"I use the key." The crone's eyes flashed up toward Una. "For the cemetery." Trembling fingers reached for the collar of her shirt and pulled out a string, upon which dangled an old-fashioned-looking key.

Una stood up a little straighter and held out a shaky hand. "Give it to me."

Jaga clutched at the key. "But, milady! You cannot ask this of me."

Una quirked one eyebrow at the old woman and frowned with displeasure. "I *cannot*?" Peter didn't like to see this side of Una. Whether she was pretending or not, he wanted to grab her by the elbow and drag her out of the ramshackle shop.

The old woman tugged sharply, and the string snapped in two. "I live to serve, milady," she said as she handed the key to Una.

"Very good," Una said, and with a twist of her wrist, the key was hidden away in her cloak. "You needn't come to my castle again," she said. "I will return when the time is right." She wouldn't meet the old woman's eyes. Instead she brushed past the torn curtain that shaded the window and out through the wooden door. Peter gave the witch an awkward bow. He paused at the doorway, and as he looked back, he saw the bent form of the old woman. Her shoulders were shaking, but no noise was coming from her toothless mouth. Even so, Peter was sure of it. She was weeping.

Chapter 7

Una set her mouth in a grim line and turned down yet another snaking alleyway. The quill Jaga had given her was safely tucked away in her cloak, and with every step she took, she could feel the key's weight in her pocket. Peter and Indy seemed to think the quill was a fake, some Dystopian trick to make money, but whether it was real or not, Una knew one thing. Her parents *were* hunting for the Lost Elements. Why else would her mother have servants like Jaga collecting quills that might be the silver one?

"The Hollow's no place to be after nightfall," Peter said for the millionth time as he caught up with her. "We don't even know if Jaga was saving the quills for Duessa. It could have been some other Lady."

Una elbowed her way through a cluster of hobgoblins,

leaving a flutter of angry pixies in her wake. She wasn't about to tell them that the reason she knew it was Duessa was because Jaga had confused Una with her mother. *She thought I was her.* Una tried hard to remember what Duessa had looked like from that brief moment in Alethia's garden, but all she could picture was her violet eyes. *Eyes like mine.*

"Una might be onto something," Indy said. "The original Elements were used to write the whole land of Story. With that kind of power, the Enemy could do"—he ducked under the cloud of swearing fairies— "just about anything."

"Aren't you always complaining that the grown-ups never let us do anything?" Una glanced back at Peter. "Well, here's the chance to do something. Imagine how happy everyone will be if we come back with news that we've found a secret way into Duessa's castle. That could really help the Resistance."

"They *would* be less mad about us sneaking off. . . ." Peter shrugged. "As long as we're back before bedtime."

They were in the center of Horror Hollow now, and the brightly painted buildings on either side of them gave off yellow pools of light. The doors nearest them burst open, letting out a sound of brash laughter, and a

brawling pair of gnomes tumbled into the street. The
bigger of the two pinned his companion to the ground
and punched him hard in the face. Their greenish skin
almost glowed in the eerie lamplight.

Peter grabbed Una by the elbow and whisked her
away from the brawl. "Do you see now why the Hollow's dangerous? Messing around in the Villainous
parts of Story is risky stuff."

"I get it," Una said. She really did, but hearing
Peter's warning didn't change her mind. Being afraid
wasn't an option. The disaster at Heart's Place made it
clear that the Enemy wasn't sitting around waiting to
make his next move. And she wasn't going to either.
First, she'd find her parents. Then she'd find out what
they were planning.

All day Una had clung to the flicker of hope that
she could stop the Enemy before he found all the Elements, before he did something horrible. And maybe
that would make up for setting him free in the first
place. Learning that Duessa was looking for the Silver
Quill had fanned the flicker into a roaring flame. Her
father had the Dragon's Ink, she was sure of it. Why
else would he gulp it down? He was planning to do
something with the Elements of Story. And this was

Una's chance to find out exactly what.

If she was very lucky, she'd be able to spy on her parents and learn something useful for the Resistance. And if she got caught . . . *Well, being their daughter has to be good for something.* Una had no dreams of her parents welcoming her with open arms. But she was sort of hoping that they wouldn't kill their only child on the spot.

"Everything looks different at night," Peter muttered. "If I can just get us to the main street . . ."

"I think we should have turned right at the haunted house," Indy said as he swiped the hair off his forehead.

"I'm pretty sure I've got it covered," Peter said in a tight voice. "Just keep your eyes open, Indy."

"We've just got to find an inn or something like that where we can casually talk to people. The characters who live here will know if there's a castle and a cemetery nearby," Una said.

The streets were growing crowded. The Hollow had more than its fair share of mysterious cloaked figures, but as Una wended her way through the narrow streets, she saw more and more masked faces and heard faint strains of music. A couple with grinning gold masks was dancing in the middle of the street, and Peter made a wide circle around them before coming to a standstill. Around the next corner, the street opened up into the main square. The music was wild and loud here. Masked characters were everywhere, as crowds of people filled the open space with dancing and merrymaking. Blazing torches lit the street corners but also filled the air with a hazy smoke.

"Winter's Eve," Peter said. "How could I have forgotten?"

Una peered over his shoulder into the masses of people. "What's Winter's Eve?" All the characters in the square had their faces covered. Some with masks that looked like exaggerated frowns and others with hideous grins alternated among the whirling figures.

"It's the longest night of the year," Indy said. "Every district celebrates a little differently, but all the characters do something to welcome in the new season. When we traveled with the caravan—"

Peter stifled a yawn. "*We* gather in Fairy Village to hear songs and children's Tales."

Una laughed. "Oh, Peter, you sound like such a snob." A giant danced by Una and leered at her through a distorted mask. His features looked like they were melting. Una much preferred the sparkling masks some of the ladies held up to their faces. It was nice to see characters enjoying themselves. Maybe news about what had happened at Heart's Place hadn't yet reached this part of the Hollow. Or maybe Villains just didn't care.

The music swelled, and the mass of dancers pressed closer. "Do either of you know how to dance?" Una asked.

Peter groaned. "You have got to be kidding me, Una."

Someone about Indy's size wearing a black mask that left only his eyes uncovered appeared in front of them and removed his feathered hat with a bow. "Such poor manners, my lad." He shook a finger at Peter. "Never insult a lady." He reached for Una's hand and swept a kiss across her knuckles. "And *never* miss a chance to dance." He stood up, reached behind Una's ear, and pulled out a tiny little white flower. "For you, milady."

"*Una.*" Indy's warning was a whisper.

"I can ask him questions," Una hissed back as she tucked the flower into the top of her braid. "I'll be fine. Who's going to do anything with all these people around?" She offered her hand to her dance partner and whispered one final instruction. "You guys find out what you can, and we'll all meet back at Bramble Cottage, okay?"

Before Indy and Peter could do anything, her partner had whirled Una away into the crush of dancers. The music was riotous here, and the rhythmic thumping of the drums set Una's feet flying. She didn't know the steps, but her partner expertly led her where she needed to go, spinning her in circles that left her quite breathless. The laughter around her was infectious, and the booms of the fireworks that were bursting overhead underscored the drumbeat.

After the dance finished, the masked stranger took her hand and dodged through the festive couples toward a brightly painted building. "Are you hungry?" he asked.

Una looked back over her shoulder. Peter and Indy were nowhere to be seen. "And thirsty." Whoever the stranger was, Una felt safe. For the few moments she had been dancing with him, she had forgotten who she was and what she was about to do.

"Do you know if there are any castles nearby?" As soon as Una said it, she realized it was an odd question, but she plowed ahead. "Or cemeteries?"

Her companion stopped just short of the inn door.

"Now, what would a lass like you want with a cemetery?" he asked.

"I'm . . . um . . . looking for relatives," Una managed. Let him think she was looking for their graves.

"I think I know where you might find them," her partner said. "But first come have a bite to eat." When they pushed through the swinging doors into the busy common room of the inn, the smell of roasting meat made Una's stomach rumble.

"Why, Kai! I didn't know you were back in town," the innkeeper said as they sat down.

An old witch seated on the other side of him raised her pint glass in the air. "To Kai!" The entire room erupted in a shout, and Una's companion turned to face them with a grin. His black eyes twinkled, and he stood on his stool and gave them all a comic bow.

"To my friends!" He pumped his fist up in the air. "To Winter's Eve!"

The room might never have stopped cheering for Kai, but the innkeeper came over and began loading their table with platters of fresh bread, fruit, cheese, and a dish of the roasted meat that set Una's mouth watering.

While Una ate, she watched a checkered assortment

of characters greet Kai. There was a grizzled dwarf who didn't eat any food but instead propped his muddy boots up on the table and chewed an old pipe stem as he talked about the grave conditions of the underworld. A man with dark skin and a very pointed beard sat across from Kai and debated the merits of the New School of Sorcery. A nearly silent fox perched nearby, picking genteelly at chicken bones and adding his opinion when needed. At different points in the meal, a witch, a harpy, and a watchful Siamese cat joined them.

"Tell me what I've missed since I've been gone," Kai said as he scooped a generous spoonful of roasted vegetables onto his plate. "How fares the Hollow?"

Una learned that Kai had been traveling through the far reaches of Story for some time, but she discovered little else besides that. Kai dodged every question that his companions put to him.

"Did you see aught of the Endless Sea?" The dwarf recrossed his ankles, and a powder of dirt fell onto the tabletop.

"You mean the Blue Pools of Summer? Talk is that they are no more. What say the dwarf scouts?"

Then the dwarf was off on some long story of his latest journey to find a rumored stash of quicksilver.

"Impossible," the sorcerer scoffed. "Quicksilver consumes everything it touches. If someone had discovered it, we'd all be dead."

And so it went—from debates about the rumors from the Scorpion Desert to bickering over who had, in fact, discovered the Lost Princesses—with Kai laughing over it all.

Even when Una's least favorite of his companions—a beautiful woman who sat on the other side of Kai, very nearly draping herself across him—asked, "Have you found another siren, Kai?" he didn't actually answer, only tilted back on two legs of his chair, gave a hearty laugh, and said, "There are no other sirens like you, Lorelei."

By the time she had finished her meal, Una had come to several conclusions. First, she was sure that Kai would do her no harm. The way he treated the other characters made Una think he had more Hero in him than Villain. Even the way he avoided answering a question by asking one of his own didn't seem malicious. Secondly, she determined that Horror Hollow wasn't nearly as scary a place as she had once thought. In fact, the characters seated at the table with her were quite possibly the most interesting ones she had come across in Story. And finally, she was absolutely positive that she would have to find the cemetery soon—before she fell asleep. The effort of dancing and her full stomach made her fight to keep her eyes open.

Until she heard what the witch was saying. "The Tale Master's going to make a big announcement at Perrault tomorrow. About the Tale station being shut down and all. Did you hear that out in the Badlands, Kai?"

"He's shut down the Tale station?" Kai set his chair down on the floor with a thud and rubbed his chin thoughtfully. "But what good have the Talekeeper Tales ever done us anyway?"

"That's for sure," the sorcerer said. "Better Tales when the Muses were around."

"And less bossing," the crone cackled. "My mam had some Witch in her, true enough, but she was a Romantic at heart. The Muses would've written her a witch's love story instead of the same-old same-old witch-who-eats-children nonsense she got from the Talekeepers."

There was much nodding all around, and then Kai raised his tankard with a grin. "To Villainy! And to Villains being whoever they want to be!"

Una didn't join the toast, but she took a sip from the mug of tea in front of her. She eyed the group around the table. Maybe the Resistance had been looking for support in all the wrong places. Hearing Kai's friends go on about the Talekeepers and the shoddy way they were running things made her think that some of the Hollow folk, at least the Villains seated around her, weren't falling for Elton's lies.

"What we need is some new leadership," the dwarf said around his pipe. "No more of this Talekeeper non-sense." He chewed the stem. "Copies of Tales and all that rubbish. My granddad wouldn't have stood for it, I tell you that."

"What we *need* is a Villain running things, not some puffed-up Hero." The sorcerer was smiling as he said this, but the way he bared his pointed teeth made Una sit up a little straighter in her chair.

"What we need is the return of the King." The fox had spoken very little the entire meal, and Una was surprised at how deep his voice was. "What say you, Kai?"

"Sure, the King'll return someday." Kai waved the fox's words away. "The same day foxes fly." A loud chorus of laughter followed this statement, and the

innkeeper began serving giant slices of chocolate cake
to everyone. As Una took her first bite, Kai bent down.

"I know of a cemetery that leads to a castle," he said
in a near whisper. "But it's very dangerous."

"Oh, I'm not going there tonight," Una said. *Unless
I can find Peter and Indy first.*

"And why not?" Kai asked. "I didn't say you
shouldn't go. Just that it was dangerous." He leaned in
close. "All the more reason *to* go, if you ask me. At least
if you want an adventure. Do you?"

Una swallowed the cake and then tried out Kai's
tactic. "What do you know of the Lost Elements of
Story?"

"Depends on who's asking." Kai's face split into a
broad grin. "And if they're telling the truth." Una liked
how friendly his eyes looked.

"My name is Una Fairchild," Una said, "and I need
to find the Lost Elements to make something right."
There. All true.

"I see," Kai said, and, impossible as it was, Una
thought he really did see. "The cemetery's half a mile
south of here. Take the last right before you come to
the Pit of Doom."

Una had thought she'd be pleased to have the

information. Instead, she felt like she was going to
throw up. Kai must have seen it on her face.

"I don't know if you're in some kind of trouble, lass,
and I don't care." His words were barely more than a
whisper. "I make it a rule not to get involved in other
characters' messes. Much more interesting that way."
He pressed something into the palm of her hand. "But
if you have need, put on this ring. It will help you see
clearly when things seem confused. From the look on
your face, I'd say you might need it."

The ring felt hot in her palm, and Una uncurled her
fingers to look at it. She glimpsed a solid gold circle
before Kai folded her hands up again.

"Not here, lass," he scolded. "Don't be a fool. Only
use it if you have great need."

Una slipped the ring into her pocket. "Thank you,"
she said. "For everything."

Kai waved a hand in his now-familiar gesture, and
Una knew that his moment of seriousness was over.
The others at the table were watching them, and he
raised his voice. "As you like. Thank me if you like. Or
not. Stay if you like. Or go." The lines were obviously
part of a well-known song, for as soon as he said them,
his companions joined in, and soon the little room was

filled with the sound of their singing.

"I will then," Una said, something no one heard over the noise. But Kai gave her the faintest of nods as she pushed back from the table and slipped out the door.

Chapter 8

The madman kept singing some stupid song about the man in the moon eating a bowl of porridge, and Snow felt like smacking him. Her mother had said they were looking for an Ivory Gate, whatever that was. Snow was keeping a safe distance from her, not that it would do any good. Snow knew she was no match for an Enchantress. Snow wouldn't even learn how to properly deflect an enchanted voice until third-year Elocution, and she wasn't very good at Elocution to begin with.

Suddenly, the madman stopped before a section of the wall that looked identical to every other stone they'd passed before. He turned and surveyed the desert behind them. Snow didn't know what he was looking for, but after a minute, he appeared satisfied.

"Come see," he said, as he let the sand trickle through his fingers.

Her mother dropped down by his side and touched the ground. "Look at this, Snow," she said.

Snow's skin felt crawly. Was her mother trying to enchant her? Snow didn't feel the compelling wish to do whatever she said, like she had when they first learned about enchanted voices in Elocution. In fact, she still felt the ambivalence toward her mother that she always did. Snow took that to be a good sign. "What is it?" she asked, and tried to keep her tone neutral. Maybe her mother hadn't enchanted her, but it still wasn't a great idea to make her angry.

"Feel here," her mother said, pressing her hands down into the sand. Snow reached to touch the silvery-white granules, but her fingers felt only air. It was the queerest sensation. For all her eyes saw, she was running sand between her hands, but there was nothing there. She looked up at her mother, who had something close to a smile on her face.

"We've found it, Snow," she said in a whisper. "The way out."

"Out where?" The old man drew closer. "This is the door to Nowhere Else. It doesn't go out."

"Yes, of course, kind sir," Snow's mother crooned. "But the dreamers must be waiting for you. Shall we look for them?"

The man wagged his head up and down and grinned. "Yes, yes." His gnarled fingers traced an arch across the face of the wall. "Wait and see." And then he stood back and stared at the spot.

Nothing happened. Or at least it seemed that way. But when Snow looked up at her mother and then glanced back, it was different. Parts of the stone were fading away, the dark gray rock melting to reveal a yellowed surface beneath. After some time, the wall was entirely gone, and in its place were two towering gates, covered with creamy carvings of sleeping creatures.

"The Ivory Gates. They mark the boundaries between sleep and waking, enchantment and reality." Her mother ran her fingers across the surface. "This is the way through the illusion."

The old man reached out to stop her hands.

"Not for you, kind sir," her mother said. "Why don't you have a seat?"

As though she had pushed him, the old man plopped down to the ground.

Snow stepped around him. "I've never heard of any

Ivory Gates," she said, peering at a carving of a weathered gnome dozing under a spreading tree. "Why are they all sleeping?"

"Sleep is the symbol of illusion," her mother said. "'Let this be but a dream,' remember?" Snow thought of the carvings in their cell.

"We are the sleepers." Her mother took a deep breath. "But now it is time for us to wake. Are you ready?"

Snow's throat felt dry. Who knew what they would find on the other side of those gates? The Red Enchantress? The clawed guards? A way home? She licked her lips. "I'm ready."

Her mother nodded and pushed each of the sleeping figures as though they were buttons, tracing a clockwise circle around the carving. Then, she placed both hands on the twisted knot of carved thorns that stuck out from the center. She spread her fingers wide and leaned her weight against the door. There was a great whooshing sound, and a crack of flickering light broke the darkness of their unnatural sky. Snow squinted against it as they passed through the Ivory Gates into a decrepit castle interior. Snow whirled back to the desert, which she could see through the archway. The mounds of sand melted into a forgotten garden of dry grass and scraggly weeds. As the illusion disappeared, the red landscape became clear. Beyond the garden the land dropped off out of sight, and across the gap, a dense forest grew.

Snow's mother didn't waste any time. "Stay close and keep quiet," she ordered the madman as she closed the Ivory Gates, shutting out the forest and leaving the trio alone inside the castle. "That goes for you too, Snow," she whispered. "If I'm to get us out of here in one piece, I need you to obey without question."

Obey? Snow's temper flared. "Why don't you just enchant me?" she said. "You seem so good at it."

Her mother arched an eyebrow. "I will if I have to," she said, which made Snow swallow more angry words, but she still glared at her mother's back as she followed her out of the empty room and into a crumbling corridor. As they crept down abandoned hallways, Snow wondered why the Red Enchantress had even bothered with an illusion in the first place. The actual castle was almost worse than the empty desert. It looked like no one had lived here in ages. The stones underfoot felt as though they would crumble into dust, and the same decaying smell of mildew that had filled their cell permeated the air.

Snow didn't know how her mother decided which way to go, or if she was just as lost as Snow felt. At the doorway to the next room, Snow's scalp prickled, and she stopped. The musty odor was stronger there, making her gag. Snow covered her mouth with her elbow and tried to calm her roiling stomach. When her mother noticed, she spun around, hooked Snow by the elbow, and dragged her forward, one finger up to her lips to command silence. The madman was pulling at Snow's mother's dress, whimpering and trying to tug them back the way they had come. But with one well-placed whisper, her mother drew him after her.

A few steps in, they passed a low table, shrouded in darkness. Snow could make out the shape in the center. She would have to be a fool to mistake it for anything other than a dead body. Cocooned in some gauzy substance, the arms and legs were wrapped tight like a mummy's, and the slender shape looked as though it was waiting for something. Her mother's sharp yank on her sleeve made her realize she had stopped moving again. She allowed herself to be pulled forward, past several more of the awful coffin-tables, until they reached another door.

After that room, the madman didn't bother to

contain his whimpering. Every sniffle wound Snow up tighter. She didn't know how much longer before she'd explode. They had already gone up two staircases, and it was at the corner landing of the third flight of stairs that they heard the voices. Her mother froze, one hand extended behind her in warning. Not that Snow needed it. She grabbed the madman around the neck, clasping a firm hand over his mouth. If her mother's enchantment couldn't stop his mewling, Snow would.

The voices were growing louder now, and Snow froze when she recognized one of them. "We will celebrate tonight," the Red Enchantress said. She sounded happy. "Heart's Place has fallen. This so-called Resistance will crumble, and the characters of Story will welcome your rule, Fidelus."

"There will be time for feasting later." The words were ordinary enough, but the gravelly sound of Fidelus's voice made Snow's mouth go dry. "After we find the last Element."

The footsteps stopped. "You worry too much." The Enchantress's voice sounded coy. The hall grew quiet, and Snow tightened her grip on the madman. He had stopped squirming. In the silence, Snow was sure her breathing would give her away. She heard the whisper of words. A giggle. Snow thought she knew what they were doing. Her cheeks flamed. More kissing.

"Later, my Duessa." The man's voice again, but there was no laughter in it. "Any word of the Scroll of Fire?"

Snow's mother's spine stiffened, and for her, it was as good as a gasp.

"None of the Taleless can say. All the Villains who once knew the Warlock say he never found the Scroll," Duessa said. "We did discover his grave, though." She was very close to the staircase now, and Snow shut her eyes tight, hoping against hope that the Red Enchantress and her lover were headed anywhere but down the stairs.

"Did he have a family?" The man asked as the pair drew even closer. Snow felt like crying. All she could think of was the sound of her mother's scream when the hooded guards had begun to torture her. The footsteps were right around the corner. Snow could feel the wind of their passing as they continued on down the hall.

"They died long ago," the Red Enchantress said. "Don't worry, my love. We will find the Warlock's Apprentice. And we will find the Scroll." She gave a low chuckle. "I can be very persuasive. All will be well."

"Yes. It will be well," the man said. "After we rewrite Story."

All of a sudden, the madman began thrashing in her arms, and it was all Snow could do to keep hold of him. Her mother whispered something in his ear, but even the charm of her words couldn't overcome his distress. He screwed up his eyes and whipped his head from side to side. The next moment, Snow's mother made the same movement she had in the desert, and the man went limp and silent. Snow held her breath. Had he given them away?

"Take me to the Tale Master," Fidelus was saying, "so I can question the newest Taleless." Snow let out the breath she had been holding.

The Red Enchantress's laugh was low. "When they see you . . ." Her words were drowned out by the sound of a door closing. Snow's mother waited a few heartbeats, then she crept up to the top step. Snow followed, tugging the limp form of the madman with her, and peered over her mother's shoulder. They were alone.

Snow's mother stared at the pair of black doors at

the end of the hall and seemed to come to some sort of conclusion. "We'll come back for him"—she nodded toward the old man—"but you must follow me now. Silently." Snow didn't like the sound of that. She liked it even less when her mother led her the way the Red Enchantress had gone, but Snow knew better than to make a sound.

The hallway on the other side of the black doors was just as desolate as the ones they had been through earlier. There were fewer windows here, and the handful of sconces in use did little to brighten the way. Snow was about to risk it and tell her mother they should be going in the opposite direction, but then she heard the sound of people talking. The Red Enchantress and her companion had joined another, and Snow had no trouble recognizing his voice. *Tale Master Elton.*

Whenever someone spoke, Snow and her mother inched forward a few quiet steps. They didn't dare do more. Not with the stone floors and not with their enemies so close. Finally, they reached an archway and, after a few moments of silent gesturing, situated themselves at an angle from which they could peer into the room without being seen. The Red Enchantress stood at the opposite end of a large space. Elton knelt on the floor at her feet, and the man who must be Fidelus circled around them, his form a mass of shadows that kept shifting in and out of view.

"Someone in Story is telling tales," Fidelus said as he scanned a piece of parchment. "They are writing about your broken oaths and the lies Tale Master Archimago told them."

Elton sighed heavily. "My office has been mobbed with questions about the Muses' oaths. Now the characters will want proof that what I say is true."

"Nonsense. The characters won't have time for questions, once we write Story's End." The man tore the paper in two and handed both halves to Elton. "I am nearly ready, but you must complete the second phase immediately."

"*I* must?" Elton looked as though someone had slapped him across the face. "But it is you who—"

"Don't be a fool," the man said. He lifted his index finger, and the strips of paper burst into flames.

Elton dropped them with a whimper.

The Red Enchantress began a low laugh. "You want to be their savior, don't you?" she asked. She drew Elton to his feet and pointed at something out of Snow's view. "Don't you remember how it was after the first Unbinding? They adored Archimago. Made him their Hero. When we save them from Story's End, who will they look to next?"

"You never said I'd have to slaughter characters." Elton shook his head. "You didn't tell me the Taleless would destroy Heart's Place."

"Let the Taleless do as they will," Duessa said. "The more trouble they cause, the better. When the Taleless come for them, the terrified characters will flock to King Fidelus."

"Frighten them; yes, I can do that." Elton shook a strand of greasy hair out of one eye. "But must the Taleless kill them?"

"Oh, come now, Elton. Don't be squeamish." Fidelus's laugh sounded like steel scraping over stone. "Are your hands not already red with spilled blood?" He grabbed Elton firmly by the chin, and squeezed his cheeks hard so that he couldn't look away. "You belong to me, and you will do as I say. Send the Taleless to the Ranch, so that we can squash this insufferable rebellion once and for all." He pushed Elton's face away with a sound of disgust. "But first. How many Tales do we have today?"

"Ten, my lord," Elton said, his words nearly a

whisper. "The number of Taleless we have already ripped out is many. And that's not counting the others who now roam our lands." He licked his lips. "The laws of Story say—"

"Curse the laws of Story." Fidelus's voice was hard as broken ice. "Do you think I care about any of it?" He thrust out a hand, and a stream of black fire shot through the air and scorched the stone wall next to him. "That is what comes of the laws of this Story. Do not think to question me. You are the only WI left." He snapped his fingers. "You must work harder."

Elton licked his lips. "But I'm also Tale Master." He wiped his forearm across his brow. "And with the destruction of Heart's Place and all the questions, I am doing the best—" The sound of glass shattering on stone cut him off.

"Enough!" Fidelus's anger sliced the air. "One Villain still lives who knows where Amaranth hid the Scroll. Find me the Warlock's Apprentice, or I'll give you to the Taleless and be done with you."

Elton looked from Fidelus to the Red Enchantress.

"Have you brought the book?" the Red Enchantress asked.

Elton nodded and drew out a tiny book from his

coat pocket. The binding glimmered in the darkness of the room. He laid a piece of paper atop the glittering book and examined it closely. Snow could see his hands shake.

"Now. Perhaps we will find the Apprentice today," Fidelus said in an eerily calm voice. "My sources tell me the Warlock was a regular visitor to the Villain in this Tale. Rip it open."

"Yes, milord." Elton pulled a white cloth from his pocket and blotted his forehead. He opened the book, and a faint glow shone around him, much like the light Snow remembered from entering the examinations. Elton began to read from the book aloud, but it was some strange language, and Snow couldn't understand the words.

There was a resounding crash, and the room filled with a blinding glare. Snow covered her ears, but she couldn't block out the echoing sound. Her eardrums throbbed with the ringing. When she could stand 'it, she looked up. A shimmering sphere hung in the air in front of Elton, who clutched the book to his chest.

Fidelus sighed with delight. "Excellent, Elton. Excellent." He ran a finger across the smooth circumference. Then he brought his hand back, and gave a loud cry as he smashed his fist into the circle's center. The luminous surface shattered into a shower of pieces, leaving a ragged, gaping hole. Tendrils of silvery mist seeped over the edges, trickling down to the floor.

Snow could see Fidelus's countenance now. His profile was striking: a strong face, a high brow that sloped to a straight nose. Angled cheeks and a chin that looked unnervingly familiar. The face creased into a smile. He pulled hard and drew out a misty shape that slowly came together into a silhouette.

"Hello, there," Fidelus said. "Who do we have here?"

The mist solidified into the shape of a woman, who, if not for the glowing light, might have looked like any ordinary character. But Snow's mouth went dry with horror. She knew with certainty what the man was doing. Elton was right. It went against all the laws of Story. Fidelus wasn't just ripping open already bound Tales. He was ripping characters out of them.

"I am Morgana," the Taleless said in a haughty voice. "And *who*, may I ask, are you?"

"Well met, Morgana." Fidelus laughed, a low, rough sound that grew louder. "We will find you a woman's body, but first you must tell me why the Warlock of Amaranth was a frequent guest in your castle." He turned toward a low bench under a window, the shade drifting along beside him.

The Red Enchantress hissed in her breath. "Someone is coming through the forest," she breathed as she stared off into the distance. "It must be Jaga. I should've killed her the last time she brought me fake quills." She glanced over to where Fidelus and Morgana sat. "You'll have to continue without me. That stupid hag has unlocked the enchanted door."

Snow's mother jerked hard on her elbow. "We've seen enough," she whispered, and then she jolted into action. With the next breath they were through the black doors and back at the sleeping madman's side. Her mother touched his face and woke him with a word. Pressing one hand on his spine, she propelled him along in front of them. "Hurry!"

Snow picked up her skirts and ran after her mother. Her own fear at what she had just seen was magnified by the wild-eyed looks her mother was casting back over her shoulder. *Who was this Fidelus?* "They're ripping open Tales?" Snow gasped as her mother paused at the place where two hallways met and quickly led them down the smaller one.

"No time for questions," her mother said sharply. "I told you to obey. Do you want to get us all killed?"

Whatever anger Snow might have felt was swept away by the fear in her mother's voice. The only other time Snow had seen her mother look this afraid was when the Red Enchantress was about to torture her.

A great clanging sound jolted through Snow, and she nearly screamed. Her mother, too, was frozen in her tracks.

When Snow could find her voice again, she gasped out, "That's the sound. I heard it before, when I arrived. We must be close."

They raced toward the noise, sprinting through one huge room where a skeletal throne towered over them, leering skulls perched in a row atop it. And then they were out. An open courtyard stretched off to a portcullis that led to freedom. The grating sound came from an ancient drawbridge, which they saw was even now being raised, inch by mechanical inch. Two misshapen men stood at the wheel, pushing with all their weight to bring up the heavy gate. They were so engrossed in their task, Snow's mother was on them before they saw her.

A twist of her mother's wrist, and the men crumpled

to the ground. The bridge clattered down with a thud. Her mother went first, then the madman, and finally Snow, as they all raced out of the castle and into the blackness of the night.

Chapter 9

*P*eter leaned against the building wall. He had never been so embarrassed in his life. After Una had danced off with some stranger—how could she *be* so foolish?—an Evil Stepsister had snatched him up, and he had spent the last half hour with Esmerelda, who stomped on his feet and prattled on about what a good partner he was. He had been lucky to get away from her, and now he would be happy to never dance again. Peter was rubbing an aching foot when he heard a familiar voice.

"Nice dancing." Indy did a bad job of stifling his laughter. "Oh wait, is that your partner coming this way?"

Peter whirled around so fast he felt dizzy. The last thing he wanted was for Esmerelda to trap him again, and then he saw that Indy was making fun of him. "Go ahead and laugh," Peter said with a scowl. "Where's Una, anyway? This was her dumb idea to begin with."

"I haven't seen her since she left," Indy said. "Unless she had such an *interested*"—Peter didn't like how he emphasized that word—"partner like you did, I bet she's already on her way back to Bramble Cottage. Did you learn anything from your new friend?"

Peter felt his face flush hot. He had been so desperate to get away from Esmerelda, he hadn't thought to ask her about any castles. Or cemeteries. "Nope," he said. "What about you?"

"No one I talked to knew about Jaga's cemetery," Indy said. "But the Enchanted Forest is apparently filled with castles; fat lot of good that is."

Peter sighed. The Enchanted Forest ran along the east side of the Hollow and stretched for miles. It had a reputation worse than the Hollow, and no reputable character roamed freely there, certainly not at midnight.

"I wouldn't mind asking a few more people, though"—Indy nodded toward the lit building in front of them—"if it meant we could get something to eat. I'm starving."

They pushed their way into the common room,

where a young bard was sitting by the fire playing a song. Indy stopped short in front of a crew of unsavory characters. They were crowded around a masked man.

"That's the guy who danced with Una," Indy said.

Peter and Indy were trying to decide what to do next, when the man gave them a friendly little wave. The next moment, the rogue himself was next to them, ushering them to a table, scraping up additional chairs, and gesturing to the innkeeper for more food.

Peter took the chair to the left of the man. Indy pulled his sword from the scabbard on his back, sat down on the right, and laid the blade flat across his knees.

The masked man glanced down at the blade, but instead of looking threatened, he merely gave Indy an encouraging smile. "You can call me Kai," he said as the innkeeper served them. "You're Una's friends, aren't you?"

Peter and Indy exchanged glances. "Is Una still here?" Peter asked at the same time as Indy said, "Where's the nearest cemetery?"

Kai smiled lazily at them. "You young people and your cemeteries. Una left for home not long ago, and I imagine she's arriving there as we speak."

Kai answered all of their questions, but not in a very satisfactory way. Peter had the distinct impression he wasn't taking them seriously, that he thought cemeteries and castles were a big joke. Yes, Kai knew of many castles around the Hollow, but none very nice to visit. Yes, of course, there were cemeteries in the Hollow, and some of them were lovely to visit. No, Una hadn't seemed in any trouble when she left, but he rather thought she was a capable girl. She might have said something about a place called Bramble Cottage. And he had asked her to dance because she wanted to dance. He shoveled in a heaping mouthful of stew after he said all this, and Peter found he had run out of questions. It seemed that Una was long gone, probably already tucked up in Trix's kitchen.

Kai called the bard over, and the other Villains were soon bickering about which song should be performed next. A sorcerer asked Kai something about the tune he had used to fiddle his way past the ogre at Falls Landing. The innkeeper was listening intently, and a group of curious onlookers had gathered around their table. Whatever Peter thought of Kai, the Hollow folk clearly worshipped him.

Indy leaned in close and whispered to Peter, "I

think we should tell Kai."

"Tell Kai what?" Peter asked.

"About the Enemy." Indy was leaning in so close that Peter could see the firelight reflected in his dark eyes.

"You think he'll believe it?" Peter asked.

"I think he'll more than believe it," Indy said. "I think he'll help us.

When the bard began his next song, Peter saw his opportunity. "Kai"—he beckoned the man closer—"we have something important to tell you."

"You are serious for one so young." Kai steepled his fingers and looked at Peter over them. "Don't worry about Una." He tapped his thumbs together. "She seemed ready for an adventure."

"It's not about Una or about having adventures." Indy bent forward across the table. "It's about finding the right adventure." Indy shot Peter a look as he dropped his voice to a whisper. "Did you know that Story has a great Enemy? And that this Enemy is even now plotting Story's ruin?"

"Is that so?" Kai gave a low whistle, and leaned back in his chair.

Indy told Kai about the Enemy's return, then handed

him a folded-up broadside from his pocket.

When Kai had finished reading, he looked up.

"We think he's looking for the Lost Elements." Peter explained what they had discovered so far.

"And how do you plan to stop him, lads?" He pricked a finger on Indy's sword point. "Run him through with that?" He wiped the drop of blood off with his thumb. "You boys are serious enough to try it, I'd wager."

Peter didn't like the way Kai's words sounded like he was laughing at them. The Enemy was no laughing matter. "And what about you, Kai? Are you serious enough to do anything?" Peter swept a hand out over the table of overfed Villains. "Will you stay here feasting or will you help us?"

Kai threw back his head and laughed. "I'd like nothing better." One minute he looked like a cat drowsing by the fire; the next he was up, cloaked, bow and arrows strapped on, and traveling sack slung over one shoulder. He offered a hand to Peter. "But only so long as helping you means an interesting adventure for me."

Peter didn't see how he could promise Kai that, but he got to his feet anyway. Indy slid his sword back into its sheath and stood.

"Do you think I could pass for a lad?" Kai interrupted the two women at the next table. "Without this, of course." He swept the feathered hat off his head and tucked it under his arm. He slid the black mask off, and rubbed at the skin around his eyes.

"You can pass for whatever you want to, Kai," the witch said, and grinned at the pretty enchantress sitting next to her.

Kai bent low and whispered something to the enchantress, who looked up at Peter and blew him a kiss. Peter felt the heat on his face until Kai's bony elbow in his ribs drove it from him. Without the disguise, Kai did look remarkably young. His nut-brown skin had a few fine lines, but he was the same height and build as Indy.

"It's very late," Peter said as he pushed the front door open and led the way into the night. "Maybe we should go home and sleep first."

"I believe that you promised me an adventure." Kai tossed his hat up into the air. "And by *adventure*, I mean something interesting. Stirring things up among those boring old Talekeeper farts for starters." He caught the hat and swooped it back onto his head. "I hear the Tale Master himself is making a big announcement in the morning. Do you have any more of those papers?"

Peter hesitated and then did the unthinkable. "What do you say?" he asked Indy. "Should we make sure Una got home okay?"

"Una's not a foolish girl. And she doesn't always need a hero." Indy looked between Kai and Peter. "If Elton's giving a big speech, it's the perfect place to hand out the broadsides."

Peter scowled. He knew he shouldn't have asked for Indy's advice.

"Aw, don't worry about your friend," Kai said, spreading his arms out wide. "The girl will be fine. She's a smart lass, and she could dance well enough. Besides, she won't have much of a Tale if we don't leave her to sort it all out herself, will she?"

Peter didn't waste much time deliberating. Once Una arrived at Bramble Cottage, she would tell the Resistance members about the Lost Elements, and the grown-ups would take charge. When she discovered he had been out this late, Peter's mother would have him scrubbing the whole house for sure. No more helping the Resistance. No more looking for Elements. No more adventure. Peter tightened his belt, checked that his sword was strapped properly, and hurried to catch up to Kai and Indy.

Chapter 10

The cemetery gate moved on protesting hinges, but Una finally wedged it open enough to squeeze through. Una had always liked cemeteries. She had spent hours drifting between churchyard stones, reading the inscriptions and wondering about the forgotten histories of those buried under them.

But this graveyard was not meant for wandering. The brick wall enclosed a square plot that had been overtaken by a shiny purplish plant covering everything but the tombstones. The black onyx markers seemed to suck in what little light the night offered, and, even though the moon was nearly full, it was very dark behind the cemetery walls. Una reached into her cloak and pulled out Jaga's key.

She could have found Peter and Indy first, but Kai's

comment had got her thinking. Sure, it was dangerous, but that wasn't any reason not to go. Besides, if
she found out something important, maybe she would
also find the courage to tell them all what she had done
back in Alethia's garden. And she needed some time
alone before she'd be ready to do that.

Una followed the crumbling brick wall. Where was
the door? Jaga's key hadn't fit in the iron gate, so unless
Kai was wrong, there was another door. Someone
had erected a sinister-looking angel over a cobwebby
vault. Una gave it a wide berth, and that was when she
found it.

The marker looked like a pile of tottering stones,
barely anything worth stopping for, but Una felt a
quickening inside that she couldn't ignore. Besides,
the key was growing hot in her hands, heat radiating
through her palm, as though it knew it was close to
where it belonged. She walked around the stone cairn
and stopped.

Creeping ivy had covered most of the door, making
it nearly unrecognizable from the bricks that surrounded it. Una bent closer, brushing the foliage out
of the way with the tip of her dagger. There seemed to
be carvings on the door, made out of some yellowed

stone, but it was too dark for Una to make them out. The key slid into an ancient-looking hole with a click, and Una gave it a fierce twist. The door opened a crack, and a gust of dry wind whirled around her. Una gritted her teeth as she pushed hard on the door with her shoulder and made her way through. The wind was stronger now, and it plastered Una's hair to her forehead. She was in a tunnel of some sort, and pale, silvery moonlight filtered through the branches that covered the tunnel's exit. Once Una passed through them, she found herself on a path that zigzagged up a steep hill. Over the top, a long walk away, she could see the outline of a lone turret.

This is it. It had to be Duessa's castle. Una was in enemy territory now, and she wouldn't leave until she had discovered the Enemy's plans. *My father's plans.*

Tangled vines grew thicker here, and the path soon disappeared, but Una kept walking in the general direction of the castle. The way was steep, and soon Una's muscles burned with the continual effort of climbing. From somewhere up ahead, the sound of rushing water grew louder, and Una guessed there might be a river close by.

She angled left, but she hadn't gone very far before

she heard the sound of movement in the undergrowth. Someone was coming. She ducked behind the shelter of an old willow and peered out from the veil of brittle leaves. A red-cloaked figure moved silently through the forest. *The Red Enchantress.* Una stood motionless as she watched Duessa. *My mother.* Soon, she was nearly out of sight, a muted spot of color in the black and gray of the woods.

Una hesitated for only a moment before tiptoeing after Duessa's retreating form. This was what she had come for, after all. The Enchantress's red robes swirled around her as she made her way over the twisted foliage. Una blinked back unexpected tears. The closer she got to Duessa, the more she wanted to meet her mother. She pictured her eyes, the moment their hands had touched in Alethia's garden.

Una stopped behind a thick tree and peered out. Her throat felt tight. What would she say if circumstances had been different? If her mother had been someone like Mrs. Merriweather? *Hello, Mother.* The words felt foreign, like reading aloud a name she didn't quite know how to pronounce.

The red cloak was in a constant state of movement, the fabric rippling behind Duessa as she walked. Una was careful to stay out of sight, to move only when Duessa moved, to creep along from tree to tree. Which was why she wasn't prepared when Duessa whirled around and pointed her raised arms at the spot where Una was hiding.

"Show yourself," Duessa commanded.

Chapter 11

A branch slapped across Snow's cheek, but she couldn't slow down. Her mother was setting a fast pace, despite her wounded feet, and the madman stumbled next to her, pointing the way through the thick underbrush. The Red Enchantress's castle was situated at the top of a hill, and the first route they had taken had led to the edge of a scorched field. "Too open," her mother had said as they retraced their steps. The ground they now traveled angled down toward a densely wooded valley. Snow supposed there might have been a view to her left, where the land dropped off, but the mist and the blackness of the night made it impossible to see very far into the distance.

"Is this the way home?" Snow asked her mother as they came to the edge of the forest.

"No," her mother said absently as she scanned the woods. "We have to go somewhere else first."

"What?" Snow stopped running. "What can be more important than getting out of here and going somewhere safe?"

The madman was hopping up and down on one foot, muttering something about a dog sailing on the ocean.

"Finding the Enchanted Swamp," Snow's mother said. "It's not very far from here."

"No way," Snow said to her mother's back. "Why in the world would we go there?" Snow had never been to the Swamp, and she would be fine with it staying that way.

"There's something we need to get," her mother said in a weary voice. She looked at Snow over the top of the madman's head. "Something Fidelus and Duessa want."

At first Snow thought she meant the Taleless, but then she realized what her mother was talking about. "You mean the Scroll of—"

"Not now, Snow," her mother said, eyeing the madman, whose sailor dog was now eating oranges.

"Seriously?" Snow asked. "You're worried about *him*?"

"People aren't always what they appear to be." Her mother seemed to have decided on a path. "Let's just say, the less we speak, the better, hmmm?"

"Okay," Snow said as she followed her into the darkness of the forest. "But how do you know about"—she paused—"*the thing* everyone's looking for?"

The madman twisted hard and took two steps away from them.

"I said *not now*," Snow's mother said through clenched teeth as she caught him in an iron grip.

The madman began to beg, assaulting her with so much flattery that Snow found herself laughing in spite of Duessa's castle towering on the hill behind them. She had never heard anyone call her mother a "lovely little flower" before. When he realized that wouldn't work, he began to threaten her.

"Milady will kill you, see if she doesn't." He squinted at Snow. "Start with your girl first, perhaps." His mouth twisted down at the corners. "Hot steel can burn more places than just feet."

"Maybe you can instruct me in the technique," her mother said with the tiniest of smiles. "When I begin to work on you." She wrapped her hand around his neck and gave it a slight squeeze.

Snow knew her mother had been missing for thirteen years, that she had lived in the Enchanted Forest and learned whatever it was that qualified her to be the Villainy professor at Perrault. But Snow had always thought the biggest mystery about her was why she had abandoned her infant daughter. Snow had been wrong. There was a lot she didn't know about her mother, and, for the first time, Snow felt she might be okay with that. The only thing worse than being captured by the bad guys would be to discover that you were actually on the side of the bad guys.

"Don't." Snow didn't want to see her mother choke anyone, even the crazy old man.

Her mother stopped and let the madman squat down on the rocky terrain. His forehead was beaded with sweat, and he was wild eyed. "Don't hurt me. Please don't hurt me." He darted glances in several directions as though enemies surrounded them. "I know things. Things that will help you."

Her mother circled behind the man's cowering form as she spoke. "You have told us nothing." She stopped in front of him and used one finger to tilt his chin up so she could examine his neck, as though he were an animal she was about to slaughter. "You live only because you may prove useful." She ran the back of her hand gently across his neck, and the man whimpered. "You will not try to run away again."

"Stop it!" Snow was surprised to hear her own voice sound so strong. "He's doing what you said. He's coming with us. Why do you have to keep torturing him?"

Her mother released the man and eyed Snow speculatively. "You pity him." The madman looked up at Snow with hopeful eyes and gave her a grin. Shiny threads of spittle stretched from the corners of his mouth. It was disgusting.

"Don't be foolish, Snow," she hissed. "You do not know who we are dealing with." Her mother leaned in close and whispered in Snow's ear. "You think I am enjoying this? That I like to see another creature's fear?" She sounded like a different woman. "Do you think so little of me, Snow?"

When Snow didn't answer, her mother shook her head slowly. Her voice grew hard. "It doesn't matter. This madman, pitiable though he may be, dangerous though he certainly is, has lived for a long time in Duessa's lands. What he knows of the Enchanted Forest may mean the difference for us between life and death."

"But your enchanted voice. He'll do what you say without you threatening him."

Her mother laughed. "We shall see if he is"—she patted the man's head—"willing to cooperate."

The madman seemed to think Snow was the one more likely to help him. "You're a good girl, I can tell you are." He wiggled in her mother's grasp. "She's hurting me. Help a poor man, won't you?"

"Leave my daughter alone." Her mother's voice was steel. Snow felt a warm flush come over her. She had never heard her mother say those words before. "No more games," her mother said in that same hard voice. "I can free you from Duessa's enchantment."

The man stopped wiggling.

"If you tell us the truth," Snow's mother said.

The old man's tongue darted out over his lips. "How do I know you will keep your word? How do I know you won't betray me to *him*?" He rolled his eyes toward the trees. A sour smell filled the air, and Snow stepped back. The man had wet himself.

"Listen well, old man." Her mother reached forward and grabbed his shirtfront. "Trust me or not; it's your choice. I give you my word in truth: If I betray you to Fidelus, let death come for me. And if you lie, it will go ill with you. Let Story witness our oath."

The man's eyes were open too wide, his expression like that of a fey animal. "You know the old ways," he said.

"Do you agree?"

The man was very still for a moment. Snow didn't understand what exactly was happening, but it seemed to be more than a simple promise. She hoped with all her heart that her mother knew what she was doing.

The old man's voice was soft when he answered. "So be it."

Snow wasn't sure what she expected. Another spell, perhaps. Or some outward sign of the solemn vow the pair had just taken. But there was nothing. Just the same unending forest and the rasping sound of the man's breathing. Snow's mother's face was pale, and the half-moons under her eyes had deepened into purple. Her voice cut through the silence. "Now tell me truly. Who are you?"

The old man sat up. The film was gone from his eyes, and he had stopped trembling. "My name," he said, and even his voice sounded different, "is Archimago Mores."

★ ★ ★

After Archimago had told them what he had done as the old Tale Master, her mother had walked in silence for some time. Snow wished she would say something. She couldn't believe the story Archimago had spun. The discovery that all she knew about the Unbinding was a lie. The knowledge that Fidelus had betrayed Story back then and was planning to do so again. The upending of everything Snow had ever thought about the Muses. *The Muses!* Despite her exertion, she felt chilled at the thought of it.

Her mother had seemed unsurprised when Archimago described how he and the Red Enchantress had lied to all of Story.

"Does Fidelus really have the Silver Quill and the Dragon's Ink?" her mother asked, but Archimago didn't know the answer and had no memory of the conversation they had overheard in the castle. The old man seemed confused about the time. He remembered nothing of their journey or the prison and kept talking about the Unbinding as though it had just occurred.

"We need to recirculate the old Tales," he said. "It was wrong of me to lock them away. Once the characters read what the Muses actually wrote, they'll trust them again." Explaining to him that more than fifty years had passed and that Duessa and Fidelus had succeeded in defeating the other Muses shook his new-found clarity of thought.

"What do you know about WIs and their power to rip open Tales?" Snow's mother asked.

"The Muses should have never brought WIs from the Readers' World into Story." Archimago shook his head and ducked under a low branch. "Even the WIs who remained loyal to the Muses were not smart or careful enough to wield the power that would rewrite a bound Tale."

"Is that what Elton was doing?" Snow interrupted. "Rewriting Tales?" The fact that WIs could rip open a bound Tale was shocking enough. Snow had been taught little of WIs or any of the things from before the Unbinding, but she had thought that no one in Story could change a Tale—until now.

"It's possible." Snow's mother was looking at Archimago thoughtfully. "Ripping characters out of Tales would change the entire plot and influence all the other characters in the Tale. The repercussions are endless. Which is one of the reasons it is forbidden."

A cunning smile appeared on Archimago's face. "You are very clever, milady. Rewriting a Tale would be a powerful feat indeed, would it not?"

"And one that threatens the very fabric of Story," Snow's mother said coolly.

"Quite true. Quite true," Archimago said, nodding his head. "Rewriting. Editing. Erasing. Powers best left to the capable. And not all of the WIs are capable. The newest one is a complete idiot." Archimago pushed a clump of stringy hair off his face. "He has no idea how to assist the Muses. In fact, he was such a little boy when he first was Written In that he could barely write a word. Fidelus is training the WI himself; oh, what is his name?" But the detail escaped him, and the only other thing he could tell them was that Fidelus had killed all the other known WIs one day in a forest. No matter how else Snow's mother phrased the questions, he had no more information to give.

They didn't say much after this, only stopping once for a brief rest. Little sleep and no food did not make hiking through a forest, let alone a densely overgrown one, easy.

Snow had a brief reprieve when they came to a quick-flowing river that cut across the path. Archimago thought there was a stone bridge, but he was having trouble finding exactly where.

"Is he telling the truth?" Snow asked her mother after the old man disappeared through a thicket of brambles.

"I believe that what he is saying is true," her mother said in a weary voice, "but I don't think he is telling us everything."

"That's not what I asked," Snow said.

"I'm not sure he even knows what truth means anymore." Her mother flexed one foot gingerly. "His memory of things before his enchantment is probably reliable. Everything after that will be incomplete, like reading one page out of a Tale." She eased her foot back to the ground and worked the muscles in the other. "But you mustn't forget, Snow. Archimago was once a leader in Story. Just because he is old and frail now doesn't mean he isn't as wily as a fox."

"Do you think Archimago knows what"—Snow dropped her voice to a whisper—"*he'll* do now that he's free?"

Her mother frowned. "You mean Fidelus? Most likely he'll do whatever he was planning to do before the Unbinding." She waved Archimago over as the man stumbled back into view. "Which is why Archimago's old memories are more valuable than I could have dreamed."

"This way," the man said. "It's still there." Snow squinted at the man's dirty face as he led the way over the stone bridge. He looked nothing like the statue in the Tale station. He had no resemblance to the hero she had heard described in Backstory class. Now that he wasn't perpetually stooped over, Snow could see that the man was tall, but he was so thin that he looked frail despite his height. Snow thought she could probably knock him off into the river with one good shove. And it would only be what he deserved. Archimago had lied about everything. And all in the name of his love for his Red Enchantress.

"We're close now." Her mother's voice was muffled by the sound of the water. "I recognize this place." They passed through a clearing where three giant stone boulders leaned against each other, forming a crooked archway. Archimago looked back toward Duessa's castle, a pained expression on his face.

"You can feel her pulling you." Snow's mother wasn't asking a question.

Archimago rubbed his grimy sleeve across his forehead. "She is a strong woman."

"She is an Enchantress."

The Tale Master closed his eyes, and with what

looked like a great deal of effort, turned away from the forest behind him. "She is my true love," he whispered.

Snow wished she had pushed him into the river when she had the chance. "How can you pretend that makes any difference? Loving her is no excuse." Snow felt hollow inside. "Because of you, people died."

Her mother laid a quieting hand on Snow's shoulder. "People do all sorts of foolish things for love."

"The girl speaks truly." Archimago looked at Snow with red-rimmed eyes. "But she's also never been in love." His voice was bitter. "Duessa stole my heart, and then used me up. And yet I would do anything to win her favor."

"Take courage." Snow's mother said. "If you wish it, you will yet live free."

"Some freedom that would be." Archimago's laugh was forced. "I know what I've done." He threw a hand out toward Snow. "She's right. I'm responsible for so much destruction. Many deaths." He covered his face with his hands. "And even after all of that, I still want her." His voice broke. "It would be better if I was dead."

"Death is never better than life." Snow's mother gently pulled his hands away from his face and looked into his eyes. "And the restoration of things is best of all.

Don't give up hope. You may yet make things right."

Archimago didn't have a chance to answer, because once they were farther from the sound of the river, they heard voices. Two cloaked forms were standing some distance away. The taller figure's back was to them, one arm extended toward the girl opposite. For a heartbeat, Snow thought she recognized the girl's face. *But that's silly.* Una wouldn't be wandering through the Enchanted Forest. She was no doubt snug in their room in Grimm Dorm. Then, the other face came into view, and any thought of Una flew from Snow's mind. *The Red Enchantress.*

Archimago whispered a pained, "Duessa!"

Quick as a flash, Snow's mother yanked them both off the path and into the thick undergrowth. They raced through the woods, any pretense of silence gone, hoping only for speed. The trees were older here, looming up to the dark canopy.

Snow hadn't noticed when it began, but a misty fog appeared at her feet and snaked through the surrounding undergrowth. The air was wet on her throat, and she knew she would have to stop and rest soon.

The fog was rising, and Snow felt like she was running through webs of smoke. She found an extra spurt of strength and barreled forward after her mother's form. As she reached the top of the path, a thick cloud wrapped around them both. But this wasn't smoke at all. Snow struggled vainly to free herself. Every move she made bound her fast. No matter which way she pulled, no matter how she kicked and fought, she knew they were stuck, wrapped tight in a stringy white web.

Chapter 12

Una stood only an arm's reach away from Duessa. Time seemed to slow. She could hear the distant rush of a river and the crash of scurrying creatures in the underbrush. Mixed in with the panicked thought that she had been caught was a desperate desire to please the owner of the voice. She had to say something. Had to give the Enchantress some reason she had sneaked through her secret door. Which was when Una remembered the old woman and what she had given her. "Um," Una managed. "Are you Duessa?" She pulled out the painted quill she had hidden in her cloak and thrust it toward her mother. "I've brought this for you. From Jaga."

Unreadable emotion flickered across the Enchantress's face. Una stared at her features. Her mother had the same pale skin and violet-colored eyes as Una, though Duessa's were a different shape, more catlike. Her long, dark hair fell back in waves from the pointed peak at the top of her forehead. Her very red lips were pinched together as she considered Una.

Una wished she hadn't listened to Kai. This had been a bad idea. She should be back at Bramble Cottage. Duessa didn't care who Una was. She didn't know that her own daughter stood in front of her. A spell would shoot from her hands and destroy Una before she could explain. She gripped the dagger she held in the folds of her skirt.

There was a calculating look in Duessa's eyes. "This isn't the Silver Quill, as you well know." Duessa dropped the quill to the ground. "What is your name, girl?"

Una's mouth opened before she could stop herself, and the words tripped willingly off her tongue. "I'm Una," she said. "Your daughter."

Duessa stared at her. A tiny smile flickered along Duessa's perfect lips, and her pointed eyebrows arched up. Una saw something strange in her eyes, but the moment passed, and Duessa's whole face softened.

"My daughter?" Her voice was a gentle whisper.

"My Una?" One wet tear trickled down her cheek, as Duessa let her hands fall to her sides. "Come here," she said, and opened her arms wide.

Una could see beyond Duessa, could see faceless figures who hovered under one of the ancient trees, but it all looked so, so far away. Everything around them faded beside the vision of her mother's perfect face. Una wanted her mother to speak to her again, wanted to hear her lovely voice. Una wanted to tell her all her secrets, all the things she'd wished she could tell the mother she'd never had. And underneath the impulse, Una's heart skipped with happiness. Her mother did want her. Her mother *wanted* her. The dagger fell forgotten to the forest floor as she rushed toward Duessa and into her red embrace.

"I've missed you so," Duessa said, in just the way Una had always desired to hear it. "Ever since they took you from me, I've longed for this day."

"Really?" Una asked as her mother patted her on the back.

"I couldn't find you." Duessa released Una and looked into her eyes. "I was all alone. Your father—" Her voice tightened at this, hardened for a moment, and then was soft like liquid again. "I felt mad with grief and despair. I ran through the forest as hard as I could, until I couldn't run anymore. I wanted to scream and shout and reverse time so that I could stand next to him once again." She sounded sad, and she drew the back of one hand up to her eyes. As she looked away, Una could see her profile: straight nose, unlined skin. "I had made you a little nest nearby in the woods." She hooked her arm through Una's and began to walk. "I didn't mean to leave you, dear girl. You were every-thing to me. You were ours, together." Her eyes were earnest, begging Una to understand.

And Una found herself patting her mother's hand and smiling back at her. How lovely it was to know her mother and father loved each other so. Had wanted to be together. Had wanted her. She nodded. "Go on."

"I found the place easily enough—the soft feathers that lined your cradle, the pine branches I had laid care-fully just so. But you were . . . gone." Duessa led Una across a bridge that arched over rushing water. For a fleeting moment, Una had the thought that they were going in the wrong direction, that there was somewhere else she should be heading, that someone was going to be mad she was out this late. But her mother called her name gently, and the nagging feeling evaporated.

"And what happened next?" Una wanted to be able to ask all the questions she'd always wondered. What had she been like as a baby and when had she first started crawling and what were her favorite foods and what did she say that made her mother laugh? The things she had heard other kids recount in those horrible classes where you had to bring pictures and tell everyone about your family. She clasped her hands greedily. "Tell me what it was like, when we were a family."

Her mother took the edge of her sleeve and dabbed her eyes. "It pains me so to talk of it, child. Must you ask so many questions?"

Una bit her lip. Of course she had been thoughtless. She had barged into her mother's private memories to satisfy her curiosity. She had poked at her poor mother's bruised heart. She squeezed her arm. "Oh, I am sorry, Mother." The word felt nice on her tongue. "I don't mean to pry. We don't have to speak of that."

Her mother gave her one of her rare smiles, and Una thought she understood how an immortal had fallen in love with her. Her mother was everything Una had hoped she would be: charming, beautiful, and happy to see her.

"Let's talk about you, dear," her mother said. "Tell me how you came to Story." In front of them, a many-turreted castle perched on the hilltop like some giant bird brooding over her nest. The towering structure glistened wetly in the moonlight, and the path in front of them widened to a road that ran straight toward it.

Una wasn't sure what to say. Wanting to know about her family was one thing; telling her mother things about other people was quite another. Faces flickered through her memory: a boy with dark skin and hair that flopped over one eye sitting across the campfire from her, a furry cat cuddled in her lap contentedly, a friend arguing with her in the middle of the Hollow District. *Peter.* More images flashed before her mind's eye. She was at Bramble Cottage with Peter; he was hovering protectively at her side while they walked by the harbor; he was examining the door of Elton's study, trying to break in; his hands were reaching into the compartment under the floorboards to pull out Archimago's confession—it all came back to her.

This wasn't just her mother before her. This was the Red Enchantress, Duessa. The one who had destroyed all of the Muses' books. The one who had scripted the countless lies about what had happened. The one who had worked tirelessly to bring the Enemy back to Story. And she had used Una to do it.

Una pulled back from her mother in horror. "You made me open the book."

Her mother's laugh was a little trill of affection. "Why, Una, dear. No one can make you do something like that." She looked deep into Una's eyes. "You know I'm right, child, don't you?"

Una's mind went blank. What had made her say such a thing? She had been silly. Her mother was right. Una was the one who had opened the book with her own two hands. She had been curious to know about Father in the same way she had come here finally to meet Mother. She had done it. She alone.

They were almost to the castle now, and a great drawbridge dropped with a thud, spanning the protective moat. Until now, any memory of that moment in the garden had filled Una with guilt, but here with her mother she felt nothing of the sort. In fact, she felt proud. Because of Una, Father was alive. Because of her, he was free again. She did a happy little skip as she followed her mother across the bridge and into the castle.

Chapter 13

$\mathcal{I}$t had only been a few days since Peter had been on campus, but things were already much different. After a short nap in the woods, he, Kai, and Indy had made their way across Perrault's grounds toward the Weaponry Arena, where Elton planned to give a speech later that morning. They heard the sound of the rioting before they saw the crowds mobbing the Talekeeper Club. Characters jostled one another in an attempt to get at the solid front door.

In the quad, things were scarcely more orderly. Angry-looking Moderns had formed a line and were marching up and down demanding Tale Master Elton's resignation. Others sat in a circle around the fountain, shouting, "MIGHT ISN'T RIGHT. WE WON'T FIGHT."

Peter wondered who they had decided they wouldn't fight. A woman dressed as a warrior was standing on a tall wooden platform. "Down with the Muses!" she cried. She pointed at Peter and Indy and waved her sword over her head. "You boys look brave," she called. "Come join the fight of your lives!"

Peter gave the woman several of the broadsides. The Resistance could do with some reinforcements like her.

"You want a fight?" a soldier in a bright-red uniform said. "Join forces with us. We prepare for war." His troop kept marching, long-nosed rifles swinging from their shoulders.

It wasn't unusual to see ninjas going through their forms, but Peter had never seen so many at one time. And he certainly hadn't seen them actually sparring with one another. There was even a group of witches and wizards practicing their offensive spells with their familiars.

"Excellent," Kai said, rubbing his hands together. "The whole air crackles with the energy. With characters getting ready to *do* something."

Some people looked like they were too frightened to do anything. The Dystopians had seen their opportunity, and they paced around the perimeter with their

apocalyptic banners PREPARE FOR THE END and JOIN A
NEW TALE.

Peter felt like dueling the brother who held out a
coffer to them as they passed. The man actually looked
like he was enjoying himself.

Kai and Indy had stopped to talk to a cowgirl wearing chaps, and Peter vaguely recognized her from his
Elocution class. "How do things fare on the Ranch?"
Kai asked as Peter handed her one of the Resistance's
notices.

"We've seen worse," the cowgirl said, squinting up
at them as though it were high noon instead of early
morning. "But a storm's on the horizon. A few scouts
have seen bands of strangers, and the air smells of danger." She spit on the ground, and Peter had to step aside
to protect his boots. "Just how we Westerns like it."

Kai clapped a hand on her shoulder. "Couldn't have
said it better myself."

The cowgirl was one of the few characters they met
who didn't seem to be shaking in her boots. Peter tried
to ask discreet questions, feigning the same look of
concern that everyone wore, but all he could get out of
the other characters was their fear of what was coming
next. The End of Story was upon them. Hadn't they

heard? The Tale station was malfunctioning. The Taleless had been seen. Characters were being kidnapped.
Killed. Sold into slavery. Heart's Place was already
destroyed. Who could say what district would be next?
Some of their theories sounded straight out of a Tale.
Some of them, like the one repeated by a woman who
whispered about the Muses being behind it all, hit close
to the truth. But in the end, it didn't matter what their
theory was; every character reached the same conclusion: only the Tale Master could save them now.

"The characters are so frightened, they'll believe
anything Elton says," Peter said as they neared the
Weaponry Arena.

"Fear makes characters do foolish things," Kai said.

"But fear also leads to moments of bravery." Indy
handed a broadside to a pair of worried-looking Vil-
lagers. "My dad says that true courage is carrying on
even when you're afraid."

Kai studied Indy for a moment and then nodded
slowly. "Your father is a wise man," he said. "I've often
said something similar myself."

"Wisdom *and* bravery?" a voice asked from somewhere near Peter's knees. "You must be thinking of a
cat."

"Sam!" Peter knelt down and gave the cat a friendly pat. "What are you doing here?"

"Reconnaissance mission." Sam blinked at him. "The Resistance needed a spy."

Peter gulped. His parents must be furious. "How are things at Bramble Cottage?"

"No idea. I left as soon as that lot from Heart's Place showed up." Sam arched his back into a lazy stretch. "Certain humans I can handle well enough, but I have my limits."

As they made their way through the crowds, handing out broadsides and stopping to speak with some of the characters, Peter noticed that everywhere he went, Kai made friends. He applauded the dogs that were play-tackling each other outside the Eating Building. He whistled at the Sci-Fis who were having target practice with their laser guns. And he even sang a pretty little song to a group of fairies who were stringing tiny arrows on cobwebby bows near the fountain. Peter secretly wondered if Kai thought this all was some big joke. Story might seem a whole heck of a lot more interesting now that the characters were training for battle, but the Enemy's return was no laughing matter. He said as much to Kai when they passed the fountain.

"The Plot thickens," Kai said as he nodded to a beautiful princess. "But you're quite right, my lad. Evil is never funny. Even so, you can't deny that the best, rip-roaring Tales come about when the Heroes have to overcome a great evil." He clapped one hand on Peter's shoulder and the other on Indy's. "We're in the middle of such a Tale, lad, right at the heart of it. I wouldn't miss it for the world."

They neared the entrance to the arena, joining other characters who were filing toward the main entrance arch, the same one Peter used for his Weaponry classes. The normal routine of Perrault felt ages ago, even though it had been less than a week since Peter had been going through his swordsman drills with the weapons master. Peter, Indy, and Kai took their place in line, while Sam ran over to a pack of cats that sat sunning themselves on the garden wall. A serious-looking Dystopian was standing outside the front doors with a cracked clipboard. Even from their place in the line, Peter could hear his somber voice. "Name, please," he said to a cluster of girls. "And district."

"Of course Elton would put that lot of nitwits in charge," Peter whispered to Kai, who raised an eyebrow.

"End-of-the-world types?" He stroked his chin thoughtfully. "Always gnawing at the bone of impending disaster, aren't they? Well, if the Enemy has his way, they'll have their fill of it soon enough."

Sam galloped back toward them. "He's taking attendance," he said. "Rumor among the other cats is that there's a roster. Certain characters are to be reported immediately to Tale Master Elton. Happens that yours truly is on the list." Sam pulled a paw across his whiskers with pleasure.

"Cheers, Sam." Kai gave him a thumbs-up. "You must've done something right."

Peter pulled the others out of line. "If you're on that paper, I'd bet anything the rest of us are as well. Probably near the top."

Kai grinned at him. "Best place to be, mate." He pointed over to the cats. "Why aren't they practicing for battle, or whatever it is everyone else is doing?"

"Cats," Sam said as he squinted his eyes, "never do what everybody else does."

Kai rubbed his palms together. "Excellent. Tell me this. Is there another way to get inside?"

"The animal entrances are around back," Sam said.

"Perfect," Kai said. "Sam, go get your friends and meet us there. And tell them they won't be doing what everybody else is doing. Peter. Indy. Come with me."

What would have been a problem for Peter and the other humans was not a problem with Sam as their leader.

"The Rodent Entrance," Sam said as he led them to a small round door. "Humans always underestimate the animals." The cat was right. No Tale Master minion stood guard here. Sam slipped through easily, but Peter, Kai, and Indy had to crouch on hands and knees to make their way down the tunnel. Once Sam saw the humans were inside, he slunk away to join the other cats. Peter silently crawled through the Rodent Wing to a miniature crossroads that opened up into the main hallways that ran around the circumference of the amphitheater. The curved rows of stone seats were already full of characters, and Peter had to squeeze past them to find spots in the uppermost row. A thick wall ran behind them, with pillars that held banner flags spaced every few feet around the arena.

Peter had been here many times—both as a partici-pant in Weaponry challenges and as an observer—but the usual excitement had been replaced by a buzz of worried energy. Soon, even the concerned whispers died down to an uneasy silence as Tale Master Elton made his way to the center of the stage at the bottom of the arena. Elton wasn't wearing a suit like he usually did. Instead, he wore a long green cloak, under which Peter could see the sparkle of battle armor, and he had a very grave expression on his face. The usually ridiculous-looking Tale Master for once appeared very fierce and very in charge. Behind Elton came a parade of other Talekeepers, a few Perrault professors, and, at the very end of the line, as though it was the most ordinary thing in the world, was Horace Wotton.

Indy must have seen Horace then, because Peter heard him suck in his breath. Horace held a clipboard importantly in front of his chest, and when he reached Elton, he shook his hand vigorously. Peter squeezed his fingers together. He wanted to leap over the group in front of them, shove aside the teachers, and wring Horace's traitorous neck. Elton's too, for that matter.

Kai must have known what Peter was feeling, for he leaned in close and whispered into Peter's ear. "Easy, lad. There will be time enough for action later. First we listen. Then we ambush."

Elton cleared his throat and moved forward to address the characters. "We gather here where Heroes-in-training fight their practice battles," he said. "A real battle is coming, and I call each of you to find the hero within yourself." Elton's voice wasn't his usual grating volume. Instead, it was strong, comforting, and solid as a rock. The rage Peter felt toward Elton's treachery oozed slowly out of him. He found himself wanting to listen to Elton and wondered whether the Tale Master might actually have Story's best interests at heart.

"Some of you may remember the horror of the Unbinding." Elton thumped his chest with a fist. "These dark days have come again."

Peter nodded his head without thinking. *Elton is right.*

"Character lives have been lost," Elton continued. "Our Tales are threatened. I promise you, people of Story, that, as your Tale Master, I will protect you and ensure your safety."

Someone on the fringe of the crowd started clapping, and it was contagious. Soon, the same people who had been terrified were cheering and shouting Elton's name. Peter clapped so hard his hands stung.

"I'm so glad Elton's here," Indy said with unusual

cheerfulness. "He'll save us."

"Cleverly done," Kai said in a low whisper. He fumbled around in his cloak and pulled out a handful of dried green leaves. "Chew on this." He handed some to Peter and then to Indy. "To clear your head."

Peter wished that Kai would stop talking. He wanted to hear what the Tale Master was going to say next. But he took the leaf and crammed it into his mouth. Immediately, the flavor of cool mint filled his senses. It was as though a fresh wind had come and blown a foggy mist from before Peter's eyes. All thoughts of Elton's truthfulness evaporated.

"Why, that dirty—" he began.

"Elton's enchanting everyone." Indy spit the words out as though they were poison. "The characters don't stand a chance."

Peter looked around at the crowds of people hungrily waiting on Elton's every word. He had learned in Elocution what kind of control an enchanted voice could hold over people, but he had never seen one so powerful before. He shook his head. If not for Kai's leaf, he would be gazing hopefully at Elton along with the rest of them.

"This is it," Indy whispered to him. "This is the

moment when all of Story begins to believe Elton's lies."

And then Elton did the last thing Peter would have ever expected. He told the truth. "The Muses were never defeated." Elton scanned the crowds as he said this. "In fact, they are still in Story." There were gasps. The girl next to Indy screamed. The cheers that had been there the moment before transformed into a low rumble of panicked questions.

"Be brave, good people of Story. Be brave. Heroes aren't afraid." Elton spread his hands out wide. "The Muses are evil, no doubt about it. They have not changed since the Unbinding. They want to trap us in our Tales, binding our every move. They will not rest until every character in Story is under Muse control. We expect more attacks like the one at Heart's Place any day." The murmur of voices increased, but Elton spoke over them. "It is as I have long feared: the End of Story is upon us." Elton paused then, waiting for the full effect of his words to take place. He must have known how hearing the Tale Master voice their worst fears would terrify them. Some of the Dystopians began waving their signs. Characters were crying. A few set their faces into looks of stoic determination.

Peter could almost taste the fear in the air.

"Now," Elton continued, "the moment we heard of the attack on Heart's Place, we knew it was the work of the oath-breaking Muses. Immediately, I sought out records from the Unbinding so that we could learn from Tale Master Archimago's heroic deeds. Tale Master Archimago kept a sealed record of the actions he took to secure Story's borders. In these writings I discovered a surprising fact. Not all the Muses turned against Story. There was one who vowed to uphold his oaths, who, at his own peril, fought to save the characters of Story."

Peter took another bite of Kai's leaf. Even though he knew Elton was twisting the truth, he wanted his wits about him for what he thought Elton might say next.

"I have been working night and day to plan for the defense of our districts. Story *will not* suffer the same casualties we saw in the last Unbinding. You have my word on that." Even with the leaf, Peter had a hard time disbelieving Elton. If he hadn't known better, he would have said that perhaps the Tale Master really did care about the fate of Story. "To increase the security in Story, I have sought out and found someone who will provide you with all the protection you need."

A ripple of expectation ran across the arena.

"Tonight," Elton said in his newly strong voice, "you are all invited to a coronation ball. We will gather at the Red Castle in the Enchanted Forest. Fidelus, the last faithful Muse, is prepared to uphold his oaths to Story. He is an immortal warrior. Our savior. And the new King of Story."

The characters leaped to their feet, and loud cheers erupted. Peter chewed hard on the piece of minty plant Kai had given him.

"Do you have enough leaf for all of Story?" Peter whispered to Kai.

"In a manner of speaking," Kai said with a wink. "Not to worry. We'll reveal the full truth in time. But for now: just a glimmer. Are you ready?"

When Peter nodded, Kai shoved a soft parcel into Peter's hands and clasped first his and then Indy's arm. "Once the characters see clearly, they will fight for Story. You're brave lads, and I'm glad to have met you."

Kai hopped up onto the uppermost wall of the arena, did a few heart-stopping handsprings, and a final flip that landed him on one of the banner pillars.

"But isn't a King in Story just a child's Tale?" Kai said in a loud voice as he gave Elton a dramatic bow.

"Well, I—" Elton began as he motioned to two burly-looking figures off to the side.

Kai kept moving. He hopped along the circumference of the wall, and, as he went, characters swiveled to look at him. It made it seem as though Kai was leading the characters in some strange dance. Elton's face had gone a deep shade of purple. He was whispering wildly to Horace and pointing to the far end of the stage. Peter didn't doubt that more guards were about to come bursting into the crowd.

"The thing I like best in the world is a good story," Kai said, as he leaned up against a banner pole. "But lies make a bad Tale."

Elton was pushing his way up the center aisle toward Kai now, and the guards had spread out, as if they meant to squash Kai between them.

Kai kept talking. "The Muses *are* still in Story. But they aren't your enemies."

"Who is he?" Elton screamed, but his voice had lost some of its enchantment. "Catch him!" The crowded amphitheater stood between Elton and Kai. Down near Horace, another guard appeared, leading two snarling beasts at the end of a long chain. They were bigger than the ones Peter and Sam had battled that day on the dais. Matted fur stood stiff on their necks. Their yellow eyes glowed as they scanned the arena for their prey, and their distorted snouts dripped with saliva.

Kai was unperturbed. "Oh, you wouldn't know me, Tale Master Elton, though I know all about you." He leaped and skipped along the wall, calling out in a loud voice. "And what you hunt." Elton's head jerked back, and Kai continued. "But that's not part of my speech. I wanted to warn the good people of Story about their real Enemy." Kai stood on his tiptoes, cupped one hand over his mouth, and shouted in a loud whisper, "And let me just say his name rhymes with *Ridelus*." One final leap, and he was on the highest banner pole. "The characters need to know the true Backstory, and then they will be able to fight their true Enemy." He looked straight over at Peter, and Peter knew their moment had come.

He sprang to his feet, Indy beside him, and they began throwing rolled-up broadsides into the crowd. Kai hadn't given the people any of the leaf, but his words seemed to free some of them, at least, from the enchantment they had been under.

"Who is that?" someone cried.

"What does he mean that Fidelus is our Enemy?"

"We want the truth!" the cowgirl Peter had talked to earlier yelled.

At that moment, Sam's clowder of cats poured into the arena. Some slunk in over the top of the wall. Others galloped through the side doors. One even dropped down onto the stage. On the cats' necks rode tiny pixies, arrows taut in their silken bows. They simultaneously released their smoldering arrows, straight up toward the sky. With a great explosion, the air filled with sparkling pixie dust, which snaked and twisted to sketch a shape Peter had seen not that long ago. He thought Elton might have recognized it, too, by the astonished look on his face. There, right in the middle of Elton's big meeting, sprouted a huge, beautiful outline of the Kingstree.

Chapter 14

Snow rubbed her eyes and blinked up at the grubby face hovering two inches in front of her own. Beady black eyes twinkled out at her over a pointed beard. Then Snow rubbed her eyes again. She wasn't dreaming.

The thing was shaking her by the collar. "Wake up!" it said in a thick voice. Snow sat up and saw the creature was barely a foot high. *A leprechaun.*

"Best not to stay in the Red Lady's traps," it said.

"Where am I?" Snow's head felt foggy. "Who are you?" Another leprechaun had a tiny sword out and was sawing Snow free from the sticky web that still bound her feet. It was all coming back to her now. They had seen Duessa in the forest and had run away—

"Wait. Where's my mother? And Archimago?" Snow

tried to sit up, but only her arms were free. She kicked her legs to no avail. The rest of her was stuck fast.

How long had she been asleep? It had been night when they left the castle, and daylight filtered through the treetops now. "There were others—a tall woman with silver hair and a crazy old man."

The leprechaun nearest her jumped back, both knobby hands outstretched. "Pull it together, kid." He darted a look over his shoulder. "You're making too much noise."

Snow grabbed the leprechaun by his shirtfront. "Where is the woman who was with me?" Her legs were still trapped in the sticky web.

The leprechaun's eyes grew wide. He kicked his legs back and forth. "Calm yourself. The Red Lady will hear."

Snow didn't release him. Leprechauns were tricky creatures. They could be helpful, like the kind that sneaked into houses and tidied up for the owners, or not so helpful. She hoped these were the first kind. She didn't have time for riddles and impossible quests that always ended badly.

"There was also a man. Old and filthy."

"Do you see any man?" This leprechaun had a

nasty-looking hook, and he waved it around in the air until it pointed at her. "I don't see anyone else. Do you, Tuck? Besides a fool human girl, that is."

Snow ignored the barb and set the leprechaun down. She had no doubt Archimago would do anything to save his scrawny hide. But even with all her mother's faults, Snow knew she wouldn't abandon Snow in the Enchanted Forest, no matter what. So where was she? Could the Red Enchantress have followed them somehow? Taken her mother back to that awful castle? "Wait. You said something about the Red Lady."

"May she sink into the bottomless swamp and burn forever." The one called Tuck spit on the ground. "She passed this way not long ago. The whole wood reeks of her."

Snow stopped struggling in the trap. At least the creatures weren't in Duessa's service. "We were running from her when we got caught in your web."

"Not our web," Tuck said as he sliced the last piece of web from Snow's ankle. "*Hers*, may her food rot in her mouth. To catch unwanted visitors."

"I was traveling with a woman," Snow said as she flexed her one free foot. "I need to find her." As soon as she had seen the fog, she should have known. It was one of the reasons no one ventured into the Enchanted Forest beyond the Hollow. The woods were riddled with traps. Some were set by the more sinister Villains who lived there. And some, apparently, were rigged by Duessa herself.

Tuck looked at his companion. "What say you, Tumbler? Friend or foe?"

Tumbler scratched his chin with the pointy end of his hook. "Hard to be sure. But, either way, the War-lock's Apprentice wants to see her." He cut the final cord on her net, and Snow was free. "You'll have to come with us."

"The one Fidelus is looking for?" Snow flexed her leg. Fidelus was ripping open Tales to find this guy, and the Apprentice was in Duessa's backyard? Snow had to find her mother and tell her. She took two steps and found herself surrounded by Tuck and Tumbler's companions. The leprechauns were filthy, their clothes hardly recognizable beyond tattered rags. And they smelled. From the looks on their faces, they had no idea what she was talking about. Something sharp pricked her in the calf.

"Ow!" Snow frowned down at the leprechaun who had poked her with his stupid hook. He held a worn

net in his other fist, and his friends also wielded an odd
jumble of household tools that had been fashioned into
weapons.

"No need for all that." Snow lifted up her hands. "I
want to meet this Apprentice anyway." It was a good
thing, too, because the leprechauns weren't giving her
much of a choice as they herded her through the forest.
With any luck, the Apprentice lived outside the woods,
and, once she had talked to the Apprentice and found
her mother, she could get far away from here. "As long
as you're sure the Apprentice isn't a friend of the Red
Lady's, that is," she added almost as an afterthought.

There was a minute when each of the leprechauns
spit on the ground in turn and cursed Duessa to rot
under the still water, whatever that meant. It was good
enough for Snow.

"Excellent," said Snow. "Let's get on with it, shall
we?"

The leprechauns were fast, and their light weight
gave them the advantage as the land grew swampier.
Snow had trouble keeping pace with them, and each
step forward into the gooey mud took more and more
effort. She had to pull hard to fight the suction against
her soles, and half the time her foot came straight out,

leaving a mud-clumped boot stranded in the mire. Snow wobbled on one foot and yanked hard on her shoe. *The Warlock's Apprentice better be worth this.*

The air was thick with moisture, and the stillness of the forest had been replaced with sounds of hidden life. Mosquitoes buzzed hopefully around her ears, and a chorus of bullfrogs provided a mellow background for the leprechauns' constant bickering.

"I say it weren't alive before, and then it was. I saw it with my own eyes." Tumbler appeared to be the leader of the group, even though none of the others seemed to accept his word as true.

"Well, I say you had been in your cups too long," Tuck argued. "Didn't the missus give you a whole tankard to take with you?"

"A tankard's nothing," Tumbler snorted. "You'll wish you had a whole tableful of tankards if the half-dead creature I saw comes for you. Bunch of yellow-hearted cowards." He swiped his hook through the air. "Even *she* couldn't make them look whole."

"You've seen the Red Lady?" Snow realized her mistake as soon as she said it. The spitting ritual took even longer this time, as each leprechaun tried to trump the others' curses. After the Red Lady had been condemned to a bath of thickest mud, sand that would come out of her nostrils, and the poison bite of the swamp rat, Snow finally got her answer.

"Aye," Tuck said. "I did once from afar, may she rot in the fetid springs of waste."

Snow lost her balance, and one foot landed in a soggy puddle.

"Are you mad, girl?" Tumbler demanded when Snow asked how far Perrault was from here. "You'd have to pass right by the Red Castle, and she'd see you coming a mile away. And there's beasts and worse in her dungeons. The whole castle stinks of the Taleless."

"Now, you never said afore that it was the Taleless you saw," one of the oldest-looking leprechauns said to Tumbler. His floppy hat kept sliding down over one eye, and he finally whipped it off with a huff. "The Taleless are near enough the walking dead themselves, and I wouldna put it past the Red Lady to try and bring the dead to life if it served her cause."

The other leprechauns nodded sagely, and one even went so far as to give Tumbler his net, but he shoved it away. "No need for all of that. Keep your net. And your wits about you. Dark things are afoot in these lands."

"That's the understatement of the age," Snow said as her boot sank down into the muck yet again. She was putting together what the leprechauns were saying with what she had overheard when Elton was ripping open the Tale. "You're telling me that Duessa is—"

The leprechauns hawked up their spit in preparation.

"Now cut that out, will you?"

The leprechauns watched her silently, their mouths shut tight.

Snow found it hard to stay balanced on one leg, and her stocking foot wobbled as she tried to yank the offending boot out of the swamp. "Bringing the dead to life is more than a 'dark thing'! It's insane!"

The leprechauns said nothing.

"Oh, forget it. Go ahead with your stupid curses." Snow managed to get her foot reshod while the leprechauns revealed the grim depth of their repertoire of curses. She hoped Tumbler had been drinking too much. Snow wasn't all that familiar with the dark ways, and she knew even less about the forbidden magic that played with life and death, but from what Elton had said and what Tumbler had seen, she thought she knew how the Taleless were being given new bodies. She felt sick to her stomach. As much as she despised Heart's

Place and hated her aunt and uncle, she couldn't wish that on them. She hoped they had escaped the Taleless's clutches.

The leprechauns were moving forward again, this time with a load of harsh words for the oldest leprechaun and his choice of hat. How were they able to put aside their worry over Duessa's minions so easily? Snow wondered if there wasn't something to their strange ritual. Feeling stupid even as she did it, Snow spit on the ground. She didn't feel altogether better, but some of the weight that had fallen on her since she had left the dungeon lifted, and she whispered under her breath, "May her own deeds come back to haunt her."

The other leprechauns began trickling away to return to their own dwellings, but Tuck and Tumbler were determined to escort Snow all the way to the Warlock's Apprentice. She was more than glad for it when she saw the piles of smoking quicksand. Snow wouldn't be any help to her mother if she died in the Swamp before she could even talk to the Warlock's Apprentice.

Tumbler thumped one foot on something that sounded solid. "There's a boardwalk there." The leprechaun's pointed shoes skipped over the top of the grime. "Unner there, see? Just step lively."

Snow was doing her best to oblige. She had traded conversation with the leprechauns for strategizing where to take her next step. Fireflies hovered nearby, lighting their way through the gloom, and the buzz of mosquitoes was a constant hum. Snow had never been to the Enchanted lands before. *Maybe because they're not fit for human existence.* She slapped at a bug feasting on her arm, and the blood smeared across her skin.

Everything in the Swamp was miniature in size. Tiny rowboats no bigger than her shoe navigated the puddles of water that trickled around little mud islands. Most of these were piloted by wrinkled brownies, one of whom cut Snow off while she was busy tugging on her blasted boot. The brownie expertly docked below a hut crafted all of twigs and perched on stilts. The farther Snow went, the more such dwellings she noticed. She was encountering more of the Fairy Folk than she had seen in her whole life: the smiling sprites who peered out of mossy logs, the very ugly nix who swung wildly at her with a club, and the kelpie who, fortunately, didn't notice her passing.

Every few feet, Tumbler turned around to wave Snow forward with his hook. "This way now," he called out, in what Snow supposed he thought was an encouraging voice. "Just a wee bit more."

"This is it?" Snow asked when Tuck finally stopped in front of a jumble of sticks that made a low dome over the mud.

"Aye." Tumbler tucked his hook back into his belt. "That's the place."

Tuck had explained that the Warlock's Apprentice was a person of mystery. Many underground passageways led from different districts to this secret hiding spot, and the Apprentice passed to and fro without detection. "Stealthy as a cockroach, that one." Tuck said this as though he meant it as a compliment. "Can sneak into just about any place unseen. And darn near hard to kill."

"Haven't seen her in these parts in many years." Tumbler bent down to wedge a stick under the bottommost row of branches. "But it's good to know she's back in the Swamp, keeping an eye on things. Seems especially keen that we don't lose track of you."

"The Apprentice is a woman?" Snow asked. "And she knows about me?" Snow didn't like the sound of that.

"The Apprentice knows about all the goings-on in the Swamp," Tuck said. "Just you wait. You'll meet her soon enough." He joined Tumbler, and, together, they heaved until the thatched pile folded back like the top of a trap-door and revealed a huge stone pipe that delved down below the mud. Tumbler put two fingers in his mouth and whistled hard. A troop of lightning bugs appeared and swarmed after the leprechauns. Snow hesitated only a moment before following them inside the pipe.

"Handy little fellows, these," Tumbler said, as the bugs busily lit up the dark passageway. The pipe snaked its way deeper and deeper into the earth, and Snow had to crawl on her hands and knees. *Why does everything have to be in some gross underground tunnel?* After some time, the pipe ended abruptly, opening out into an earthen passageway. It was so gradual Snow didn't notice at first, but the farther they went, the larger the tunnel got. Soon she could walk hunched over, and then altogether upright, Tuck and Tumbler tripping along at her knees. As they rounded a corner, Snow saw a brightly painted green door.

"Three knocks an' a tap," Tuck said, rapping the rhythm on the door with his hook.

Snow could hear a shuffling noise on the other side of the door, and then a muffled voice called, "Who's there?"

"Um," Snow answered. "It's Snow Wotton."

There was a dreadful pause and then the click-ing sound of several bolts. The next minute the door flung wide. A hand grabbed Snow by the shoulder and yanked her inside along with Tuck and Tumbler.

"Hurry now," a stooped figure was saying. "Don't want anyone to see you."

Snow darted a panicky look back up the tunnel. No one *could* see her. No one knew where she was. What if the Warlock's Apprentice was some horrible Villain? Someone worse than Fidelus and Duessa?

The stranger slammed the door shut, and Snow let any thought of escape go with it. The only way was forward. Her guide pushed them along a poorly lit hallway, and the next thing she knew, Snow found herself seated on a very uncomfortable horsehair sofa in a dark parlor.

A figure was standing before an unlit fireplace, run-ning fumbling fingers along the mantel. "Are you the Warlock's Apprentice?" Snow asked in a hushed voice.

The man let out a hoarse laugh, one hand finally seizing on a packet of matches. "Oh, no, not me," he said. "I keep things in order here when she's away. Just a humble vampire I am." With a flick of his wrist, the fireplace bloomed into light, and the vampire flashed a very long pair of fangs at her. "Living underground suits me."

"Oh," Snow said. She was seated next to a desk covered with thick stacks of books, most of them situated to hold unrolled parchments open on the table. The room was an odd shape, with sharp-edged walls and more doors than Snow could count. There was a loud knock on the door nearest her.

"That'll be the Apprentice," the vampire said.

Snow wished she had thought to bring in one of those sticks from the pile outside. *Just in case.* Or, better yet, that she had her mother's enchanted voice. The sight of the vampire's fangs had made her think she had been very wrong to come with the leprechauns. Maybe they weren't the helpful kind after all. She should have left them long ago and braved the dangers of the quicksand rather than this. She was alone underground. With no way to defend herself. Nothing she could do if the Warlock's Apprentice turned out to be something horrible. Maybe if she caught the Apprentice by surprise, she could still escape.

The door swung open. Snow sprang up out of her chair and steeled herself to make a run for it. But then she found that she couldn't move at all. For there, standing in the doorway, was her mother.

"You're the Warlock's Apprentice?" Snow croaked.

"Thank you, Tuck and Tumbler," her mother said to the leprechauns. "I knew I could count on you to keep her safe." She came over to the desk, and it looked as though she might hug Snow, but instead she gave her an awkward pat on the shoulder. "I have tea, somewhere." Her mother nodded to the vampire. "And something hot to eat. Sit down, Snow."

Chapter 15

Peter and Indy hurried past Birchwood Hall and down the forest path. The meeting was over, and they had left Elton and his guards surrounded by a mob of angry characters who wanted to know what Kai had meant and why they had a horrible headache.

"How did Kai free them?" Peter said. "Elton's enchantment had them swallowing lies like hungry fish eating worms."

"I could do with a fresh fish," Sam said, licking his chops.

The cat was the only one of their little group who seemed content. Indy was tense as a bowstring, and Peter still felt jittery inside. They were going as fast as they could, and it still felt like they wouldn't make it to Bramble Cottage in time. Peter couldn't wait to tell

Una and the others what they had learned. The coronation ball was to be held at the Red Castle, one of the many fortresses outside of Horror Hollow. Peter didn't doubt that if they hunted for a cemetery nearby, they'd probably find it. And if Jaga had been taking her quills to Duessa all along, then Una had been right about the Lost Elements.

"But why does Fidelus want the Elements?" he asked, even though he and Indy had already discussed it to no avail. "Even if he has all of them, what then? It doesn't make sense."

"Una said that back at the Unbinding, he wanted to write his own Tale." Sam loped next to him. "Now that he's going to be crowned King of Story, maybe that's not enough." He growled. "Maybe he wants to write all of Story's Tales."

"But he's not the true King of Story." Indy was outpacing Peter. "That's nearly blasphemy. Wait until the Sacred Order hears."

"They won't be able to do anything either," Peter panted, "if the Enemy enchants them like Elton just did all of us. But for Kai's leaf, we'd have believed him, too, and would probably be out shopping for something nice to wear to the Red Castle tonight." Peter's heart was pounding, and it wasn't just because Indy was setting a fast pace. "Let's hope there's enough of the stuff to go around." The packet Kai had given him before he left was full of dry leaves, but they would need more to save all of Story. "I'm not even sure how we're going to sneak it into the Red Castle," Peter said.

"The Resistance will help us." Indy pointed back toward Perrault. "Perhaps more will join us after they read the broadsides."

As Peter stopped to untangle a clinging vine from his calf, he had the knowing feeling that someone was watching him. He reached over to his boot and silently eased out his dagger. In one fluid movement he swirled around. But instead of one of Elton's guards, he saw a tabby, flanked by a fierce-looking Siamese and an all-black cat.

"Put that away," Sam hissed from behind him.

"You've been following us this whole time?" Peter tucked his weapon back into his boot.

"You're as loud as a dog," the Siamese said as she bared her teeth at the scimitar Indy had pulled out. Peter wasn't sure if it was supposed to be a threatening look or some sort of feline joke, so he just shrugged and looked at Sam, but Sam only blinked at him.

"As loud as a dog who lets his master lead him on a leash," the black cat said.

"As loud as a pack of dogs who hear their dinner bowl being filled," the tabby said, and licked a paw. "As loud as—"

"Okay, I get it," Peter said. "We're loud." The trio of cats looked at him expectantly. "*And* you guys are quiet."

Sam crouched low to the ground. "Esteemed felines, we give you honor," he said in a very grave voice. "Thank you for your work at the arena." The cats seemed pleased with this, and the tabby twined her tail around her paws with a throaty purr.

"Human enchantment disgusts us, and we despise those who use it to control others." The Siamese primly sat back on her haunches. "We are happy the enchantment failed."

"You knew Elton was enchanting us?" Indy asked.

The Siamese blinked her crossed eyes at him. "Of course."

"Well then, you've got to help us," Peter blurted. "At the coronation tonight, they'll use the same enchantment, and if you can—"

"I am tired of talking." The Siamese flopped down

on her side and squinted at Sam. "The loud ones must leave."

"No, you don't under—" Peter began, when Sam hushed him with a growl.

"She said no," he hissed.

Peter ignored him. "But you helped before."

The Siamese gave a great yawn and licked her paw. "Where is the one with the pesky feather in his hat? Him I would speak with."

"Yes," the tabby purred. "Feathers are fun."

"He's gone, but he would want you to help us." Peter knew he sounded desperate, but he didn't care. The cats seemed to be impervious to the Enemy's lies, and the Resistance needed all the clear-thinking characters they could get—especially now.

Sam swiped a paw at Peter's ankle. "Stop talking," he ordered. He turned to Indy. "Get him out of here," he said. "And, both of you, leave this to me."

"Good luck, Sam," Indy said as he began to back away, but Peter could only stare at the little cat.

Sam turned and made the same funny bow again. "Perhaps if I were to request an audience with the Feline Quorum," he said.

"I cannot refuse your request." The Siamese flicked

her tail back and forth irritably. "But the loud ones must leave immediately."

Peter tucked his head in an awkward bow. What was it Sam had said? "We give you honor," he said back to the cats, but the cats only made a strange wheezing sound. Peter had heard Sam do it often enough to know the cats were laughing at him. And then Sam was gone, loping away through the underbrush, and Peter felt as though a great portion of his courage was going with him.

Peter joined Indy back on the main path, unfolded the pouch Kai had given him, and looked at the pile of crumbling herbs. For a moment, he felt the folly of their plan. It was something his brothers might think up. Waltz into the coronation of an immortal Muse and—what?—force some of the herbs down everyone's throats? Peter had an awful vision of a ballroom full of pointing and laughing characters. Of an angry King Fidelus who wanted him dead. He turned to Indy. "What if Kai is wrong? What if the characters won't fight for Story, even if they see clearly? They might even decide to crown Fidelus king. Or maybe we won't be able to get them to eat the leaf in the first place." He shoved the pouch into his cloak pocket. "Doesn't seem like much against the forces of the Enemy." He wasn't sure if he was talking about himself or the plan. The cool fragrance of crushed mint filled the air.

"No," Indy said. "It doesn't." He breathed deeply. "But sometimes it's the smallest things that end up making the biggest difference." Indy reached out and clasped Peter's arm. "And you're not alone. No matter what happens, Peter, we do this together. And we do this for Story."

Chapter 16

Una pulled the red thread through the thin cloth. After she had slept in her very own bed in a suite prepared especially for her, she had been escorted to one of the castle's lavish sitting rooms. They had tea while her mother waited for a messenger to arrive. When Una had asked if it had anything to do with her father, her mother had pulled out the sewing basket. Una had never embroidered anything in her life, but, under her mother's careful instruction, a red rose was blooming on the handkerchief in front of her.

"Just tie it off like so," her mother said, leaning over and expertly knotting the string. "Then you can begin again here."

Una smiled up at her. She could sit and listen to her mother talk all day. The sound of her voice made Una feel all soft inside. She had to focus on trying to keep her stitches even. Every so often she would hand the fabric over for her mother's inspection, waiting breathlessly for the smile of approval that would show what a good job she had done. Finally, Una was making up for all the lost years.

"Was I born here, Mother?"

Her mother buried her face in the sewing basket. "So many questions, darling!" She pulled out a spool of green thread. "Try this for the stems."

"Thank you." Una unwound the top thread. "I just want to know everything about our family. What about my aunts and uncles?"

"What about them?" her mother said carefully. She set the basket on the ground and clasped her hands in her lap. "Una, you must know that your father and I loved his brothers and sisters very much." Her eyes filled with tears. "Try to understand, darling. We didn't *want* to oppose them. We had to."

Una stopped poking the green thread through the needle's eye. Something about what her mother was saying felt significant, but when Una tried to remember, her mind felt blank. Oppose who? Why did that make her heart beat faster? "Of course I understand.

But why did you have to?"

Her mother frowned and then quickly relaxed her face. "It wasn't the Muses, darling. It was the King. He means only bondage and servitude for Story. Surely you know that."

Una dropped the spool of green thread. Someone's face flashed before her mind. Someone who was looking for a King. A boy. *Indy.* She was standing in a forest with him, and he was talking about wanting the King to return. "But the King promised to return to Story."

Her mother narrowed her eyes. "Yes, dear. But his return is a *bad thing for Story*. Isn't that right?"

Whatever spark Una had felt at the mention of the King was gone now. It was replaced with the sure knowledge that her mother spoke the truth. It would be a Very Bad Thing if the King returned. "It was brave of you to fight the Muses like that."

Her mother's smile was back in place. "Yes, dear. And hard for your father." She picked up the wayward spool and handed it to Una. "Even so, he always does what is best for his people. For Story."

Una began to rethread the needle. She had an idea. "Father should be the King!" She looked up at her mother. How had no one thought of this before?

"It would be wonderful for Story! And you could be Queen."

Her mother gave an embarrassed-sounding little cough. "Now, Una. The very idea." She smoothed out her skirts and said thoughtfully, "But whatever is best for Story . . ."

Una began to work on a dainty leaf. Of course it was best for Story. They had a castle already and everything.

There were footsteps in the hallway, and her mother stood up, her sewing forgotten at her side. Una glanced at the doorway, and what she saw made her prick her finger with the needle. A man entered the room and held out a book to her mother. Its cover was battered, like it had been torn in many places. Something about his mustache and his glasses was familiar. The man twisted a ring on his finger, and then Una knew him. *Mr. Elton!*

Half-remembered glimpses of the fight in Alethia's garden flashed through Una's mind. Mr. Elton chasing them with wild beasts. His hand cuffing her face. Hot anger boiled up inside and she nearly cried out that he was a miserable traitor, but an overpowering soothing sensation drowned out the emotion. She felt like she was looking at everything from a great distance. Una sucked on her pricked finger. Mr. Elton's meanness was her old life. The old Una didn't know the truth about Story. That old Una didn't know her mother. Now that she knew the truth, what did a little mistreatment done by Elton matter? If what happened in The End was the best for all of Story, the Tale Master's imprudent mistakes were just tiny bumps on the road. She made another stitch. It was the perfect length. Her mother would be pleased.

"There were complications," Elton was saying. "I had to double the enchantment to restore order. We'll have to use more control at the coronation."

"We can discuss that later." Her mother's voice was like silk. "And the Scroll?"

Una paused midstitch. Something about a scroll was important. Someone was looking for it.

Elton shook his head.

"That's not good enough. We have the other Elements," Una's mother said. "You will bring me the Scroll by nightfall, or you will pay with your life."

Una set the cloth aside. She was good at looking for things. "I'd love to help, Mother. Oh, please, let me."

Elton gave her a funny look and then turned back to her mother. "Mother?"

Her mother swept across the room to Una's side. "Mortimer, this is my long-lost daughter. The one I've spoken of nearly every day since she disappeared." She rubbed Una's shoulder lightly. "We've had a lovely reunion this morning, haven't we, dear? Nothing will make me happier than having you stand next to us tonight"—she gave Una a knowing smile—"when your father is crowned King."

Una beamed up at her. She could think of nothing better than for Story to have such a King. When she looked back at him, Mr. Elton's face had gone a sickly gray color.

"A daughter," he choked out, and then his mouth twisted into an ugly frown. "Fidelus must be pleased."

"Enough," her mother hissed. Then she laughed. "Don't ruin our morning with silly jealousies." She bent low so that she could whisper into Una's ear. "My dear, I think it's time you met your father."

Chapter 17

*Y*ou're the Warlock's Apprentice?" Snow said to her mother again. The underground room felt pleasant after the swamp's humidity, and she sat in the chair across from the crackling fireplace. Hopeful sounds of the vampire rummaging around came from the kitchen.

"Yes," her mother said shortly. She was pawing through the rubble on the desk, tossing aside crumbling scrolls and mysterious-looking maps. "Now if I could just find his book of spells, I could release the Scroll of Fire. Even on its own, it is very powerful, and it may give us the upper hand against Fidelus and Duessa."

"You know where it is? How?"

"Because long ago I helped discover it." Snow's mother frowned as she reached underneath the old desk and ran her hands back and forth. "And with luck, we'll have it in our possession soon enough."

Snow felt like she was looking at a stranger. She knew nothing about her mother's past. And her mother had made no effort to change that. "Okay," Snow said. "Let's see here . . . you know where to find one of the Lost Elements, you're some warlock's apprentice, you have an *underground house* in the middle of the Enchanted Swamp, you're an enchantress. Anything else I should know about you?" Just when Snow thought she was beginning to understand her mother, she dropped another bomb like this one.

"Which reminds me," her mother said, grabbing an old piece of paper and scribbling something down. "I need to send a message to the Resistance."

Snow frowned. *She's not listening to me.* "Everything you've told me is a lie. How do I know if you're good or bad? Hero or Villain?"

"You are keen on making hasty judgments, aren't you, Snow?" Her mother shook her head and gave a low chuckle. "Just like your mother."

"I'm nothing like you," Snow mumbled. They might have reached an uneasy truce during their mutual imprisonment, but that didn't mean Snow had forgotten what her mother was. An enchantress with lots of secrets. Not to mention a lousy mom.

Her mother blinked twice, turned back around, and finished her note. The sound of a pot lid clattered from the kitchen, followed by the crashing noise of pans hitting the floor and the leprechauns shouting wildly at the vampire. Her mother brushed by Snow in icy silence and started giving the leprechauns instructions about how to get to Resistance headquarters.

From the sound of it, the Resistance was part of some underground rebellion. *More secrets.* Snow pushed aside the feeling of guilt that was blooming inside her. A couple of days together didn't make up for thirteen years. "Where is Archimago, anyway?" she asked when her mother came back into the room.

Her mother peered into the darkness below the desk. "Gone," she said. "He wasn't caught in the web. My best leprechaun trackers are looking for him. They say there's no trace of him, no evidence of him returning to the castle. Perhaps he is still close by."

"You think he'll go back to Duessa?" Snow sucked in her breath. "I *knew* we should have left him behind. What if he turns on us? It wasn't safe to take him with us."

"Living isn't safe," her mother's muffled voice said. "And living with other characters is least safe of all." She emerged with a tattered shred of paper. "You can't control everyone in Story, Snow, and you will have a very sad Tale indeed if you try. Leave Archimago to make his own choices, and we will make ours." She got to her feet, and met Snow's gaze. "I gave my word, Snow. He deserves a chance to make things right."

"And if he doesn't?" Snow hissed. "A second chance is well and good for him, but what if he betrays us? Think of what he's already done!"

"The difference between good and bad, between hero and villain, is not so clear, Snow." She was talking in her teacher voice. "You think Archimago is all bad because he has made mistakes? Which of us is without error? Have you done everything the way you wished? The way you ought to have done?" She looked at Snow with tired eyes. "Whether you agree or not, he *will* have his second chance."

The last thing Snow wanted was a lecture. She didn't care if part of what her mother said made sense. Sure, she had made mistakes, and she didn't have any trouble admitting it. But calling Horace names or making fun of Una wasn't quite the same thing as watching other characters die. Or lying to all of Story.

"Whatever you say, Warlock's Apprentice," Snow said, and didn't care that she sounded surly. "Is *that* the spell book?"

Her mother had cleared off the desk and put the tiny shred of paper right in the middle of the flat surface. "No more questions, please," she said without looking at Snow. "There are many traps around this, and they were all intended to kill enemies."

Snow eyed the scrap and risked one question. "How do you know?"

Her mother's voice was hard. "Because I set them myself."

Of course you did. Snow scowled at her mother's back as it bent over the desk. *Between learning your enchantress spells and hanging out with warlocks, you had time to set stupid booby traps in some underground hut.*

Despite all her glaring, Snow did as her mother said. She sat quietly as the vampire brought her a tray of beef stew.

He stood across from her, his gaze sharply following each dip of the spoon as she ate. *Creepy.*

The vampire seemed eager to talk. He had learned a lot about Duessa living in the shadow of her castle. The more Snow heard the vampire talk about Duessa, the more she despised her. Duessa's crimes seemed to have no limit: practicing the forbidden arts, dark rituals that left the denizens of the forest paralyzed with terror, underground excavations that turned acres of Story's land to ruins, unnamed prisoners being taken to and from the castle at all hours.

He licked his lips hungrily as Snow reached for a slice of buttered bread.

"Do you want some?" she offered, then felt stupid when the vampire waved it away. Of course he didn't want any. Snow asked if there was any recent news of Duessa.

"She's taken a hospitable turn," the vampire said. "All of Story is invited to a coronation ball at the Red Enchantress's castle tonight. There's a new King in Story."

Snow looked sharply at her mother, who was muttering under her breath and making little circular movements in the air over the paper. Either her mother wasn't listening, or the ball was old news to her. A tiny web of light shot out from her mother's clasped hands, and wherever it touched, the paper flickered. There was a click and the sound of steam escaping from a hot kettle. What looked like a scrap of paper wavered, and Snow caught a glimpse of something big. The air shimmered, and the paper disappeared altogether, revealing an enormous leather-bound book.

Snow let her spoon drop to the edge of her bowl. "How did you do that?"

Her mother glanced at her and laughed. "Haven't you learned yet?" She wiped beads of sweat off her forehead and pointed toward the book. "Story is rife with illusion. Enchantment and deception are everywhere."

"Maybe so," Snow said. Or maybe it was her mother that was full of deception. There was a crash from somewhere beyond the doors, and the vampire hurried away, muttering something about leprechauns not doing as they were told, leaving Snow and her mother alone.

"Oh, Amaranth, if only you were here," her mother murmured as she flipped through the dusty pages. "How much I've missed you."

"Who was he?" Snow asked in a dull voice.

"You haven't been taught about Amaranth the Brave?" her mother said as she ran her finger down a column of spidery script. "The one who studied quicksilver?"

Snow shrugged. "Maybe I learned about him in

Backstory." Maybe not, seeing how she at best pulled a C last term.

"It would have been in Heroics, though I doubt that Heroics professor teaches anything useful," her mother muttered. "Quicksilver is a substance found in the Enchanted Swamp. It's why we built this"—she waved her hand toward one of the many doors—"chamber, I guess you could call it." She stood up and looked around the room fondly. "Amaranth and I spent an entire year studying the organic composition of quicksilver. Then there was the matter of the right conditions. Too careless, and it would consume any vessel we used." Snow's mother strummed her fingers in the air to explain. "Too soft, and it would evaporate."

Snow was watching her mother's description in stony silence.

"During one of our digs," her mother went on, "we came across an ancient chest. It had been buried in the Swamp's quicksand for generations. Amaranth knew at once it was the Scroll of Fire. Worse men would have stolen the Scroll. Used it to write ruin on their enemies. Even alone, the Scroll is a powerful weapon. Whatever is written on it will instantly come to pass. Used in combination with the other Elements . . ." She shook her head. "It's undefeatable." She leaned back against the desk, the spell book momentarily forgotten. "But Amaranth wasn't power hungry. He was a good man. We brought it back here where no one would look for it." She barked a sharp little laugh. "Even Duessa wouldn't deign to visit the Swamp, though it's on her very doorstep. We never finished the quicksilver work. We didn't complete proper testing before—" She dropped her hands to her sides, and all the energy went out of her voice. "Well, before we stopped the project."

Snow didn't care about the proper testing. Or the quicksilver. She hated it, in fact. *A stupid project? That* was why her mother left her with her aunt? What about all the business of her heart turning to ice and naming her Snow? Was it all just a show? "Did you love him? The Warlock of Amaranth?"

"You pry too much, Snow."

"Too much?" Snow made her voice hard. "You tell me nothing. Was he my father?"

Her mother visibly stiffened. "Your father is dead to me now, Snow," she said in a tired voice. "And I will not speak ill of the dead." She turned back to the book and tore out a page. "But no. The Warlock of

Amaranth was not your father. He was my friend. And I found him when I most needed a friend." Snow's mother came toward Snow, and her smile was soft. "We discovered some incredible things together, he and I." She brushed by Snow and knelt before the fireplace, the paper spread out in front of her.

Snow stared speechlessly at her mother's back as she began to perform the spell. Snow had always wanted to know why her mother had left when she was a baby, but now that the truth was in front of her, she wished it was still a mystery. Part of her had always wondered if her mother had run off for love of Snow's father. But then why were her words about him so hard? Was it really just the excitement of working with the Warlock? Any possible answer left Snow feeling hollowed out inside. Was this what her mother had chosen over her?

The fire was changing colors. The flames were red, or perhaps gold, or maybe even black. There, in the center of its swirling darkness was what they were looking for. A glowing parchment hung suspended in the middle of the magic blaze. "Beautiful, isn't it?" Her mother's words sounded rapturous.

"Amazing," Snow said in a sarcastic voice, but her

mother didn't notice. "Just amazing that you could remember exactly where something was all those years. Especially since it was so hard for you to remember your own daughter while you were off with your precious Warlock." Snow spit all the venom she felt into her words. She was through with pretending.

Her mother's form froze in front of her. Her head dropped down, but then her spine stiffened, and she spoke as though she hadn't even heard Snow. "The Scroll of Fire. Right where we hid it."

"When would that be?" Snow pronounced her words carefully. "Before you had a kid, or after you left her on someone's doorstep?"

Her mother jumped to her feet and faced her daughter. Her hands were shaking. "What do you want from me, Snow? To pick a fight? To punish me?" Her eyes glistened wetly. "Believe me, I've punished myself." Her voice broke, and she wiped hard at her eyes.

Snow blinked back her own unexpected tears. "Just tell me why you didn't want me."

Her mother stood very still in front of Snow. "I wanted you, Snow. How I wanted you." She held her hands out as though she was embracing the air around Snow. "But you weren't safe with me. After"—her mother looked down—"you were born, I was very confused. And broken. I had wanted to be a Princess, and your father . . . well, after what he did to me, I felt like the worst Villain." She blinked furiously. "If I had known . . . To me, you were just the reminder of a terrible night. I didn't know *you* then. I was angry. I don't like to remember those years. At the end of them, I found the Warlock. He took me in when I had nowhere else to go. He gave me something important to do." She pulled Snow to her feet, and her eyes were wet. "I came for you as soon as I was well again." Her hand wavered, and then she drew Snow into an awkward embrace. "I don't expect you to understand, Snow. How could you? What I did was unforgivable."

Snow wanted to believe her mother, wanted what she was saying to be true. But she kept her arms at her side. Tears or no tears, she didn't want her mother's hugs or her apologies or excuses. She wanted those thirteen years back.

The room all of a sudden felt very quiet. No sounds of vampire and leprechauns bickering came from the kitchen. Only silence. Snow's mother froze. "Someone else is here."

As they whirled around, they saw that Archimago

was already at the fireplace. With a shout of triumph, he snatched the Scroll of Fire from its hiding place. "Oh, how touching," he sneered, as he twirled the Scroll through the air and slid it under his raggedy cloak. "Mother and daughter reunited at last. Just in time, too." He withdrew a slender wand and pointed it straight at Snow. "Say good-bye to Mummy, puppet."

Snow stood frozen to the spot, but her mother had no such problem. She leaped in front of Snow, and a web of glistening light shot out from one hand. She spun Snow around and propelled her through the room toward one of the doors. "You have to believe that I did what was best for you, Snow." She pressed her hand against the door, releasing a lock, and shoved Snow through. "Just like I'm doing now."

Snow didn't know what kind of spell her mother had thrown at Archimago. Whatever it was, it hadn't stopped him for long. The sound of an explosion rang out behind them, a rush of heat whistling over Snow's shoulder.

"We can't leave the Scroll," she cried. From behind them came a sound like a roaring fire followed by the pummeling of a driving rain. "If he takes it to Fidelus, he'll have all three Elements!"

"That is the sound of our hideout's alarms." Her mother pushed Snow through the dark tunnel. "Archimago has not come alone. The Scroll is lost to us for now. We need help to stop him." Her mother paused at a tangled crossroads. Passageways snaked off in every direction. With only a moment's hesitation, she chose one.

"But what about Archimago's promise?" Snow asked. "Won't something bad happen to him now?"

"Something bad already has happened to him." Her mother was sprinting. "Poor Archimago. He is beyond the hope of second chances. He has given himself over to the schemes of the Enemy."

Chapter 18

*U*na leaned back in the leather armchair. The heat
from the fire in front of her weighed her eye-
lids down and made her sleepy. She missed her mother
already. A servant had appeared with an urgent message only moments after their arrival in the cozy room.

"Wait right here for just a minute," her mother had
said, and now Una was alone in the castle library. A
chair that matched her own was across from her, its
leather surface reflecting the shadows cast by the flickering flames. Lit sconces affixed to the wall revealed
floor-to-ceiling empty bookshelves. Una wondered
where all the books had gone.

Mother said that Father had been waiting to see her,
that Una had been one of the first things he asked for

when he was set free. But now Una wasn't so sure she believed her mother. Una's head felt strange, like it did when she was recovering from a cold and parts of her that had been stuffed up popped open. This was all wrong. She should be able to remember things. How she got here, for instance. Una looked down at her lap. A scrap of fabric sat there, covered with a knot of badly done stitches. *Embroidery? Is this* my *handkerchief?* Una stood up and shoved it into her pocket. Her fingers touched something hard and cold, and she pulled it out.

The gold on the ring looked dull in the firelight. The thick band met in the middle of a flat square panel. She felt a flicker of interest. Someone had given this ring to her. For a specific purpose. Una slid it onto her index finger so that the panel faced up, and it warmed with heat. A shimmer ran across the surface. As Una watched, a tiny tree blossomed with white light. The dull metal was transformed into golden brightness, and, in that moment, Una remembered everything.

I'm in Duessa's castle. She spun in a circle. *Waiting to meet the Enemy.* The events of the morning flashed through her mind. Why hadn't she punched Elton in the face when she had a chance? Was that really her, sitting beside her mother and begging for her smiles? While all of Story was in danger, she had been busy with a *sewing lesson*? Una ran to the library door, and pulled fruitlessly on the handle. *Locked!*

She let go of it as though burned. The next person who would come through that door would be her father, the Enemy himself. Una felt light-headed. They would know. As soon as they saw her, Duessa would know that her enchantment had worn off.

Wait. Maybe she could play along. She wished she knew more of how soppy she had been when under Duessa's enchantment. Had she really hugged the Red Enchantress? Would she have to fake-hug the Enemy? Una looked at Kai's ring. It had stopped glowing. *I can do this.* Now was her chance to learn something useful. She didn't know how she'd escape, or if she'd be able to, but she would be ready. And when she returned to Bramble Cottage, she would be armed with information that would help the Resistance.

The low desk in the corner was surrounded by stacks and stacks of papers. Una crept over and sifted through some of them, but all of them were smudged and blank, as though someone had written a Tale and then erased it. She was reaching for a second stack, when the sound of footsteps echoed outside the door. She scurried back to her chair, spread her skirt beneath her, and tried to slow her breathing. The next moment a figure appeared at the doorway. Even before he stepped into the room, Una knew that it was him.

Fidelus brushed past her and sat down in the chair opposite without a word. He looked at her with gray eyes. Una stared back at him. A square jaw and firm chin framed a handsome face. His skin was lined, but he didn't look old. His hair was dark like her own, and it shone in the flickering light.

He didn't smile. "Una," he said as he stretched out his hands to clasp her trembling hand. "I'm so glad you've found us."

Una did her best not to flinch at his touch. She kept the hand with the ring hidden under a fold in her skirt. "Me, too. Mother said you were resting." She tried to imagine what this reunion would be like if she didn't know what her father had done. If she didn't know that he was the Enemy. It wasn't hard. Part of her had been waiting to meet him for her entire life. She took a deep breath. "I've wondered about you both for so long."

Fidelus patted her hand and released it. "We've missed you, too." He leaned back in the chair and put both hands behind his head. "And what do you think now that you've found us? Now that you know my Tale?"

Una forced herself to look into his gray eyes. "I want to know how the story ends. What happens next?"

Fidelus laughed. "Those who are with me have nothing to fear. We'll get our happy ending." He had none of Duessa's softness, none of the lilting words that made Una forget who she was. Instead, his voice was hard, and he was looking at Una as though she were a piece of food he was about to devour. "Are you with me?"

"Of course I'm with you." Una twisted her mouth into a bitter smile. "I freed you."

He folded his hands across his stomach. "A good answer."

Una needed to take control of the conversation. Her mother's voice had enchanted her. Who knew what her father could do? "What's all the paper for?" she asked.

"Some Tales need a lot of revising." A slow smile crept across his face. "Especially the drivel that pathetic old King wrote for the land of Story. Once I rewrite

Story, I will get the ending I deserve."

"Rewrite?" Una willed herself to remember the details. The slightest turn of phrase could be valuable to the Resistance. "Wouldn't that change all of Story's past?"

"You *are* a clever thing, aren't you?" Fidelus watched her like a hawk. "The new Story will be mine. Those who oppose me?" He snapped his fingers. "Unwritten. Those who serve me"—he raised one eyebrow—"I think they might come to a good end."

Una's mouth went dry. She thought of the legend of the beginning of Story. "Can a Muse really unwrite someone?"

His laugh came out low and menacing. "Don't worry, Una. It won't be painful. It will just be over. They won't feel a thing. Because they won't have existed at all." His eyes narrowed thoughtfully. "The more obliging characters will remain and be my happy subjects."

"Oh?" Una tried to make her voice casual, as though it was the most normal thing in the world to have a fireside chat about an evil plan that would make everyone she had ever cared about unexist. "So will you use the Silver Quill to rewrite Story?"

Fidelus didn't say anything. He rubbed his index finger and his thumb together in tiny circles.

Una tried a different approach. "You must have all the Elements if you're crowning yourself King tonight."

He gave her a polite little clap. "Very good, Una. I knew you weren't a fool." His voice grew unpleasant. "But then, neither am I. You think me a stupid Villain who would disclose his whole plan to anyone who wants to listen? You test my patience, Daughter."

"I don't think you are a fool," Una lied. She wanted to shout the truth in his face. Only a fool would betray his family. Only a fool would break his oaths. Only a fool would come back to try again.

"We shall see." Fidelus leaned forward and let his hands fall between his knees. "You might be a simpleton, of course, not to realize after you read my true Tale that I stole the Ink." His eyes were calculating. "But I don't think so." He gave her a hard laugh. "Dissembling doesn't become you, my dear daughter. You should try truthfulness."

Una looked into the fire. "And betrayal doesn't become one whose name means 'loyalty.' Why did you do it? Why couldn't you have just listened to the other

Muses?" Una had a momentary flash of the way things could have been. Her father wouldn't have broken his oaths. He would have been a faithful Muse, one who welcomed the King's return instead of fighting against it. He would have been like the other Muses, excited to finally have their own Tale. Then the King of Story would have written a Tale for them all. Her mother, her father, and her, together in Story from the beginning. Happy. "Why didn't you just let the real King write your Tale?"

Her father struck her then, and her eyes watered with the sting of it. "Do not speak of him in my presence," he said.

"Fidelus?" Duessa's breathy voice came from the doorway.

Una lifted a hand to her cheek. It didn't matter. She couldn't rub away the shame of it. Duessa floated into the room in a cloud of red, but she didn't come over to Una. She draped herself across the back of Fidelus's chair, and kissed his forehead. "Things are going according to plan. Elton has commanded the characters to attend you here at nightfall."

Fidelus stood and grasped Duessa by the shoulders.

"And my brothers and sisters?"

"Sleeping soundly. I sealed their dreams with my blood. When they next wake, they'll have horrible ends in the new Story. Or perhaps they won't be there at all. Aren't you pleased?"

He gave Duessa a low laugh and wrapped his arms around her. "How could I be anything but pleased with you?"

Una sat very still in her chair. Maybe they had forgotten her.

He rested his chin on Duessa's head. "The only thing that would please me more is to begin writing now."

Duessa pulled back and stared up at him. "Didn't I tell you? I sent that old fool Archimago to spy on one of my"—her tongue flicked out over her teeth—"uncooperative prisoners, and he stumbled across the Warlock's Apprentice. She wasn't in a Tale at all, the clever thing." She gave a hard little laugh. "But all her cleverness won't do her any good now. Archimago sent word that he is bringing the Scroll here tonight." She traced Fidelus's jawline with her finger. "Too bad I've already found my true love." She kissed him on the mouth.

Una looked away. When she was a little girl, she had

dreamed many things about her parents. That they had been crazy in love with each other. That they were rich. That they were royalty. That there was some tragic, secret reason they had disappeared. Now that she knew all those things were true, it only made her feel like throwing up.

"And Elton? It would be useful to have a WI present. Someone to come up with the right turn of phrase. A muse to inspire the Great Muse," he chuckled.

"Elton is tiresome. He cares too much for the old Story." Duessa tugged on Fidelus's collar. "But I have a better idea. Have you forgotten that our little daughter was Written In? She lived for many years in the Readers' World and could prove a valuable assistant."

"No," Fidelus said in a bored voice. His eyes found Una's. "This girl may be our flesh and blood, but she is no daughter of mine."

Una sucked in her breath. It didn't matter that he was the Enemy of Story. It didn't matter that he was a horrible man. He was still her father, and the sting of his words was worse than when he had hit her.

"Ah, I see that I have been gone too long. Our Una has come to her senses." Duessa's laugh was like a song, and even though Una knew she was an Enchantress, she still felt the overwhelming urge to please her. She twisted the ring on her finger for courage and tried out a weak smile.

It seemed to work.

"Look how pliable she is. So naive. So trusting." Duessa looked up at him with a coy smirk. "Nothing like her mother, hmmm?" She walked toward Fidelus. "With the old Story's End, the new Story can begin with the three of us. One happy little family."

Una kept the empty smile pasted on her face and stared past her parents while they embraced. The only thing she could think of worse than being unwritten with her friends was being doomed to a lifetime with these two. She had to figure out a way to escape. What had she been doing while she had been enchanted besides acting like a complete idiot? *Sewing!* She fumbled in her pocket for the handkerchief and pretended that her mess of stitches was the most interesting thing in the world.

Her mother seemed to remember that Una was in the room. She snapped her fingers, and a cloaked figure slid into view. Its hooded head bowed before the pair across from Una.

"I have other things to think about now," her mother

said, without a glance at Una. "She will sleep until the coronation." She waved her hand in Una's general direction. "Put her with the other one."

The guard stood silently by Una's side. Her mother looked up and peered strangely at Una.

"She is still awake?" She sounded irritated and repeated the hand gesture.

It took Una a moment to figure out that her mother had cast a spell on her. She was supposed to be asleep. And it sounded like it was supposed to happen immediately. She let her body crumple beneath her, and sank into the corner of the chair. Duessa turned back to Fidelus, and then the cloaked creature had its claws on her. It scooped her up in powerful arms and swept her out of the room and down a long hallway. Una kept her eyes mostly closed, peering out from behind her lashes, but all she could see were the castle's stone walls. Her captor smelled like smoke, and its grip on her felt like iron. *What kind of creature does Duessa's bidding anyway?*

The thing climbed a staircase that twisted up, up, up for what seemed like an eternity. Finally it opened a great door and moved quickly through it, its gait so smooth it felt to Una like she was gliding through the air. She was in a dark corridor. Una had the fleeting thought that if she could break free from the creature, she would escape. *But then what?* She'd be alone at the top of the castle, and she didn't doubt that the guard would have her back in his iron grip in no time. The creature came to an abrupt halt, and Una heard the creaking of a door. Up more stairs and through another door. The guard was none too gentle about depositing her on the cold stone floor. Then, the door slammed behind her, and, with a click of the lock, she was alone.

When Una was sure that her captor had really gone, she risked a peek. One barred window filtered a few squares of pale afternoon light into the round room. Una pushed herself up to a sitting position.

There was a rustle of movement from the wall opposite her.

Una froze, peering into the darkness.

Someone groaned. Una grabbed for her dagger, but the belt at her waist hung empty. She crept forward, fumbling against the wall in the dim light. Her hand brushed the edge of a table. She felt blindly until her fingers found the handle of a pan. She held it above her head like a club and inched closer to the corner.

A boy lay there, either unconscious or fast asleep—

Una couldn't be sure. But there was no mistaking that spiky hair. Una set the pan back on the table with a thump.

"Horace," she said as she aimed a none-too-gentle kick at his gut. "Get up."

Chapter 19

I thought you said tunnels led from Amaranth's hideout to every district in Story," Snow said to her mother as they crouched at the end of the tunnel. "Why did you pick the Ranch?"

"This is the place where Fidelus sent the Taleless, remember?" her mother said in a tired voice. "We need to save the Westerns and defeat the Taleless." She laughed. "And we need to finish our work before we can go to the ball."

Snow scowled. Was her mother making a joke? There wasn't anything funny about their predicament. *We lost the Scroll.* The gratification of being right about Archimago's treachery had paled with the certainty that Archimago would take the Scroll directly to his one true love, Duessa. And the Enemy.

"*We* are going to save the Westerns?" Snow put a hard edge in her voice. Her mother had brought them straight to a place where they'd be in danger. "How are we supposed to fight the Taleless?"

"I have seen much in the world that I wish I hadn't." Snow's mother looked up at her. It wasn't sadness Snow saw in her eyes, but anger. "There was a sorcerer. He discovered a way to clothe the Taleless with bodies. But the bodies didn't make them whole. The Taleless who tried this were clothed with flesh for a time, but those bodies wear out, and they must keep finding more." Snow's mother got to her feet. "A twisted magic. And one expressly forbidden in Story."

Snow remembered what the leprechauns had been talking about in the forest, how Duessa was doing something with dead bodies. It was all true. "You mean," she said hollowly, "the Taleless are here to take the Westerns' bodies?" It sounded like a bad Zombie Tale straight from Horror Hollow. Find a shade. Give it someone else's body.

"The good news is that once they wear bodies, they can be destroyed. Perhaps no one else knows the fate Fidelus plans for the Westerns." Snow's mother was watching her carefully. "Knowing what you now know, could you really leave a whole district to the Taleless?"

Snow shook her head silently. She didn't particularly like the Westerns she knew at Perrault, and the way they bragged about how brave they were annoyed her, but that didn't matter now. "No one deserves the Taleless." Her mother gave her a brief smile and then led the way out of the tunnel's mouth and into the heart of the Ranch.

Snow wiped a hand across her sweaty forehead. As if the humidity wasn't bad enough, a fine dust coated her skin. Freshly laundered sheets were flapping on zigzagged clotheslines, and Western girls bustled to and fro. Two Indians popped out in front of Snow, shouldering a pole that had a bucket of boiling water swinging from the middle. Snow ducked under the nearest sheet to avoid being burned. Her mother had told her to wait there, to keep her ears open and her mouth shut. Which Snow had no problem doing. Fantasy folk and Westerns got along all right, but Snow had the creeping suspicion that they might mistake her ragged cloak for Horror Hollow's Villainous apparel. Which would be a problem. Westerns and Horrors were always getting suspended from Perrault for dueling with each other, and the feud ran deep. Snow took care to stay hidden behind the drying laundry as she peered out at the crowded scene.

Across the way, a fire heated cauldrons to boiling, after which the water was dumped into a huge vat. Three cowgirls stood around it, stirring clothing with long wooden poles.

"My pa said that there's a fancy-dress ball tonight. All of Story's invited." A big-boned girl pushed down hard on the pole. "I'd wager that's why the Tale Master's messengers want all these clothes cleaned."

"Talekeeper mumbo jumbo don't mean anything, Effie Lou; you oughta know that." The short girl next to her carved some soap peelings into the water. "Won't have no peace with outsiders. And those aren't no *messengers*." She spit on the ground. "There's an evil air about them worse than the stench around Horror Hollow."

"Don't I know it? Wasn't it a Horror who cheated my brother? Took off Billy's leg, and I won't forget it." Effie Lou's biceps bulged as she scooped up a large pile of clothing on the flat part of her pole. She dumped the load onto the wooden table next to the pot. "The day

I follow any Horror, whatever she's called, is the day my body lies cold in the ground. If we don't figure out a plan soon, I'm going to bust out of here and kill the first one I see, whatever the Tale Master says. Hang the consequences."

Her friend grabbed a wet garment and swiped it twice with the soap. Then she began vigorously scraping it back and forth across a washboard. "That's what I think about that *Tale Master*. Would cut his lying tongue out if I had the chance." *Plunge* went the girl's red-knuckled hands. *Rip* went the fabric as it brushed against the rough board. "Rounding up all our menfolk. Penning 'em up like cattle. Won't let me see my ma neither."

Snow shrank back behind the clean sheets—she didn't want to take her chances with Effie Lou's ability to identify whether Snow was a Horror character or from the Fantasy District—and bumped straight into her mother.

"The Taleless are already here." Her mother pulled Snow close.

"I know." Snow told her mother what she had overheard.

Her mother was eyeing Snow's clothes. "They've got

the Westerns trapped out where the cattle are supposed to be. We have to hurry." She grabbed a clothespin off the nearest line and knelt down to shake out the hem of Snow's skirt.

Snow squawked a protest. "What are you doing?"

"Fixing you up." Her mother sighed when she saw the tattered remains of Snow's petticoat. "The Westerns will shoot me as soon as speak with me—they hate Horror Villains, you know—so I need you to talk to them." Her mother clamped the clothespin in her mouth so that she could work with both hands.

"Me?" Snow brushed at her mother's deft fingers. "Why on earth are they going to listen to me?"

"Because"—her mother twisted the fabric into a neat fold and spit out the clothespin—"you're going to be very persuasive." She clipped the makeshift seam. "There. It'll have to do. You still have a touch of Fantasy, but, with a little luck, you may pass for a Western. And at least you don't look like a Horror. Now, put on my petticoat." Snow didn't know how she did it, but with the tiniest movement, her mother's undergarment sat in a neat heap on the ground. "You need some ruffles."

Snow stared at it. For some reason it felt absurd to

think of her villainous mother wearing a frilly lace shift under her villainous black dress.

"Snow, we don't have time for this." Her mother's voice was firm. "Do it. Now."

While Snow wriggled into the slip, her mother disappeared and then returned with a bar of lye soap and a wet rag. "Now wash your face."

When she was done, her mother looked her over appraisingly. "Good enough. Get them to come with you—I don't care how you do it"—she held up a hand to forestall Snow's questions—"and meet me at the Old Red Barn."

"But I don't know where that is." Snow had no doubt that those girls meant every word they said about killing Horrors. And they looked strong enough to do it.

"They will," was all her mother said, and then she was gone.

Snow took a deep breath and tried to think of anything she knew about Westerns. The trouble was that she knew next to nothing. There had been a few cowgirls in her Elocution class. But the impression she had of them was that they would have lassoed anyone who tried to put them in a lace petticoat. The closest thing she could come up with was the Saloon Girl who helped some of the customers at Lady Godiva's. The salesgirl was a complete flake, but she had nice taste in fabric. Snow gave her skirt the tiniest flick for practice, took a deep breath, and then made her way over to Effie Lou and her friend.

"Well, howdy-do." Snow's cheeks burned as she said it, and she fervently hoped the blush looked like face paint. Was that drawl really her own? No matter how Snow spun it, there really was no good way to convince two Horror-hating Westerns to come have a little chat with the Villainy professor.

Effie Lou jabbed her pole hard into the pot with a grunt. The scrub girl didn't even look up from her board.

Snow tried again. "I'm looking for Billy's sister. He said she'd be in the laundry." That got their attention.

Effie Lou dropped her stick and glared at Snow. "Is that so?" She folded her beefy arms across her chest.

Snow held the side of her petticoat and twitched it back and forth like she remembered the salesgirl doing. "Yes, ma'am. I've got a message for her." Effie Lou snorted, but Snow plowed on. "Billy told me that you should meet him at the Old Red Barn."

"Take over for me, will ya, Pearl?" Effie Lou clapped

her friend hard on the back. "I gotta go get my *message*."

Snow gave a little dip and another toss of her petticoat. That had been remarkably easy, and Effie Lou was even leading the way out of the warren of clotheslines. *Piece of cake.* They were near the outskirts of the laundry area, when Effie Lou grabbed Snow's wrist, twisted down on it hard, and yanked her into a tent.

The next thing Snow knew, her back was on a table, and Effie Lou's hands were at her neck.

"What's your game, chit?" Effie Lou's breath smelled like onions. "Billy's been in the ground for nigh on three years, and don't you tell me he's crossed over from the dead just to see li'l ol' me."

Snow worked her mouth, but no sound came out.

Effie Lou shook her. "I'll give you to the count of three to tell me the truth. Then, I'll wring your scrawny Horror neck."

Snow's eyes bulged and she waved her hands.

Effie Lou released her grip, and Snow gasped for air. The Western girl pulled hard on Snow's shoulders until she was sitting on the table.

"Now talk," Effie said.

Snow rubbed at her throat. "I'm not a Villain."

Effie Lou cracked her knuckles.

"I'm *not*. I'm from Heart's Place."

Effie Lou's face broke into a wide grin. "A Romantic. Even better."

Snow didn't like the glint in her eyes. "Fantasy, actually," she managed, "but it doesn't matter." She mentally cursed her mother. *She* should be here dealing with this. Not Snow. What could she say to make this half-witted girl understand? "A great Enemy is back in Story." Her mouth and throat were dry.

"Oh?" Effie Lou was chewing on something, and Snow couldn't look away from the bulge in her jaw. The Western girl squinted at her with her beady eyes.

Snow forced down a swallow and continued. "Well, the Enemy is bad." She was trying to think of how to explain it simply. "Very bad. And he's the one controlling the Tale Master."

"So that paper Pearl brought back from Perrault was truthful-like?" Effie Lou's mouth turned down at the corners, and she spit something black out onto the floor. "And the messengers the Tale Master sent? Friend or foe?"

"They're the Enemy's helpers." Snow sounded more confident than she felt. *Please don't let Effie Lou ask any more questions.* "They're planning something."

How could she convince the girl this was very serious? "They mean to destroy the Ranch."

Effie Lou's face was unreadable. She seemed to be evaluating Snow. Then she said, "Well, why didn't you say so in the first place, girl? I'm just itchin' for a fight."

Snow let out a shaky breath.

Effie Lou wasn't exactly friendly after that, but she did lick her palm before shaking Snow's hand. Snow willed her face to be poker smooth as she felt the slimy wetness on her fingers.

Effie Lou led the way to the barn, but it wasn't easy. Two guards strolled around the perimeter of the laundry area, their cloaks black as night against the white washing. Effie Lou doubled back, circling a different fire, and the hot steam hid them from sight. There was clothing on the lines in this section, but it didn't look Western. Snow recognized Villainous dresses, capes of varying shades, and at least one sorcerer's robe.

Effie Lou snorted when Snow asked her about it. "The newest arrivals. They ain't natural. No lie." She swiped some clothes off the line, and ducked under to the other side. "Hoity-toity things can't even do their own laundry." She grabbed another wad and shoved it at Snow. "Put that on."

Snow was getting tired of people telling her what to wear. She dropped the bundle onto the ground and shook out each garment. The black tunic and tight fitted pants looked like something her cousin Horace might pick out, right down to the barbed chains that were sewn up and down the legs.

"You wanna get to the barn in one piece?" Effie Lou wrapped an emerald-green cape around her hefty shoulders. "Gotta look like 'em."

Snow didn't want to tell Effie Lou that she didn't exactly look like a wizard in her stolen cloak. She looked more like an overgrown Western wearing a green bathrobe. But Snow thought better of it. Instead, she slipped into the stolen black outfit and followed Effie Lou out onto the dusty streets of the Ranch.

Chapter 20

It didn't take Snow's mother long to convince Effie Lou that they could work together. And it required almost as little time to multiply their numbers. Effie Lou had been a lucky choice of ally. She was the sheriff's daughter, so many of the girls followed her lead without question.

"Duessa's *Protectors*"—Snow's mother spit out the word with venom—"are going to regret this day." The Western girls had told them that the Protectors had come into town that morning, rounding up all the grown-ups and the boys, and forcing everyone else into servitude. The Western girls had not been happy about this, to say the least. The Ranch felt like a pile of straw that only needed a small spark to turn into a raging fire. And Snow and her mother were that spark.

"They're keeping the grown-ups in the branding pens," Snow's mother said in a low voice. "But all of them are unarmed."

"Westerns are always armed," a small Indian girl said. "With or without weapons." This set off a chorus of hoots and hollers.

"Shut your big bazoos." Effie Lou silenced them quick enough. "Now ain't the time. Wait for it, girls, wait for it." Her eyes had a wicked gleam to them, and Snow had a momentary flash of pity for anyone foolish enough to underestimate the Western girls. Finally, the Western they had been waiting for, the scrub girl Snow had first seen talking with Effie Lou, appeared. Her name was Pearl, and she looked like anything but.

"I got the stuff," she said as she set three bulging sacks and a pile of clean cloths in front of Snow's mother.

"Thank you." Her mother gingerly moved the sacks apart from each other. "Now who will volunteer to set off the explosives?"

Snow kept her arms firmly by her sides, but she needn't have worried. Every other hand went up.

Her mother's laugh sounded genuine. "Very well. Effie Lou, pick your team." While the Western girls fought over who got to blow up buildings, her mother handed Snow one of the cloths and showed her how to fold it into a small pouch. "I need one scoop of this for every packet. Take care, Snow. This isn't ordinary salt."

Snow held the cloth between two fingers. Her mother didn't need to tell her to be careful. Everyone knew gunpowder was the farthest thing from stable. The Weapons Master at Perrault didn't even have any in his storeroom. Snow unwound the tie around the biggest sack, painstakingly measured out a level scoop, and poured it onto the clean fabric. Her mother worked along behind her, completing the concoction by mixing in the rest of the ingredients.

By the time the others had sorted themselves out, Snow and her mother had crafted a row of tiny mounds. Effie Lou hovered over Snow's shoulder as her mother gave them instructions.

"We'll circle around the pens and wait for your signal, Effie Lou." Her mother began folding the fabric over the explosives to make little packets. "Divide these up among your team. Don't let them brush against each other. And don't let them get too hot."

Effie Lou's friends had to have heard her mother's warning, but they didn't seem to care. They jostled around the stockpile and began stuffing packets into their pockets and down the sides of their boots; a few even shoved them under their shirt fronts.

When all the bombs were stowed away, Effie Lou and her band of merry girls crept silently out the back of the corral. Each of them had stolen Villainous apparel off the laundry lines, but it didn't do any good. They looked exactly like what they were: Western girls dressed up as Horrors. Snow gave them about two minutes under close scrutiny before a Protector called them out on the spot. But two minutes might be enough.

In Snow's group, she and her mother were the only two who looked Villainous. The small pack of girls that were sandwiched between them bumped and shoved one another, acting like the mutinous lot they were. There was a chance that Snow and her mother would be able to pass unnoticed, that they would look like two Villains rounding up more Westerns for the pens. It wasn't a great plan, but it was the best they could hope for. Even if they did pull the deception off, it wouldn't do much good if Effie Lou and her crew weren't able to finish their assignment. It was bad odds against them. But, as Pearl had said, "We'll do our darnedest, and that you may tie to."

Snow was playing the role of rear guard. There were more than a few pairs of chaps and jangling spurs on the girls in front of her, but there were also printed dresses and bonnets, the whisper-soft footfalls of leather moccasins, and even one brightly colored frilled petticoat. She had been wrong about the Westerns. Sure, the brash way they acted got on her nerves, but they were refreshingly frank. After spending so much time with her mother, the queen of not saying what she was really thinking, the brutal honesty of the Westerns was a welcome change. Besides all that, Snow admired their bravery. Even members of this group, who were at the greatest risk of joining their families in the prison of the holding pens, were in good spirits, laughing and bickering among themselves.

Snow gathered courage from their example. The least she could do was play her part well. "Stay in line!" she barked at the girls as she tried to swing her hips to match the way Horace used to saunter around Heart's Place. Her mother's brief pep talk hadn't done much to calm her nerves, but she ran the phrases through her mind anyway. *Horrors are devil-may-care. Act like you own the Westerns.* She glanced up at her mother, who was surveying the street like she ruled it. She sailed past painted storefronts and swinging pairs of saloon doors. No sound of conversation or plucky piano music seeped out of them. Silence had fallen over the Ranch.

Snow was uneasy. The streets were completely empty. The lines of imprisoned Westerns she and her mother had expected were nowhere to be seen. A tumbleweed drifted down the main thoroughfare as if to underscore the point. Snow had no idea if Duessa's Protectors were peering out at them from behind the shuttered windows, but, if they were, their plan was a failure. There was no way Snow and the others were going unnoticed. The Western girls seemed aware of it, too. They stilled their feigned resistance and now crept along like cats bristling for a fight. As her mother turned down the alley that led to where the animals were kept, Snow felt a faint glimmer of hope that they might get through all this without encountering a single Taleless.

And then it was gone, replaced with the dreadful certainty that they were about to get caught. None of the Taleless were patrolling the streets, because they were all here at the branding pens.

One of the cowgirls swore.

Snow's mother silenced her. "Remember why we've

come. Spread out. Wait for Effie Lou's signal. Be ready
to fight." Somehow the girls found places to hide, and
in a matter of moments they had melted into the dusty
landscape. Snow joined her mother in the shadow of a
building and looked on in dismay.

The branding pen was enclosed with barred-off
gates, which were designed to hold waiting animals. But
that would've been on an ordinary day at the Ranch.
Today, the narrow passages were filled with Westerns.
Young and old alike were crammed in close, shoulder
to shoulder and toe to toe. None of them were moving,
and they stood like frozen sleepwalkers. In the center
of the pen, a crowd of the Taleless milled about, and
presiding over all of them was a large-mouthed woman
wearing a purple robe. A gold tiara crowned her head,
and she spoke with the authority of a queen, but she
had the face of an ancient witch. Snow didn't know if
she had ever been pretty, but she looked like death now.
Wrinkled skin hung over her cheekbones, and wisps of
gray hair trailed from patches in her scalp. In her hands
was an iron wand, which she waved overhead.

"Everyone ready for another?" Her toothless mouth
opened wide, and her cackle filled the eerie silence.

The other Taleless crowded together as the witch

let loose a stream of enchantment. The Western at the front of the branding gate stirred to life, but while he was still drowsy, two guards gripped him firmly by the arms. The cowboy came fully awake, and his feet kicked as he struggled against his captors. It did him no good. In a moment he was before the witch.

Snow had been wrong about her. She didn't have a metal wand. She had a branding iron. One end flared red as the Witch twisted it in her clawed hands.

It happened fast. Too fast for Snow to look away. The burning brand sank into the cowboy's cheek. He didn't cry out. When the witch was finished, he had a fiery black *W* scored into his skin. "This one goes to the Wizards." She cackled victoriously, and a cheer rose from a corner of the pen, where a group of Taleless held out grasping bony hands to welcome the cowboy. The air smelled like barbecued beef. The next minute Snow was on her knees, vomiting into the dusty dirt.

When she was finished, her mother's arm drew her up firmly. A cluster of sorcerers whispered and pointed in their direction.

"Say nothing," her mother hissed in Snow's ear as she dragged her roughly toward the pen.

"This one's weak." Her mother's voice was cold, and Snow felt the sting of the mockery in it. "Perhaps you have a lesson that will make her stronger."

Snow felt the heat of the witch's gaze as her mother pulled her through the gate and into the midst of the others. Snow's skin was clammy with cold sweat, and it wasn't just from throwing up. Up close, she saw that all of the Taleless were in the same state of disrepair as their leader. Papery strips of flesh hung from their sagging jaws. Bloodshot eyes bulged out of skeletal faces. Snow fought down the sour taste of bile rising in the back of her throat.

Her mother seemed unmoved. "Where are the brands?"

"Who are you?" The witch looked from Snow to her mother, a greedy glint in her eye. "And why are you whole?"

"King Fidelus sent us." Snow's mother shooed aside the hooded guards as though they were pesky flies. "There's been a change of plans."

The witch stopped grinning. "Too late for that." She poked her brand into the ground like a cane. "My spirit aches for young flesh to clothe it." Her gnarled hand swept over to the enchanted Westerns, the ruby ring on her skeletal finger glinting in the sun. "King Fidelus promised us bodies. These belong to us."

The hulking figure next to Snow sighed greedily. The skin around his mouth was coming off, and she could see his jawbone. He gripped his brand, and a flake of yellowed flesh drifted to the ground.

The old witch reached out and brushed a crooked finger against Snow's cheek. "So fresh. So perfect."

Snow's knees felt weak. She willed them to support her, to stay steady.

"She's not available." Snow's mother's voice was hard. "Get your rotting Taleless hands off her." The witch released Snow. "Whatever sorting you're doing here can wait."

Snow realized as soon as her mother said it that she was right. This was some grotesque divvying up of the Westerns, a bartering for flesh and blood.

The other Taleless began murmuring angrily. A fading sorcerer raised a crumbling fist. "He promised me a castle. Where's my castle?"

"The King promised us all castles in the new Story." The monster next to Snow reached for her mother. "And new bodies."

Snow leaned in closer to her mother's side, which felt

like solid rock. Her mother raised one arm and released a stream of fire. The monster crumbled into dust.

"You want your castle?" Her mother's voice was barely a whisper. "You do as I say."

The Taleless went silent. Snow couldn't tear her gaze away from the tiny mound on the ground next to her. A gust of wind blew about them, and a cloud of the monster's ashes swirled upward. A low murmur ran around the crowd of half-dead Taleless.

"Take heed," Snow's mother said as she nudged the monster's remains with her toe. "Taleless that put on flesh and blood can die like any other living thing."

The witch eyed Snow's mother appraisingly. "Very well," she said. "What does Fidelus wish?"

Snow didn't get to hear how her mother would have responded because at the next moment, the whole world exploded into fire. The outbuilding across the way was a crater of flames and smoke. The Taleless dropped their branding irons and began scurrying out of the corral. Snow's mother raised her arm, and a giant web of light flashed out toward the imprisoned Westerns. In a matter of seconds, they were awake and storming toward their captors, faces distorted with fury. Everything was chaos. Bright trails of magic pierced the smoke-filled

air as the Taleless fought for their lives, or what was left
of them.

Another deafening blast cracked the air, this one
coming from the building closest to them. Clouds of
black smoke raced toward the branding pen. With a
start, Snow jolted into action. She scooped up a forgotten branding iron and maneuvered her way through
the dueling figures. A werewolf materialized in front
of her, and Snow lashed out hard with the makeshift
weapon. Her arm hurt with the impact, and then the
werewolf was gone. Snow sprinted through the mad-
ness, past a screaming cowboy, whose punch made a
soft squishing sound as it connected with the half-dead
sorcerer.

She leaped over the railing, but a large, cloaked figure was waiting for her. Snow brought her brand back
to take aim, when a hand reached out.

"Just hold your horses, little lady."

Snow squinted past the black soot that dusted
the girl's face. "Effie Lou," she breathed. She let her
weapon fall back to her side. The Western girl had
accomplished her task.

"The plan's working," Snow gasped. "The Westerns
are free. Soon it will all be over." Snow had meant it to

be comforting, but Effie Lou scowled at her.

"I hope to high heaven it's not over. They better leave some of them Horrors for me." She stepped over the iron railing as though it was nothing. "Land sakes, Snow," she called back over her shoulder. "The battle's just begun."

Chapter 21

Peter raced up the road in front of Bramble Cottage. Indy ran next to him, and he always seemed to be one step ahead. Peter swung open the front gate and stopped just inside, the sound of his breath loud in his own ears. Nothing looked the same anymore. Homemade tents were scattered about the front lawn, and groups of people sat clustered in conversation. Peter had never seen any of them before. He circled round to the back of the house and found more of the same. Off near the woods he saw the dryad Griselda surrounded by some Moderns, who looked strangely out of place as they brandished rusted swords and ran through practice drills. Professor Edenberry was talking rapidly to a circle of ogres who sat in the vegetable garden like giant decorative boulders. And a man Peter didn't recognize was leading a group of warriors in spear and shield drills. Peter hurried by them and burst through the kitchen door.

The homey space was crowded with people. Most were boys and girls his age, and Trix was shouting orders faster than they could follow them. She stood in the center of it all, chopping potatoes in time with her commands. She didn't stop when she saw Peter. "And where have you been? People arriving all through the night, and then a whole crowd of them just now. You'd think we were a hotel the way they've been coming on."

"Um . . . I . . . where are my parents?" Peter managed.

"In the living room." Trix nodded to the door that led to the living room.

His parents were circled near the fire, deep in conversation with Indy's father.

"One of the Sacred Order's Eyes-and-Ears reported that Elton's speech was disrupted this morning," Wilfred said. "Someone was handing out these." He pulled out a familiar-looking scroll.

"Um—" Peter cleared his throat. "We were."

"Peter!" His mother swept across the room and gave him a fierce hug. "We were beginning to worry about you."

"You mean *you* overthrew the Tale Master's speech?" Indy's father had a look of admiration in his eyes as he clasped Indy by the arm. "No wonder we have so many new recruits for our army."

Peter and Indy exchanged glances. "What army?"

Peter's mother shook her head. "They just keep coming. Most of them are refugees from the outlying districts. There have been attacks there." A hard look crossed her face. "Many characters have died. The Sacred Order's spies have been sending them here. They want to fight."

"Caravans from as far away as the Desert of Fable are arriving," Peter's father said. "It's the beginning of a rebellion."

"Good," Peter said. "We need an army."

Indy told them about their plan, and Peter showed them Kai's leaf, which they began to pass around.

Indy's father poked a finger at the packet of herbs. "And the coronation ball is tonight."

"We need to hurry if we want to ready the army in

time," Peter said. "We're going to have to fight, even if we don't have enough of the leaf for everyone."

"I have a better idea." Peter's mother fingered the minty herb. "If we brew it, like tea, it will make more."

"That's brilliant!" Peter grinned. "We can sneak it in to the coronation. If we slip it into everyone's food and drink, we won't even have to convince them to take it. Just eating Fidelus's feast will break the enchantment." He swallowed hard. "And then we fight."

A slow smile spread across Peter's father's face. He nodded slowly. "It could work."

Indy's father said, "The boy speaks sense."

It took some time for them to sort out the details of who would be in charge of what preparation, but in short order they all had a list of tasks. It was only then that Peter thought to ask after Una.

His parents looked at each other. "You mean she isn't with you boys?"

All his relief at their new-made plan melted away, and an icy hand of fear clutched Peter's heart. *Where was Una?*

"No," Indy said, speaking for both of them. "We haven't seen her since last night." His voice was very quiet. "She told us she would meet us here after Winter's Eve."

Peter realized in a heartbeat what must have happened. "Una's gone to the Red Castle to look for the Lost Elements," he said. "And she's all alone."

Chapter 22

Una didn't want to touch Horace. His body was curled up like a question mark, his chest rising and falling as he slept. The sneer on his face when he had found her at Alethia's flashed through her mind. She could almost feel the way he had crammed the handkerchief into her mouth so that it gagged her. She kicked him again in the stomach. Hard.

He whimpered. "No more. Please, no more."

Una squashed the feeling of pity that welled up within her, but she still took a few steps back and sat down on the floor.

Horace opened one eye a crack. The other was swollen shut. "Una?" His voice was hoarse. "Is that really you?"

"Happy to see me?" She folded her arms across her chest. "I wouldn't be."

Horace pulled himself into a seated position, but he stayed hunched over like a stuffed bear that wouldn't stay upright. "I'm sorry," he mumbled.

"Oh, you're *sorry*. That's nice." She stood. All the conflicting emotions of the hour spent with her parents came rushing out. The sting of their rejection. Her unwelcome secret desire that maybe they would forget it all and still be a happy family. Her fear that she would be killed. The absolute terror that she would be stuck here forever. With *them*. She wanted to kick Horace so hard he cried.

But Horace was already crying, his hands covering his face. His bare forearms were mottled with bruises, and blood, now dried, had seeped through a spot on his sleeve.

Una let a trickle of compassion creep in. Horace had lied and unleashed Elton and his beasts on her, but who was she to judge? She was the girl who had unleashed Story's greatest Enemy. It was her mother she should be angry at. Duessa was the one who had used Una to free Fidelus, and now both her parents would forget all about her again. "Oh, Horace, you have no idea what a sorry pair of losers we are."

Una walked across the little room. The window had a thick iron grating over it, but she could still peer out. Far below them, the forest stretched off until the land dipped into a misty valley. They must be in one of the castle's towers.

"*You* might be a sorry loser, but *I'm* only here because Elton's a lying traitor," Horace snarled. "I hate him."

Una made sure to keep the table between them. Just because Horace was pathetic didn't mean he wasn't dangerous. "What happened?"

Horace wiped the back of his hand across his mouth, but the dried blood remained. "Sold me out. Blamed me for what happened at the Weaponry Arena."

Una tried to keep her voice patient. "What happened at the arena?"

Horace scowled, but since one eye was shut, it didn't look very menacing. "You mean you weren't there with your little friend Peter? He and some other idiot were stirring up trouble, handing out papers saying rubbish about how the Muses were really good. And leaving clues about the old King."

The King! "Peter was there? Indy, too?" Una hadn't

heard the tiniest scrap of information about her friends, and she hoped that this meant they were somewhere safe.

"Yeah." Horace examined the bruises on his forearm. "And some other kid doing somersaults and making fun of Elton. Messed up Elton's stupid announcement something awful. And I took the blame."

Una allowed herself a tiny smile. It sounded like the Resistance's broadside was working. She felt a pang of homesickness at the thought of Bramble Cottage and Peter and the Merriweathers. Rufus and Bastian, little Oliver and baby Rosemary. Indy and Sam. Una choked back a sob. Story's End would be worse than the Unbinding. Worse than the unhappiest ending the Dystopians could even imagine. She knew the Resistance would never submit to Fidelus's rule. When Fidelus wrote Story's End, her friends wouldn't just be dead. They would have never existed in the first place. They were going to be unwritten. Her throat grew tight, but she wouldn't let the tears come. There wasn't time for crying. "Do you know anything about the coronation ball tonight?"

"Yeah. You hear about Fidelus the Muse guy coming back?" Horace worked his jaw from side to side.

"I've heard a little."

"He's going to be crowned King. And all the Tale-less will be there." Horace tried to smile, and then grimaced. He held a hand up to his swollen cheek. "He's brought back so many famous Villains. Franken-stein and the White Witch. Morgana. Mordred had the sickest-looking helmet I've ever seen."

Una couldn't tell what this had to do with erasing Story. "They're all going to be at the coronation?"

Horace nodded. "They'll come to the ball tonight and wake up tomorrow in the new Story. Fidelus is going to give a special reward to those who help him beforehand. I wonder what it will be."

So it *was* all happening tonight. Una raced over to the window and looked outside. The light was nearly gone. There wasn't much time.

"Wait." Horace dropped his hand down and stared at her. "What are you doing here anyway?"

Una felt like laughing. Horace was obviously not the smartest villain in Story. If it had taken this long for him to start asking *her* questions, maybe she could try a more direct approach. "Didn't you know?" She leaned in close to make her words more dramatic. "Duessa's my mother."

Horace's mouth dropped open.

"I'll let you guess who my father is."

His one open eye bulged out from his head. "You're Fidelus's *daughter*?" He scooted a whole foot away from her. "Get back! What are you gonna do to me?"

Una felt like a huge weight had been lifted off her shoulders after she said the words. It wasn't as hard as she thought it would be, and now she was almost giddy. Sure, it was just Horace, but she didn't care. Someone else knew who she really was. "Oh, I don't know. Nothing quite as nasty as this, I suppose." She reached out a hand and let it hover in front of the puffy skin beneath his black eye.

"Get back." Horace cowered against the wall. "Don't touch me."

"So why do you do whatever Elton says?" she asked him. "What's in it for you?"

Horace sneered at her. "I'm going to be the next Tale Master. Elton promised."

Una did feel pity for him then. Horace was a fool. She was about to tell him so, when she heard a tapping at the window. She hopped to her feet, but Horace curled up in a ball on the floor.

"They're coming back," he whimpered.

"Stop it," she hissed. She hardly expected her mother's

guards to come to the room through the window, but who knew what other threat they might face? She looked around the little room. It was bare except for a few sticks of furniture—the table, three chairs. No weapons. Nothing she could use to defend herself. She eyed the pan on the table before deciding on the heavy-looking candlestick that sat on the floor. The next moment, a cloud of dust billowed through the window. She couldn't see or hear anything. Una kept the wall at her back and gripped the candlestick hard in her hand. The air began to clear. When it did, Una saw that everything was just as it had been, except dirtier. The windows were still barred. One of the chairs had toppled onto its back. Horace was doubled over, hacking mercilessly. Something brushed her shoulder, and she spun around, candlestick held high.

The man in front of her wasn't wearing his mask, but Una recognized him anyway. He scooped up his hat from the floor, straightened the feather on it, and gave Una a comic bow.

"Kai?" Una let the candlestick fall heavily to her side. "What are you doing here?"

Chapter 23

Snow swallowed hard, but her mouth was dry as dust. The ashes from the explosions had covered everything with a thick gray coating. Including the goblin in front of her. Like the other Taleless in the corral, his skin hung in loose patches, and Snow thought it would probably flake off at the slightest pressure. But she had no choice. She had to touch him. Snow looped the glowing rope her mother had woven to contain the prisoners over his bony wrists, and pulled tight.

There weren't very many Taleless left. Once they clothed themselves with flesh, the Taleless bled—and died—just like any character. Snow hoped that she wouldn't see anything like that ever again. The Westerns had been furious when the enchantment broke and they found themselves in the branding pens. And the ones who had actually been branded! The Tale-less that the cowboys and Indians hadn't torn to pieces were tied to the branding pens until the Resistance had time to figure out what to do with them. Snow grimaced as she loosened the rope just a bit. The battle had proven that whatever flesh Duessa had given her minions was not attached very well. Snow didn't want pieces of goblin on her hands.

She looked across the corral. Her mother, the bor-rowed cloak streaming behind her, darted here and there among the Westerns. Some were dead. Others needed healing. All of them needed baths.

Snow finished linking the goblin's rope to the others and moved toward her mother. Too late she saw the circle of Western girls. Effie Lou stood in the center of them, her filthy face a mark of how close she had been to the actual explosion. She saw Snow coming and lifted her arm in the air with a whoop.

"Bully for Snow!"

The Westerns had been doing this whenever they saw Snow or her mother. They wouldn't stop until Snow responded in kind, and it was beginning to get old.

"Bully for all of us!" She waved her wrist weakly

in the air. The Westerns seemed to enjoy retelling the battle as much as they had relished fighting it in the first place.

"I lit the fuse myself," Pearl was saying with a gap-toothed grin.

"But I set the powder off." Effie Lou flexed a muscle. "Let's tell the whole tale, eh, Pearl?"

Her mother's shouted instructions drifted across the air. "Move out! Cowboys, you bring up the rear. Indians, scout ahead. Everyone else stay close and look sharp. The Enchanted Forest is no place to relax your guard."

They might have won the battle, but the war was far from over. If what the witch queen had told them was true, the Muse Fidelus was about to crown himself King.

Snow didn't know if they had much hope of stopping Fidelus and Duessa. Some of Effie Lou's friends had heard rumors about a gathering somewhere near Fairy Village, but even if there were other characters willing to fight Fidelus, it didn't matter. The Enemy would have the Scroll soon, if he didn't already. Her mother thought the Enemy would try to rewrite Story with the Lost Elements, and if the Taleless were any indication of Fidelus's plans, Snow felt sure that whatever he wrote for Story's future would be a nightmare. What good had stopping the Taleless really done? Now the Westerns might live another few days. Until the next Taleless attack. Or until Story's End. But her mother said they had to try. And for once Snow agreed with her.

"Good work, Snow," her mother had said after the battle, patting her awkwardly on the shoulder. She said it in the same voice she might have used if Snow had done well on an exam. Snow felt like laughing. Even now, after what they had been through together, her mother was all formality. *Maybe that's just her way.* Snow still didn't know everything about her mother. She didn't know why she had chosen the Warlock over her baby, where her mother had learned to incinerate half-dead Taleless, or how she had concocted the miraculous potion she had used to heal the wounded. But Snow did know that her mother was brave. And that she cared for the weak.

Her mother could have left the Westerns to die on the Ranch. Snow probably would have. She looked back up to the front of the company, where her mother's familiar form leaned in to consult with an Indian chief. Snow's mouth twisted into a bitter smile. Despite all the questions surrounding her mother, despite all she had seen that appalled her, Snow realized one thing that surprised her. She was actually starting to like her mother.

Sooner than Snow would have liked, they entered the Enchanted Forest with its dense trees looming overhead, an especially unwelcome sight now that it was nearly dark. The Westerns had spread out. Those who were unarmed had their hands up, as though their very bodies could somehow become weapons. The forest itself seemed like it was waiting for something, and the air was heavy with a cold humidity. Snow's muscles tensed at the smallest sounds. Even Effie Lou and her gang were quiet, their bragging finally silenced. Snow groped for the heavy branding iron that hung at her side. Just the weight of it made her braver.

Their whole plan depended on locating one of Archimago's tunnels into the dungeons and entering the castle that way. Back at the Warlock's hideout, her mother had written a message to the other Resistance members saying as much, but Snow didn't know if the leprechauns had made it out before Archimago attacked.

She had brought up the idea of attending the coronation ball, but Snow's mother thought it would be too
risky. "What if Fidelus enchants us with his voice?" she
had said, and the Westerns had unanimously vetoed
the plan. That left, at best, launching an unexpected
attack from the bowels of the castle. At worst, it meant
they'd be caught and have to fight outside the castle
walls.

A full-on attack against the castle was preposter-
ous. The Westerns were brave, that was for sure, but
there weren't very many of them. What had happened
at the Ranch had been lucky. The explosion had taken
the Taleless by surprise, her mother had worked some
fast charms, and the rage of the prisoners had done the
rest. But to lay siege to the castle? Against the forces of
the Enemy and the Red Enchantress? Snow knew as
well as anyone that she and the Westerns were basically
marching to their deaths.

A cloud moved away from the setting sun, and for
a moment the forest looked like it was awash in blood,
the glistening color of the bark reflecting back the fading daylight.

Snow felt the air bristle. Birdcalls sounded in the
forest as the Indians scouted the surrounding land. The

leaders of the Westerns gathered near her mother to plan their approach. Snow wrapped her fingers around her weapon and gave it a practice swing.

There was a bustle of movement in front of her, and figures began shouting out things Snow couldn't understand. Three low owl hoots, the Indians' call for *Enemy!* was the only warning they had. Snow whipped her iron through the air. There would be no sneaking around. No tunneling under the fortress with the element of surprise. No hidden advantages. It was time to fight.

Chapter 24

Kai seemed unconcerned when Una told him about Fidelus's plan to use the Lost Elements to rewrite Story. He was not shocked when he heard about Elton ripping characters out of Tales or Duessa giving the Taleless bodies or Fidelus holding a big coronation ball.

He finished lighting the candles he had taken from his satchel while she told him that Fidelus was going to unwrite anyone who opposed him. "So the Enemy has a plot brewing." He blew out the match. "Excellent."

Horace crouched behind Una. Una couldn't tell if he thought she would protect him, or if he just wanted to hide from Kai.

Kai, however, seemed to completely ignore Horace. He reached into his bag and pulled out a green cloth, which he covered the table with. Then he set two chairs in front of the table, unwrapped a chunk of bread, and took a bite. "You must be hungry," he said. "I'm ravenous." Between mouthfuls, he laid the table with some hard cheese, fruit, and more of the bread.

Una didn't know what to say. *Thanks for the snack? It'll be nice to eat before we're unwritten?* Kai didn't seem to understand the urgency of their situation. "These are the Elements that were used to create Story, Kai." She tried again. "It really will be The End."

"Well, it's smart of him to try, that's for sure." He pulled out a flask, took a swig from it, and held it out to her. "Wine?"

Why wasn't Kai taking this seriously? "Um, no thanks. I'm just a kid."

Kai laughed long and loud. Una didn't see what was so funny, and Kai wouldn't explain. "As you like," he said when he finally caught his breath. "Have something to eat at least."

Una joined him at the table and took a handful of grapes. They were delicious. She hadn't known how hungry she was, and Kai's table, though simple, felt like a feast. After she had taken the edge off her hunger, she sat back. "So what do we do now?"

"We?" Kai took his dagger and sliced off a wedge of cheese. *"We* are going to do whatever *we* want." He gave her a wicked grin as he popped the cheese into his mouth. "As I see it, the bigger question is, What are *you* going to do, Una Fairchild?"

Una snorted. "I think I've done enough." She reached over for the flask and took a swallow. The wine burned going down. "I'm the one who released the Enemy to begin with."

Kai finished his bite, chewing very slowly. "Now, that's very interesting."

Revealing her identity to Horace had been easy. Una had to work to make the words come out this time. "I'm the Enemy's daughter. And the Red Enchantress is my mother." She twisted a grape off its stem and rolled it around in her fingers. She didn't want to look directly at Kai.

Una saw Kai's hand reach out, and she thought he might comfort her. But he only grabbed an apple from the open sack in front of him and took a big bite out of it.

"So?" he said with his mouth full.

Una raised her eyes to meet his and saw no condemnation there. "So? Don't you care? I released the

Enemy! *I'm* the one who brought him back!"

"Yeah, I got that," Kai said around his bite of apple.

Una flung her hands up in the air. "No. You don't. Fidelus has the Elements, Kai. He's about to become the most powerful King that Story has ever seen. And all because my *mother*"—she spit the word out—"has been deceiving everyone in Story. They're a pair of lying murderers." She thrust out her wrist, the bluish-green lines starkly visible beneath her pale skin. "And their blood runs through my veins."

Kai slapped the table with one hand. "I. Don't. Care." He finished his bite of apple and wiped his mouth with the back of his forearm. "Thing is, Una, what's done is done. And you are who you are. But you'll sit in here and rot if you spend all your time worrying about what you or your parents or whoever else did once upon a time. The question as I see it is, what are you going to do *now*?" He spun the core in his hand and nibbled at the white flesh of the apple.

Una squeezed a grape, and the juice trickled out onto her fingers. "Stop the Enemy, I guess."

Kai threw his apple against the wall, and it burst into bits. "And that is what makes a predictable story." It was the closest to angry Una had ever seen him.

"I'll let you in on a little secret, Una." He dropped his voice to a whisper. "Lots of characters let the baddies write the Tale. The Villain acts, the Hero responds." He pulled a dagger out of his pocket and began digging around in his teeth. "But that's just boring. In my kind of Tale, the Hero calls the shots." His face lit up and he waved the knife around as he spoke. "Surprise the Villain. Unleash the secret weapon. Don't wait for your father to do whatever he wants." He wiped his hands on his pants. "You do what you want. You write the Tale, Una."

Una had heard that all before. "I know, I know, my choices matter. Characters have free will, blah, blah, blah." She didn't need a Character Method lesson. She needed help.

"No." Kai placed both palms on the table and leaned in until his face was very close to her own. "Mark my words. You write the Tale." He looked up, and it was as though he noticed Horace for the first time.

Horace had been hovering near the fireplace, never letting the food out of his sight. He was rubbing his hands together eagerly, but he hadn't moved any closer.

Kai went over to him, hand held out palm up. "Come now, lad." Kai was talking to Horace as though

he were a frightened animal. "Join us. You must be
hungry." Horace let Kai lead him over to the chair he
had been sitting in.

Horace looked like he was going to cry when he
took his first bite. "Thank you," he managed around
the mouthful. Una stared at him. The bruise around
his eye was fading. As she watched, the swelling vanished, and the purpling disappeared entirely. The cut
on his chin had healed, leaving only a tiny line of dried
blood. She looked down at the bread in his hand. "Did
you just see . . . ?" she asked Kai, who only winked at
her.

Una set down the cluster of grapes she had been
holding. "How did you find us here?" she asked Kai
carefully.

"I thought you knew." Kai tipped the other chair
up so it sat properly on the floor, spun it around, and
swung his legs over it. "You put on my ring." He rested
his chin on the back of the chair and waited.

Una tugged the ring off her finger. The carving of
the tree was gone, and the metal was cool in her palm.
She traced the smooth center. "There was a tree here."
She swallowed.

"It's my ring." Kai raised his eyebrows. "My tree."

He clasped her hand, folding her fingers back over the ring.

At his touch, that same fiery heat shot from the ring. She looked into Kai's eyes. Coal-black eyes. Familiar eyes. The long ago day when she had first been Written In to Story flashed through her mind. The boy in the library with the book. And the servant at Alethia's house. Kai's gaze drew her in, and Una saw images there: a starry sky, the ocean, a tiny baby. They flickered faster: the Kingstree, a pile of ash, a black dragon rimmed in blue, a forest. She lost track of time as the faces of her friends spun together with lights and colors . . . and then it all stopped.

She was on her knees. Everything was as it had been, or nearly as it had been. Una's hand was sticky with grape juice. Horace was shoveling food into his mouth greedily. The candles on the table flickered in the dusty air. But Kai's chair was empty. And the door to their prison was open. Una didn't know where Kai had gone. But she knew one thing. The true King was back in Story.

Chapter 25

Peter was surprised at how organized the makeshift army was. The brief training the characters had undergone combined with the gravity of the situation to fill the air with wary expectation. It hadn't taken his father long to ready the troops. There had been a tearful farewell at the gate of Bramble Cottage, for the children were staying behind. The very young would be cared for by the very old, as everyone had decided they would be safer away from the Red Castle. There still was the risk that Elton would send forces against Fairy Village, but Peter pitied anyone who dared to come against the likes of Trix. She was already up on a ladder, hammering wood over the windows for extra fortification. Rufus and Bastian had wanted to come too, of course. Only when Peter hinted that the other kids would need brave guardians had they finally agreed to stay and protect them.

"Thank you," Peter's mother had whispered, blinking back tears as the boys ran up to the attic to get their practice weapons. She was coming with the army, and Peter hadn't given it much thought at the moment. But then they started down the lane, and Peter glanced back for one final look at Bramble Cottage. His mother was crying, great shoulder-wrenching sobs. That was when he realized it. They might not ever come back. There was no second chance here. They either defeated the Enemy and his minions, or they didn't.

It had taken them the best part of the afternoon to reach the Enchanted Forest, and worry for Una was always in the back of Peter's mind. He willed the troops to hurry. *We're coming to help you.* Peter remembered how sure Una had been that Duessa was after the Elements, how Una had been looking for the castle. He had no doubt she was there now, or on her way with the other crowds going to the coronation. *But she doesn't have the leaf.* Peter glanced behind him. His father was surrounded by a group of their neighbors. Peter wasn't sure how the ranks of bakers, millers, and blacksmiths would fare against the Enemy's horrors, but they looked determined enough.

There were recruits from other districts too. By far their greatest numbers were from the International District, which was another stroke of luck, because most of them came in traditional battle dress. It would be appropriate attire for a coronation, and, while Peter and the others had to hide their weapons in their fancy clothes, the Internationals could freely carry more than one weapon apiece. It had been harder to arm the group from the Historical District—many of whom wore full skirts or tailored frock coats, ill-designed for fighting—and the worst of all had been the handful who survived Heart's Place. Most of them had never even seen a weapon, let alone had any idea how to carry a concealed one.

A mixed-up jumble of Fairy Folk insisted on following Peter because of what they had done at the arena. Some of the fairies had been there, riding on the cats' backs, and they blushed and giggled whenever Indy walked past.

Peter eyed Professor Edenberry's battalion enviously. He and Griselda didn't even need to issue commands. Their followers walked in calm pairings—solid-looking Farmers rubbed shoulders with Woodsmen and Fair

Maidens. Edenberry had been training the recruits from
Fairy Village, so they naturally wanted to follow him.

Indy's father was leading the last segment, made
up of the newest arrivals. A caravan from the Far-Off
Lands had arrived just as they were finishing their plan.
Peter had never even heard of the Far-Off Lands, and
he couldn't help but stare at their exotic dress. They
had come with camels and, despite Indy's father's pro-
tests, insisted that the camels were trained to stay calm
during battle. So the camel group brought up the rear.

After they passed the first signpost that pointed the
way to the Red Castle, a black cat joined Peter's group.
Then a calico appeared. And a pair of tawny toms. And
then animals began pouring into their ranks, galloping
alongside the clusters of characters and weaving among
the gaps between them. Dogs of all sizes. Tiny rab-
bits who might have gone unnoticed but for all the
commotion. Even the birds were joining in, swooping
down to cry out with loud voices, "To war! To war!"

The other human characters were just as astonished
as Peter, although the Fairy Folk among them cheered
for each new species. "Hooray! The foxes! Cheers for
the foxes!"

And then, just to Peter's left, a unicorn appeared.

Its silvery coat glimmered in the dusky twilight. And there, seated on the unicorn's back, was a Siamese cat. And behind her, a familiar-looking tabby.

"Sam?" Peter said as his friend leaped off the unicorn in one fluid bound.

"The Feline Quorum has met," the Siamese told the boys, "and we have decided that your cause has merit."

"Okay." Peter had no idea what to say.

"Furthermore," the queenly cat said, "it seemed good to us to rally the other animal kind in this time of great need." She licked her paw. "We are not volunteering to take orders from humans." One blue eye winked at Peter. "But we are proud to stand with you against the great evil of our common Enemy."

Sam circled Peter three times. "Don't you look fancy." Sam sat back on his haunches and blinked his green eyes at Peter's dress clothes. "I suppose I should have told the other animals to dress up." He gave a sharp yowl. "Now let's go save Story." The characters around Peter, human and animal alike, broke into cheers, and their newly formed army was soon ready to continue.

For a time all seemed to be going well. Then, the animals grew wary.

"We're not alone," Sam hissed, as the fur on his back puffed up. "The smell of a battle is nearby."

"Castle guards, maybe? Talekeepers? What do you think?" Peter asked Indy.

Indy shrugged and eased a wicked-looking scimitar out of the scabbard on his back. "Does it matter?"

Peter wondered if the other companies sensed the impending danger. He sent Sam to warn the group behind them, and the soft conversations ceased. An owl hooted near him, and Peter swung at it with his sword.

There was the crunch of footsteps off to the side, and then a cool hand on his shoulder.

Peter spun around and nearly dropped the blade from his hands.

"Professor Thornhill?"

Chapter 26

Una poked her head out of the door. "Come on," she hissed at Horace. "Now's our chance."

"Nothing up here," Horace said while wolfing down the rest of Kai's food, "but a bunch of sleeping Villains."

"You know where we are?" Una said through clenched teeth. "Why didn't you say something?"

Horace shrugged.

Una paused at the doorway. Horace could stay in the tower forever for all she cared. But there was one thing she had to do before she left him. She walked back to the table. "You do know Elton's not going to make you Tale Master, don't you?" She tried to say it in a kind voice.

He stopped chewing, a mound of food bulging out

of the side of one cheek. "I domph bmpheev ooo," he said.

Una didn't have time for this. "Think about it. Have they ever done anything nice for you? Elton blamed you for his mistake, for goodness' sake. They obviously haven't fed you." She put one hand on his shoulder. "You should go home, Horace. Get somewhere safe."

She grabbed the heavy candlestick and left Horace staring silently at the remains of the meal on the table in front of him. Una's conscience was clear. She hoped Horace got it together and left before Duessa's creatures came back for him.

You write the Tale, Kai had said. That must mean there was something she could do to fight the Enemy. A way she could take him by surprise. Una made her way down the spiraling stone staircase. Before she reached the bottom, she came across another door, and this one was covered with a thick curtain of barbed vines. She gripped the candlestick tightly and poked it into the mass of thorns. The plants started moving. They twisted and snaked around the candlestick, squeezing so tight that the metal crumpled right before Una's eyes.

Una stood for a minute. Her parents were obviously hiding something important. The candlestick was now a wad of metal no bigger than her fist. It didn't matter what was behind that curtain. There was no way Una could get to it.

Footsteps echoed in the stairwell, and they weren't Horace's. They were coming from below. Una had waited too long. She retraced her steps, but there was nowhere to hide in the curving stairwell. She pressed back against the wall, hoping that the shadows might somehow disguise her, as the hunched form of Tale Master Elton bobbed toward her.

"Rip out the characters, he tells me." Elton was muttering to himself as he stomped up the steps. "After everything I've done. What will he give me? Nothing." He reached into his coat pocket with one hand. "What has he ever given me? Just 'Read the words, Elton.'" Una tiptoed closer so she could get a better look. Elton pulled something small out of his pocket, and he gazed down at it. "I should have known. From the very beginning, it's only been what I can do. How he could use me. And then after he was gone, Duessa."

Somewhere far above her, Horace coughed, and Elton glanced up. Una held her breath, but it was no good. Elton had seen her. And now he was coming closer, his stout form blocking any room for escape. For a split second Una thought about pushing past him and racing down the stairs, but where would she go? And how would she find out what was in the secret room? Then she remembered that Elton would think she was still under her mother's enchantment. Being Duessa's daughter had to be good for something.

She stepped out of the shadows. "My mother is expecting me," she said. "For Father's coronation."

"Oh, yes. The long-lost daughter. The girl who was Written In." Elton spat the words as he ascended the stairs. "My replacement. Too muddleheaded to flee while you have the chance. They'll use you up, too, mark my words, and then they'll toss you aside like rubbish." Elton had been crying. His eyes were red and puffy as he looked up at Una. "I wish they'd kill me and get it over with. I'm tired, Una. So tired. I'm glad you're here, really, because now I can be done. It's always just been me. The last WI."

Elton was right in front of her now. "Elton, read

these words. Elton, rip into Tales. Elton, tell the people of Story this lie. Elton, tell them that one." The Tale Master's hands were shaking violently, and Una could now see what he held. It was a tiny toy sailboat that a little boy might play with.

"Elton, read the words. Elton, write the Tale. Elton, read the words, and you can go home. Read the words, and you can be Tale Master. Read the words, and it will all be over." The Tale Master was sobbing now, great tears rolling down his cheeks, as he cradled the boat in his hands. "Just one more thing, Elton. Then we'll set you free."

Una stood frozen, unsure what to do. She was prepared to bluff her way past the old Mr. Elton, the mean one who had taken her prisoner in Alethia's garden. But this broken shell of a man was another thing altogether.

Elton was staring down at the toy boat. "They killed them all. Walter and his wife. The crazy old man. Every last one of them."

Una's mouth went dry. She knew that name. *Walter.* She remembered sitting at a table in the Heroics class-room with Sam and Peter, back before everything had happened. She could almost see the crumpled packet of pages, covered with words scrawled in a childish hand. *The boy who had been Written In.* Una remembered how sad she had been when she read those letters, how frightened the boy had sounded and how much he had missed his mother. Una stared at Elton's bent form. *Elton* was the boy who had been kidnapped? *He* was the one who had wanted to go home?

"I am the last of them," Elton said as he put the boat back into his pocket. "I should have known how it would all end."

"How will it all end?" Una said, speaking softly as she would to a very young child. She wasn't afraid of Elton anymore.

"With me never being finished." Elton looked up. His eyes were bloodshot from all the crying. "Never doing enough. They'll always make me do more." His face crumpled into an ugly sob. "I'll never be free."

"But you can be free," Una said. She thought of Kai's words from earlier. "You write the Tale, Mr. Elton. You get to choose what kind of character you are."

Elton stopped sniffling. He squinted up at her.

Una held her breath. Maybe she had gone too far. Could Elton tell she wasn't really enchanted?

Elton didn't say anything for a long time. When he finally spoke, it was as though he hadn't been crying at all. "Your mother and father want to see you," Elton said in an even voice. "They sent me to fetch you for the coronation."

Chapter 27

Snow stared at Peter Merriweather and his ragtag army. There were maybe a hundred characters with him, not counting the animals, and the humans among them were shakily putting away their weapons. "You look ridiculous, you know." Snow pointed at Peter's tailcoat.

"No worse than you," Peter said as he eyed the barbed wire on her outfit. "We *are* going to a coronation."

Snow wiped at a dirty spot on her black trousers. Not that it did any good. The whole thing was covered with stains. Her heart was returning to its normal pace, now that she realized she wasn't facing some new host of Taleless.

Neither party could quite believe what they were hearing from the other: Thornhill and the Westerns, that the Enemy had actually enchanted most of Story's characters; and the Resistance members, that the Tale-less had been loosed to destroy the Ranch.

"Do you think your plan will work?" Snow asked Peter as she fell into step beside him. "You think some herbs will help everyone become unenchanted?"

The Westerns were spreading out among the other characters, filling in the empty spots in their ranks, until soon there was just a long line of characters threading their way up through the forest toward the castle.

"The leaf will help us see clearly and fight off the Enemy's enchantment," the boy with Peter answered. "Once they know the truth, Story will fight, I'm sure of it." The boy sounded confident. Almost too confident.

Snow watched him out of the corner of her eye. She had seen him before at Perrault, remembered his name was Indy, but knew little else of him. "And what makes you so sure?" She arched an eyebrow at him. "What if they still choose to crown him King, even when their eyes are opened?"

Indy scowled at her. "We have to try. Would you rather wait and see what the Enemy does next?" His dark eyes were nearly purple. "This is the best plan we've got."

"The leaf worked for us," Peter told Snow. "Everyone else believed the Enemy's lies, but we were able to
see what was really going on. We just need to make
sure that each character gets a little taste."

"How are you going to do that?" Snow asked, snag-
ging her pant leg on a brambly bush. "Force everyone
to eat it?"

"We've brewed it." Peter pulled out a little stoppered bottle. "There's enough for everyone that way.
We want it to last as long as possible," he said as he
swirled the liquid around in the glass. "We'll each take
one sip before we go into the castle, and then we just
have to get a single drop onto everyone's food."

The land began to slope upward here, little eddies
of mist swirling about Snow's boots. She could hear
the sound of low laughter among the characters. She
wondered what her mother would say about Elton's
enchanted voice and the leaf Peter planned to hand
out. But her mother was deep in conversation with
several of the grown-ups who had come with Peter,
and she barely had a glance to spare for Snow. Snow
wondered if she was telling them about the secret
entrance in the dungeons. The topmost castle turrets
rose in front of them, warm candlelight shining out at

them from the highest windows.

The leaders of the group slowed. It must be nearing the time when they would hand out the potion, and Snow was about to ask Peter how they planned to find the kitchens inside, when there was a great cheer from the group next to them. The characters were circling around a woman's form. Snow reached out for Peter's sleeve. She wanted to tell him that his plan had a fatal flaw. Who cared about how long the potion lasted? They needed it now. She fumbled for his arm. Where was the stoppered bottle? But it was too late. The Red Enchantress pushed back the hood of her cloak, smiled directly at them, and opened her mouth to speak.

eter sat back in his golden chair and sighed. Wonderful thing had followed wonderful thing ever since they had arrived at the castle. As soon as Peter had heard Duessa's voice, he had known that everything would be all right. In fact, now he wondered what it was he had been so worried about. He was seated with his friends in the middle of a ballroom lit with torchlight. Musicians were grouped near the front of the room, and the notes of their pleasant music filled the air. More tables than he could count crowded the large space, and the place settings sparkled with gem-encrusted goblets and polished silver. He looked across the table at his companions, who all seemed vaguely familiar, although he couldn't place them. The woman with the reddish hair piled on top of her

head—her name was on the tip of Peter's tongue—and
the man with the glasses and serious voice; surely Peter
knew him?

But soon his thoughts were distracted by the bril-
liance of the ballroom. Vases sprouting with blood-red
roses towered over every table. Peter had never seen so
many candles in his life. The room sparkled with the
light of a million flames, like some enchanted fairy
feast. Wide windows opened to the gardens of blooming flowers. Peter shifted in his seat, slowly rubbing the
aching spot in his side. Why was he sore anyway? His
memory felt patchy, like fabric worn thin in spots. He
had been looking for someone. No, that wasn't right.
He had wanted to do something. But what?

A platter of food appeared at Peter's elbow. Figs,
grapes, and half-moons of melon surrounded a slice of
flatbread stuffed with pale cheese. A beautiful servant
girl circled the table, pouring mugs of hot tea. The
aromatic blend of cinnamon and clove melted away his
muscle aches. Peter sighed. He had been hoping for tea.

More characters than Peter had ever seen filled
the ballroom. Characters from every district of Story.
The woman next to the man with glasses tickled his
memory. He knew her from Perrault. Was she Peter's

teacher? Peter set his tea down. Something was wrong. His memory was gone. Vague images flickered through his mind, but he couldn't solidify any of them. His head pounded when he tried to remember something new, something about Perrault or his father's voice or the feel of the wind against his face.

There was a flicker of movement off to his left. A striped cat crouched near his feet, eyes dilated wide. Peter felt a jolt of affection. But that wasn't right. He hated cats. All of Story hated cats. Peter leaned down and held out his hand. If he could trap it, the servant girl could take it away and drown it. The cat's mouth was working strangely, as though it was trying to talk. *How absurd.* Peter made coaxing noises, but the cat still worked its mouth. Maybe it was rabid. Peter wasn't sure how he knew, but he thought that cats could go wrong like that. He snatched his hand back and drew his dagger. The cat looked frantic now, panicked sounds coming from its mouth. *Definitely rabid.* Best to slice off its head rather than count on the drowning to work. Peter raised his hand, and the cat darted off, skirting the next table, and disappearing out a side window.

Peter moved to follow, but his head was throbbing now, an explosion of pain that made it hard to sort through his thoughts. The music stopped. The musicians were on their feet, bowing toward a balcony that protruded above them. A red carpet hung from the balcony's edge, and a man who Peter recognized stood there. The Tale Master of Story. Elton brought his hands together in front of his chest and proclaimed in a loud voice.

"People of Story, may I present to you King Fidelus, the master of Story, and his Queen Duessa." The next moment, the sound of trumpets split the air, and there, waving down at them all, stood the rulers of Story.

The Queen was the most beautiful woman Peter had ever seen. Her long dark hair fell in glossy waves, and her red cloak cascaded behind her. The man next to her was a towering pillar. Clad in warrior's armor, the King greeted his people with outstretched arms.

When the cheering had died down, Fidelus spoke: "Welcome to my castle." He bowed his head. "And welcome to my table."

Peter felt a tiny tug on his ankle. The cat was back, and Peter kicked sharply with his boot. The cat was fast and smooth as water, and it darted out of the way. Irritation flared within Peter. Cats were nothing but trouble.

"Eat and be merry," Fidelus was saying. "For tonight

we bid farewell to the old Story and welcome a new era."

The old Story. A pulse of pain. Something flashed in the corner of Peter's vision, a burst of bright light that shot out a rainbow of colors. But when he turned to look in that direction, there was nothing out of the ordinary.

"Some of you fear The End," Fidelus said, and the Dystopians at the next table stirred. "But the End of Story is only a new beginning. You will see."

Peter rubbed his temples. He had a parched and stinky feeling in his mouth. He tried to focus on his slippery memories. Two boys, pestering him with questions. His brothers? Why couldn't he recall the faces of his family? A spark of light roused him. Why had he been thinking about his family? He should be listening to the King.

Another flash. This one filled the whole room with colors.

"Did you see that?" Peter asked the man next to him. "That light there?"

"The throne?" The man polished his glasses. "Pretty amazing, isn't it? It's about time there was a King in Story."

The Tale Master was placing a ruby-encrusted crown on King Fidelus's head. The red gems glistened wetly in the candlelight. King Fidelus then reached for a silver tiara and situated it on Queen Duessa's glossy mass of hair. Peter felt something prickling at the back of his memory. Something about the King of Story and a feast and the coronation. But he brushed away the feeling. Things would be all right now. Now that Story had a King.

The air above the throne was shimmering oddly. . . . Now it looked like ordinary silver, but when Peter looked away, it wavered and expanded, rising upward to touch the ceiling. He shook his head. Maybe he was ill. When he looked back at the throne, there it was, stretched like taffy. No ordinary person could sit on that weightless, narrow seat. He glanced back at his companions, but they were already eating. King Fidelus and Queen Duessa were gesturing for the musicians to resume their music, and they were disappearing into the seclusion of the balcony. The Tale Master was following them, escorting a girl by the elbow.

Bright flashes flickered around the girl. Like Duessa, she was wearing a long red robe. *But her face.* Peter knew that face. Violet eyes. A long black braid. She took her place between the King and the Queen, her mouth set in a brilliant smile. Peter wanted to go talk to her. Wanted to make her laugh. But he couldn't very well go up to the King's private balcony just to talk to a girl. He shook his head. He was being ridiculous. He grabbed his cup and drank the liquid in one long gulp. The aching in his head subsided. The pleasant music calmed him. He filled his goblet from the pitcher on the table and held it up in front of his companions.

"To the End of Story!" he said.

Chapter 29

Una stood stiffly between her parents, the muscles in her face aching from her forced smile. They had done it. Her mother and father stood across from her, crowned the King and Queen of Story. And all the characters! The hall below them was full of people feasting merrily, not in the least bit concerned that the End of Story was coming upon them.

In fact, the table nearest the balcony was toasting that very thing. Una felt her smile slip. *Peter?* And Professor Thornhill sitting next to him, grinning like a schoolgirl. Una sucked in her breath. Across from her friends sat the Merriweathers. Una's heart sank. And there were Edenberry and Griselda. And the other Resistance members. *It can't be.* They all were under the Enemy's enchantment.

Peter was staring up at her with a dull, glassy look that confirmed her fears. *He doesn't recognize me.* Peter pressed a hand to his temple and set the goblet he was holding back on the table. Una felt like throwing up. She didn't know what her parents were serving their guests, but even from a distance, Una could see the flies buzzing around the rotting food. She looked at the faces of her smiling friends. None of them were aware of what was really happening.

"At last," Duessa said to Fidelus, as she escorted them to the privacy of their own table. "Story is finally ours."

"Soon, my love," Fidelus said. "Once that fool delivers the Scroll."

Una felt a quickening in her chest. The Enemy didn't have the final Element. Maybe it wasn't too late.

Duessa's lips curved into a lazy smile. "If you say so." She spread her hands over the crowded hall. "But isn't this enough for you? Look. They all adore you. The only ones who can stop you are asleep in the tower." She gave a wicked laugh. "Why go through all the trouble of rewriting Story?"

Una's father's voice was hard as ice when he answered Duessa. "Don't be a fool, woman." His gaze held none of the warmth that had been there a moment earlier. "An enchanted kingdom is no kingdom. All of this"—he waved a hand across the crowded hall—"is nothing. Except a captive audience when I unwrite my enemies." He scooped up a forkful of food and slid it into his mouth, his teeth scraping the fork. "And an invitation."

The corners of Duessa's mouth turned down. "Invitation?"

It seemed to Una like her father was working on that one bite forever. The music across the hall drifted over, the clinking of flatware on china, the low murmur of conversation. But she watched him chewing, working the piece of meat until it must have been ground down to nothing. He swallowed.

"For the King. When I use the Elements, he will come." He smiled. "And he will be the first one unwritten." Fidelus stood and stretched, moving over to the balcony and receiving the resulting cheers that came from the ballroom.

Duessa dragged her fork around the edge of her plate. "The King," she said in a very soft voice. She looked over at Una, as if she only just then remembered Una was at the table with them. "Eat, my dear. This is a feast, you know."

Una nodded, and mechanically began shoveling food into her mouth. Anything to keep playing the part of the enchanted daughter. "It's lovely," she managed. "So thrilling."

"I told you to eat," her mother said in a cold voice. "Not yammer away as if you have something important to say." Una felt the ring burning on her finger and knew Duessa must be heightening the enchantment.

Elton appeared at her mother's elbow. "Archimago is here," he said. "And he wishes to see you, milady."

"You mean, 'my queen,'" Duessa said sharply. "Bring him to me."

Una sneaked a peek at Elton's face. His eyes were dry, and there was no sign of the broken man she had seen earlier.

Elton gestured toward the doorway behind them, and the next moment a man was seated with them at the table. He was very old. His hair hung in stringy masses from his wrinkled scalp. There was a feverish light in his eyes.

"Archimago." Duessa held out both hands to the thin man. "You have impeccable timing."

The thin man grabbed one of Duessa's hands and planted a kiss on her knuckles. "My queen." With a flourish, he reached into his cloak and pulled out a wrapped bundle. The air around Una was filled with a sudden heat.

"The Scroll of Fire," Duessa breathed.

Una pretended to be scooping the last of her potatoes onto her fork and eyed Archimago. This was it. This was when the Enemy got the last Element. Archimago removed the layer of cloth, and there it was. A thin roll of parchment that glowed like a dying ember. Duessa reached for the Scroll.

Una darted a hand out to snatch it herself, but she wasn't fast enough. Archimago swept it out of reach, and Una switched course so that it looked like she was desperate for her water goblet.

"The last Element." Archimago twirled it in his fingers. "I will give it to you," he said with a cunning look. "On one condition."

Duessa arched an eyebrow. "And what is that?"

"You promised me." Archimago dropped down on one knee. "So long ago, you said you would be mine if I did all you asked." He shot a hateful glare beyond Duessa to where Fidelus stood. "Leave him. You know I've always loved you."

Una couldn't read her mother's face. It remained

smooth as she looked evenly at the former Tale Master.
Una almost felt bad for him.

"We can figure out a way to wield the Elements. We
can defeat him and rule Story together," Archimago
said, and raised his head. "You belong to me."

"Archimago—" her mother began.

"Deny me"—Archimago's voice was poison—"and
I will destroy him on my own. One way or the other,
you will be mine."

Her mother let her lips curve into a slow smile. She
reached out a slender hand and drew him to his feet.

Archimago blinked his eyes wide, as if he could
hardly believe what he was seeing. Duessa leaned in
toward him. "Archimago, there's something I must tell
you." Archimago tilted his chin up, as though he might
kiss her on the lips. When their faces were so close that
they were almost touching, Duessa whispered. "I—"

And with the speed of a viper, her hand darted up
and thrust a dagger into his chest.

Una stifled a gasp, but Archimago's groan drowned
out the sound.

He dropped to his knees, one hand fumbling at the
red dagger protruding from his torso. Duessa leaned
forward and slipped the Scroll from his grasp.

Duessa nudged him with one foot, and he toppled to the ground. "—I belong to no one."

Una felt the bite she had just swallowed come back up her throat. She fought down the sensation and willed her hands to work again. How far did the enchantment go? Should she show some emotion? Should she pretend to be happy? One hand was shaking, and she stabbed the fork into the big piece of meat on her plate. Her mother had just killed someone. Right in front of her.

Fidelus was back at the table in an instant. "He brought the Scroll?" Fidelus stepped over Archimago's body with barely a glance. He reached out both hands for the glowing parchment and held it in reverent fingers. He looked at Duessa. "And so it begins."

"The beginning of The End"—Duessa planted a kiss on his knuckles—"my king."

Fidelus's laugh started low and then built into a wild sound that made Una's bones turn to ice. His eyes looked half mad, and he cradled the Scroll like it was a newborn baby. From his cloak he drew the Silver Quill. It was nothing like the fake Una had brought from Jaga's hovel. The silver of the feather was woven with black, as though it was fringed with smoke. With a flick of his wrist, Fidelus took the sharp nib and cut a gash along his forearm. Dark blood gushed out, and Duessa caught it in a silver goblet. And then Una realized what she was seeing. *The Dragon's Ink.* Una's mouth was dry. She should do something. She should stop her father. Reach out and grab the Quill. Go over to the edge of the balcony and shout at Peter and the other characters. Didn't they know Fidelus was about to use the Elements? *Do something.* Una couldn't make her hand work, couldn't lift the fork, couldn't do anything but stare at her father's face. The space around him grew dark. The air in the room shifted uneasily, and the table began to shake beneath them. Fidelus took the Quill and dipped it into the goblet.

Una braced herself for The End.

A sliver of light shot from the floor to the ceiling, cracking open into a blinding rainbow of color. The black cloud around Fidelus was snuffed out. The table stilled. Her father's hand froze, black liquid dripping from the quill's point. And, there, balancing on the edge of the balcony, was the true King of Story.

"The Lost Elements, Fidelus?" Kai asked, leaning on a wooden staff, one ankle hooked behind the other. "An interesting move."

"You have no authority here. I am the King now," Fidelus spit. "You abandoned Story long ago." He aimed a hand toward the King. "And you are about to abandon it yet again."

"So you still will not bend?" Kai twirled the staff in front of him. "Even now, I will write you a Tale."

"You will never write another word in Story," Fidelus said, summoning the darkness with a swirl of his hand. The rest of the ballroom seemed frozen in some far-away scene. Gone was the sound of silverware on china. Gone the sound of laughter and jesting. It was as though Una alone witnessed the duel.

"You will watch The End come to all you have written," Fidelus said. "And everyone in the new Story will serve *me*. And you, the once-upon-a-time King, will be unwritten once and for all."

The Enemy blew on the Scroll, and the smoldering ember flamed into brightness. Una shielded her eyes for a moment. A square of fiery parchment hovered in the air before her father. He dipped the Quill into his Ink-blood and, with a flourish, began to write the first words of his new Story.

Chapter 30

Snow cowered behind one of the twisted trees of the Enchanted Forest and tried to catch her breath. At the last second, before Duessa began to speak, Indy had crashed into Snow and shoved his hands over her ears. Then they were sprinting away from the Enchantress's words, deeper into the forest and far from Duessa's charming tones. The stitch that had started throbbing in Snow's side was now an ever-present dagger of pain.

"Do you have any of the potion?" she asked. Her breath was ragged, but she tried to keep it under control. Indy was barely even winded. He had told her he had been chewing on the leaf ever since they entered the forest just in case, but from the way everyone else

had stayed behind to listen to Duessa, Snow thought
he was probably the only one clever enough to think
of doing that.

"Nope." Indy shook his head. "It's all sitting there
in their pockets, but they won't remember to take it."
He scuffed his shoe on the ground. "We have to get in
there somehow. Do something to save them."

This part of the forest was all too dreadfully familiar. Here was where her mother had first threatened
Archimago. Was it really only the night before that
they had raced through these same grounds? And then
Snow remembered. *The Ivory Gates!*

"Come with me," she said to Indy, and this time
she took the lead. She remembered that the wasteland
had melted away to abandoned gardens, but the castle
was huge, and they would have to find a way across
the moat if they had any hope of finding the gates.
The main drawbridge was out of the question. The
side of the castle nearest them was impenetrable. Then,
as they made a wide circle around the castle, she saw
their route. A narrow, crumbling bridge stretched like
a sliver of stone over the moat. And there, in front of it,
paced a huge, scaly dragon.

Snow tried to size up their opponent. It would not be an easy fight. Dragons were fast, even though they were large, and this one breathed fire. Indy had a scimitar, and Snow had her branding iron, but neither would do much unless they could land a blow in one of the dragon's few exposed areas, which would be difficult.

"Let's each take a side," Indy said, and Snow was grateful he wasn't going to try and play the part of a Hero. If they worked together, their odds of surviving this were marginally better. The dragon arched its neck, and a blast of heat singed Snow's eyebrows. The next moment, a volley of flame shot toward Indy, who ducked and darted out of the way. The dragon flicked its tail, and it was faster than Snow could have imagined. She rolled, and the tail's spiked barbs whistled over her head. She scrambled to her feet, cutting her hands on the sharp stones as she moved.

The dragon reared back to blast more fire at Snow, and Indy ducked in close to its body, aiming his scimitar at the dragon's exposed underbelly. It was a mistake. The dragon roared and swiped a powerful claw toward Indy.

Indy moved sideways, but it was too late. The dragon slashed across his back, and Indy howled with pain.

Snow fought back a scream as Indy dragged himself farther away.

But Snow didn't go to him to make sure he was okay. While the dragon was busy with Indy, she grabbed the biggest stone she could find and hurled it straight at the dragon's head. It reared in pain and lashed its tail from side to side. Another stone, this time right in the eye. The dragon roared and wobbled.

Indy was on his feet, his scimitar slicing through the air, cutting into the dragon's unprotected belly, and then it was done. Quicker than Snow could have thought possible, the dragon was dead.

They sped over the slender bridge, fearful that someone—or something—else might have heard the sound of their fight. The door on the other side had long since been bricked over, but a shred of a path snaked around the nearest turret. Snow pressed her back into the wall as they worked their way sideways. Pebbles shifted under her feet, dropping down into the moat under them. They rounded the corner, and the path widened a fraction and led to a rotting garbage heap. Snow gagged her way over the refuse and tried her best not to identify the soft, rotting shapes bursting under her hands. And then she was beyond it. The smell vanished, replaced by the same hollow air she remembered from the desert. A few more paces and she was there, the familiar Ivory Gates towering over her and Indy.

"She did something with this knot," Snow said as she ran her fingers over the mess of carved thorns. Next to it was a dozing princess leaning against a unicorn. And a king sleeping in his throne. What was it her mother had done? Why hadn't Snow paid more attention?

"Are there guards in the castle?" Indy asked. "Will we need to fight our way through?"

"Possibly," Snow said. "The castle was mostly deserted when we were there, but that was before the ball. If Duessa made a dragon stand guard, who knows what we'll find inside?" And then she found it. At last. There was the gnome snoozing under the tree. She took a deep breath. *What if there were Taleless inside?* Indy stood solidly beside her, and his silence made her braver. She began to push each of the figures in turn, making a circle just as her mother had done. Then, she shoved hard on the thorns, and the Ivory Gate began to dissolve.

There weren't guards on the other side. Or Taleless. Instead there was darkness. And instead of silent, deserted corridors, there was the sound of wailing. Of prisoners calling for help, the desperate cries of people who knew they were about to die.

Snow raced toward the sound. Down a staircase and around a corner. And then the awful smell overtook her. She knew this place. They were in the dungeon. Up ahead, a very old man had stuck his hands through the bars of his cell, and he was trying to wedge a piece of stone wall into the lock.

"What's happening?" Snow asked him. "Why is everyone screaming?"

The man looked at her as if she might be a ghost. "Are you real?" he croaked. "Or am I dreaming?"

"I'm real." Snow reached out and grabbed his wrinkled hands. "And we're here to rescue you."

"The Taleless are coming," the man whimpered. "They will take our flesh." Snow didn't wait to hear more. She began hammering at the lock with her branding iron.

"What's thissssss?" A hissing, cloaked creature was drifting toward her. "A ressscue?" The dungeon guard had no face, just a gaping black hood where the head should be. It reached out iron claws toward Snow. Until Indy chopped one off. Whatever the hissing beast was,

it hadn't expected an ambush, and it hadn't been prepared for Indy.

The thing's blood sizzled on the blade, and Indy
wiped it off carefully on the dead creature's cloak.
Then he took the tip and unhooked a large ring of keys
from the guard's belt.

"Would these help?" he asked Snow, and even in
the darkness she could see his smile.

It didn't take them long to empty the cells. Snow
went first with the keys, then Indy came after, helping
the prisoners out. Many of them were so old they could
barely walk, and their thin legs looked as if they might
snap under the pressure. Snow thought of Archimago
and how crazy he had become in Duessa's dungeons.
What of these poor souls? How long had they been
trapped here? And what would happen to them now?

A wrinkled woman patted Snow's hand as she passed.
"Thank you," she said. "Thank you, dear."

Snow wondered how things were faring at the coronation. Emptying Duessa's dungeons was all well and
good, but they needed to do more if they were to stop
Fidelus from becoming King. And an army of ancient,
frail prisoners wouldn't be much help. When the last
chain was unlocked and the last prisoner escorted

outside the Ivory Gates, she turned to Indy. "I have to go to the ball. My mother's in there."

Indy looked at Snow. Then he looked back at the crowd of shivering prisoners. "I'll take them as far as the forest. And then I'll come find you."

Snow gave him a brave smile. "I'll see you then." She knew as she said it that her words were wishful thinking. Whether any of them made it out of this alive was a long shot.

But Indy didn't remind her of their small odds. Instead he clasped her arm as she had seen the warriors in Heroics class do. "Fight well, Snow," he said, and then they were gone, the line of prisoners tottering toward the rocky path.

Snow raced back through the dungeon and up the stairs. She didn't know where she was going, but she could hear a crashing noise and the sound of shouting. The floor shook beneath her, sending her stumbling around a corner and straight into the arms of the last person she ever expected to see.

"Snow?" Horace's voice was a question mark as he steadied Snow on her feet. "What are you doing here?"

"I could ask you the same question," Snow said with a wry smile. "But I don't really want to know the answer." Horace had always been a bit too comfortable in the company of Villains, and Snow didn't want to find out that her cousin was on the Enemy's side. "Just tell me how to get to the ballroom."

"You don't want to go that way," Horace said, trying to pull her back toward the dungeons. "The real King just showed up, and Duessa's enchantment is already beginning to fail. There's going to be a fight in there, and you won't want to be anywhere near it."

Snow jerked free of his arm. Her cousin had also always been a bit of a scaredy-cat. "I'm going to fight, Horace." She took a step back.

Horace stared at her. "That's the dumbest thing I've ever heard." He shook his head. "There's no way you can fight the Taleless. Besides, you'll lose. Fidelus is—"

"I know all about the Taleless." Snow didn't have time for arguing. "And winning or losing isn't the point." She looked straight into his eyes. "Now's your chance, Horace. You get to choose. Be brave and fight for Story? Or run away and regret it for the rest of your life." She turned around and started walking toward the battle. "You do what you want, but I'm going to go rescue my mother."

Chapter 31

Una studied the thorny vines in front of her. As
soon as Kai had appeared, her parents had forgotten all about her. And Una hadn't waited another
minute. She had slipped out of the balcony and found
the way she had come earlier that evening. How had
her mother phrased it? *The only ones who can stop you are
asleep in the tower.* The Muses were behind that curtain
of thorns, Una was sure of it. The stones beneath her
shook with the blasts of the battle. Una leaned closer,
careful to keep a safe distance from the violent leaves,
scanning their tangled mass for some sort of clue. A
pattern. Anything.

It happened in a flash, before she could even cry
out. Her braid swung forward and caught on one of
the thorns. And then the plant had her hair. She heard

the crackle of the vines as the plant moved toward its prey. She pulled backward as hard as she could, but she was caught fast. She would have to cut off her hair. She reached for her dagger, and cried out when her hands met empty air. She didn't have a weapon.

The plant was working quickly. Una could feel something poking into her shoulder. She struggled vainly, ensnaring herself more with every movement. Which was how it happened. One of her fingers scraped across an especially sharp thorn, and a red drop of blood bloomed on her skin. The plant's response was instantaneous. The pressure on her scalp relaxed. Her braid was free. And then, the unnatural curtain spread to either side, leaving her way clear.

Una wiped her blood off on her sleeve. *It's my blood.* One of her parents had set this enchantment. Her breath came out in a shaky gasp. She was alive. Her own treacherous blood had saved her.

Una made her way into the interior, peering hard through the darkness in case some new trap awaited her. Every few paces was a miniature tableau. Closest to her, a gray wolf was flat on his back, toppled piles of bricks surrounding his still form. His jaws were open, revealing pointed teeth, and it seemed unnatural that he lay so peacefully in the eerily silent room. Una's heartbeat quickened, but she relaxed when she saw the slow rise and fall of the wolf's chest. He was sleeping.

None of the sleepers even stirred as she moved frantically around the room, studying each figure in turn. *Where were the Muses?* Next to the wolf was a woman wearing a pointed witch's hat. She was curled up on her side in the middle of a gilded cage. Scraggly white hair draped over all of her features except for an extraordinarily large nose with a hairy wart on it. A giant padlock fastened the square door to the bars.

Una hurried up to a big canopy bed and drew aside the velvet curtains that hung to the floor. A tiny woman lay in it, her dark curls fanning out from her wrinkled face. Her brow looked peaceful, if not beautiful, and her hands lay folded across her stomach.

Una recognized the scenes, of course. The classic fairy-tale touches were a dead giveaway. The cage was from *Hansel and Gretel,* and this was no doubt Sleeping Beauty's bower. She would never have pictured the princess so old, though. And wasn't it Hansel who was in the cage, not the mean old witch? The fairy tales were all backward, with the Villains trapped and bound, but how in the world could any of *them* defeat her father?

Una was at another bed now. An ax was sunk deep into the footboard. A red wolf lay beyond it, tucked under an old-fashioned quilt, with wire-rimmed glasses perched crookedly on his nose. His whiskers were neatly trimmed, which provided a stark contrast to the ruffled nightcap on his head. He was snoring softly.

Una barely stopped at his bedside, but hurried around him to a coffin on the other side. The glass was fogged, though, and she couldn't see inside.

This one had to be Snow White. Or her evil nemesis. *A wicked Stepmother?*

Una stood. She was missing something. She scanned the room. Two Big Bad Wolves, an old Witch in a cage, an Enchantress in the bed, and whoever was in this glass coffin. She peered over her shoulder at the last scene, where a wrinkled old man sat imprisoned in the floor, surrounded by mounds of golden thread.

She stooped down to peer into Rumpelstiltskin's face. He appeared to be the safest villain. It wasn't like Una had any children he could run off with, and as far as she remembered, the worst thing the old hobgoblin did was disappear into the ground.

Rumpelstiltskin's head was thrown back at an odd angle, with soft snores coming from his open mouth. She poked a tentative finger at the creature's bony shoulder, and then pulled it back with a gasp of surprise. The man's countenance shimmered when she touched it, revealing an entirely different face beneath.

Duessa had been quite clever. Not only had she enchanted the sleepers, but she had disguised them as well. Una made her way slowly around the little room, prodding each character in turn. These faces were familiar. It wasn't because she recognized them from some fairy tale she had read in her old world. They were from a different book. From her father's book.

Una had found the other Muses.

Una made her way around the room once more. The air around the golden cage shimmered oddly. If Una tilted her head just slightly, the witch's hat disappeared and the dirty blanket became a stream of long red hair. The shadows beneath Clementia's face made it seem like she had a horrible hooked nose.

Virtus dozed among the pile of bricks. His ruddy cheeks looked as though they belonged outside in the sun, not in this dim room. Una pulled back the canopied curtains to reveal Sophia's sleeping form. Her dark skin was the striking color of a starless sky, and Una thought that even under the grip of the enchantment she looked as strong as she had in the clearing.

Beyond the bed, Una saw scattered stones that looked like the ruins of a crumbling tower, and Alethia lay in the midst of them, her golden hair unbound and her chin tucked in to her chest. Una raced to her side.

"Alethia!" she cried. She grabbed the Muse's shoulders and shook gently. "Won't you please wake up?"

Una had pushed and prodded every last one of them. She had pinched their arms, whispered in their ears, and, after a great deal of deliberation, tried to kiss one of them. But none of it mattered. They were still fast asleep. The faint sounds of yelling and the clashing of metal told her that something else was happening in the ballroom. Every second mattered, and Una was no closer to waking them than when she first walked into the room.

Una began patting Alethia gently, and then harder, on the cheek. They had to wake up.

That was when she saw the sparks. Una stopped slapping the Muse. The light from the enchantment filled the room with an eerie glow. Somehow, Una's touch was changing the spell.

She tried again. Could she actually undo the enchantment? If someone who had her father's blood could affect the magic on his binding, then maybe someone who had her mother's blood could change her charms. Una's heart quickened. It had worked on the thorns.

She looked down at her hand. The blood was smeared across her fingertip, and when she placed it near Alethia's ankle, a glowing rope appeared.

Una gasped. She had been staring at the Muses' faces when she was trying to wake them. But now she let her hand hover in the air over each of them until she could determine how they were trapped. The glowing cord wrapped around Charis's neck and then over to Sophia's wrist. It looped around Clementia's waist and bound Spero's feet. Una traced the enchantment around each of them until she was back at Alethia. Now that she could see their bonds, maybe she could set them free.

Untying the enchantment was hard work. Una wiped a palm across her sweaty forehead. This thread needed to be pulled in such a way. Another had to be knotted just so. At least those stupid sewing lessons were paying off. Once, Una made a mistake and had to begin all over again. Slowly, painstakingly, she made her way through the room, until what had at first been braids of glimmering light now stretched in a cord that circled the sleepers.

The last knot was above Clementia's cage, a green tangle that pulsed with light. Una groped gently in the air. The threads felt like very fine hairs. Trying to find them was like embroidering something with her eyes shut. When her fingers touched the knot, the enchantment blossomed into brightness. Green flames flickered up from the silky threads.

Just then, there was a deafening blow from the direction of the ballroom.

Una gritted her teeth. She had loosened one of the threads. If she could just tuck the other end under there . . . A drop of sweat stung her eye, and she nearly lost the whole thing.

And then Una had done it. The last cord snapped in her hands, and the green sparks began to flash pink and silver. All of a sudden, Una could see a crackling web of light stretch over each of the sleepers. The hairs on Una's arms stood up, and she felt the energy in the air like a current of electricity.

The pink and silver sparks had turned into hundreds of loops that now encircled the golden thread. The air felt tense with the pressure. Then, the loops pulled tight, clamping down on the enchantment in one fiery collision. The room went dark. No more shimmering green, no more pink or silver, nothing but black. There was the sound of tiny shifting movements. The rustle of fabric. A yawn. The Muses were waking.

Una squinted into the darkness. She thought that was Virtus pushing back the bricks and sitting up. Clementia was stretching in her cage. Someone was pounding on the inside of the glass coffin. Una's mouth felt dry as she watched shadows move and rise to standing.

She could see Clementia clearly now. Glimpses of the scene she had witnessed in Alethia's garden played over in her mind. She thought of the cluster of Muses who had determined the fate of a little baby. The Muses were her family. They were aunts and uncles and *they had saved her.*

She wasn't afraid anymore. Soon the Muses were right in front of Una, a line of towering figures. Each of them wore a draped robe that shone faintly in the dark room. Una couldn't help herself. She found herself on her knees, head bowed. A pair of cool hands touched her cheeks and lifted her up to standing. She was looking at the most beautiful woman she had ever seen. Her dark skin was soft as silk, and her golden eyes looked straight into Una's.

Una felt that she might see all her secrets in that moment, but all Sophia said was, "Do not bow to us."

The words had barely left her mouth when there was a clap of thunder, and the stones rumbled beneath their feet.

"The King is here," Una gasped. "And the Enemy is trying to destroy him."

No sooner were the words out of her mouth than the Muses sprang into action. Spero had his broadsword out, his muscles taut with readiness. Sophia slung a pouch of arrows over her shoulder and scooped up a silvery bow.

"You have done well, Una," Alethia said as she tightened the belt around her waist. "Thank you for freeing us." She clasped Una's arm. "Now you must prepare yourself to fight for Story. The outcome of this battle will determine all of our endings."

Chapter 32

Peter clapped his hands over his ears. The sound of booming voices resounded from the balcony, and the bright lights increased the pounding in his skull. Near the thrones, two fiery figures stood surrounded by clouds of swirling colors. One, swathed all in shadow, held something afire. And the other . . . Peter shielded his eyes at the rainbow of colors surrounding him.

The bright figure was looking at Peter, and, for a moment, the confusion cleared. It was as though someone had dumped a bucket of ice water over Peter's head. His sleepiness was instantly gone. His chair began to wobble, and he glanced down at the table. The edges started to waver, like a ripple in a pond, and then the beautiful feast was engulfed in flame. But when Peter stared at it directly, it stood untouched. His chair wriggled beneath him. *What is going on?*

A serving girl appeared at his side, and reached for Peter with clawed hands. Her face was spreading thin, just like the thrones near the front. It looked like her skin was melting off. The nose stretched until it was no more, and all that was left was a horrible gaping hole where her mouth had been. Peter ducked behind his chair, which now had jagged-looking knives poking out of its surface. Something was dreadfully wrong.

The girl's face was back in place. She poured a cup of steaming-hot tea and set it on the table, which was now covered in dirt. There were no candles or roses, only cobwebs and shreds of graying cloth. The stench of mildew lay heavy in the air. A tray of molding food rotted, sending up clouds of steaming wetness. Peter whirled back to the servant, who bowed again.

"Tea?" she asked, her mouth moving unnaturally. Her loose skin hung awkwardly from her limp jaw, and her eyes stared sightlessly ahead. "Tea," she said again.

Peter's heart hammered in his chest, matching the throbbing in his head. He backed away from the table, upending the tray of spoiled food. It fell with a clang, and sparks of bright light shot through his line of vision. He kept moving, shoving hard to get past the others at his table. What was happening? Where was he? The fetid aroma of spoiled meat filled his nostrils—everything smelled like death.

Peter ran across the room, stumbling by cowboys and Indians, who stood still as statues staring up at the thrones. The stench was fouler here, and Peter fell to his knees. His stomach clenched with each spasm as he retched all over the filthy floor. He wiped a shaky hand across his mouth and got to his feet. In front of him was a table fashioned entirely of bones. The round surface looked exactly like a perfect rib cage, curved maliciously to surround the food.

The muffled silence was broken by the sound of shuffling. A bent man appeared, scraping his way toward Peter, trailing an entourage of flies and bilious scent. His skin looked papery thin, as though it was an ill-fitting garment, and his eyes had a glassy stare.

"Is aught amiss?" the servant asked. His voice was the rough scrape of metal on metal.

The pounding was back in Peter's skull. His head

felt like it was going to explode. "Get away from me!" Peter shouted as the man grabbed his arm. The servant might have looked like a shrunken skeleton, but his grip was steel.

The skin under the man's chin swayed as he looked shrewdly up at Peter. "Of course, milord," the man said, bowing slightly. "Right away." But then he pulled Peter toward him with an evil grin. His grip loosened, and the skeletal face melted into black smoke. That was when Peter remembered his sword. He reached for his weapon. This was no coronation. Under all the enchantment and illusion, Peter could see the truth. This was a deathly feast. And the feasting characters were surrounded by the Enemy's Taleless. Peter cut through the thing with his sword, and the creature exploded into dust.

Peter looked up at the balcony where he had seen the performers appear for the feast's entertainment. But that was no performer. Kai stood balanced on the railing, and across from him, the Enemy was crouched over a blazing Scroll.

"Characters of Story," Kai called out in a loud voice. "Wake up! Shake off the lies of the Enemy!" The truth of what had happened came crashing in on Peter. They had fallen under Duessa's enchantment. They had been fools, all of them.

Around him, characters were coming out of the spell, their eyes taking in the horror of their deathly feast, their noses awakening to the odor of rotten food. The whole room smelled like mulching leaves, like things better left alone that had been unearthed and uprooted and woken. And there, standing in the middle of the ballroom, was Sam.

"More Taleless are coming," the cat hissed. "While you humans have been feasting, they've been gathering outside."

Peter could see that Sam was right. The doors of the ballroom were crowded with the half-dead. And wild beasts snarled outside the windows.

From behind Peter, his father sliced the air with his sword. His mother looked like some primal huntress, her hair tangled about her face as she unsheathed her dagger and let out a fierce battle cry. The Westerns at the table next to him had a new light in their eyes, a fury awakened by the memory of how they had once again been deceived.

The full weight of the Enemy's lies took Peter's breath away. The boldness with which he had deceived them. The characters who had been killed to clothe the Taleless. The many more who had simply vanished. The dark things they had done to gain power beyond measure. A cry for justice ripped straight out of his gut. He sprinted toward the nearest Taleless.

Sam was whipped to a frenzy beside him. Peter could hear the cat's yowls for the animals to attack on one side and his father's war cry on the other. As the ranks of Taleless collided with the characters, the animals flooded over the crumbling castle walls. The whole room seethed with the battle. A sorcerer stood by the nearest opening. Peter recognized him, though his posture now was much different from when Peter had last seen him arguing with Kai at the inn on Winter's Eve. The sorcerer held out a wand. It hovered before the remains of the wall for a moment, and then the entire side of the castle blasted into bits.

"For Story!" a Village Maiden screamed, thrusting a club straight up into the air. Her action seemed to rally the rest of the characters, and they rushed out through the castle ruins to meet the Taleless.

"To the Red Lady's doom!" one of the fairies yelled,

and somersaulted off the stone next to Peter, another not far behind. A horde of leprechauns sprinted after them, cursing Duessa as they ran.

In the courtyard, cowboys were wrestling hideous Taleless. An Indian stood with his back to a wall, an arrow nocked in his bow as a rotting shade floated toward him. Then the first of Peter's allies were upon them. The sorcerer's wand was out again, shooting flaming fireballs at a pair of black cloaks. And the others sprang into action. Rifle shots mixed with the flash of enchantments. Villains fought alongside Heroes, Ladies, and Moderns, all of them battling back the half-dead creatures the Enemy had created and Duessa's wild beasts.

Peter was acting on instinct. Ducking the threatening spell. Spinning around and thrusting. His body felt like a machine, each muscle responding to his senses. A rustle of movement behind him. With a well-placed swipe, a hooded figure crumpled to the ground.

Across the way came the scream of a cat's battle cry, and Peter sliced cleanly through a beast. *That one's for you, Sam.* An arm's length away from him, Professor Thornhill shot a web of light at a line of the Taleless. She barely nodded to Peter as she ran next to him, and when they came upon the next cluster of the half-dead, it was over in a matter of seconds. *We're winning!*

The energy of the battle pushed Peter along, and he released the war whoop that was clambering up his throat. Off in the distance he saw Sam atop the great unicorn, and a cluster of humans ran next to them. Everywhere Peter looked, animals fought alongside characters, and, together, they swept the Taleless army away.

Peter wondered if Indy and Snow were still inside that room of death. Then he remembered the girl he had seen on the balcony with Fidelus and Duessa. *Una!* Peter doubled back toward the ballroom, which was a mistake.

The Taleless found him, and the next moment he was surrounded. Somehow he had been cut off from the rest of the characters. Three of the Taleless circled Peter with curved weapons pointed directly at him. The leader was floating toward Peter, blood dripping from the blade it held in its claws. An unearthly hissing came from its hood. Peter moved backward, his sword out in front of him. He reached down and pulled out the dagger hidden in his boot. If he acted quickly, he could take down one, maybe two of them. The sound of his own ragged breathing filled his ears. He bumped up against the edge of a castle wall. Behind him, the moat dropped out of sight. The Taleless pushed closer, hemming him in with predatory cunning.

Peter's sword locked with the glistening red one. He swept it aside and kicked hard at the creature's middle, and his opponent fell backward. Immediately, a second came at him from the right. Peter inched sideways. It took all of his sword skill to keep the flashing red blade at bay. Peter was lost in the dance of the fight, his senses tuned in to every whisper of movement. And then Peter saw his chance. With a flick of his wrist, Peter aimed for the Taleless's neck, but the thing was fast. With a serpentine grace, it slid to the side, and Peter's blade caught the edge of its cloak instead. The hood fell back to reveal a shrunken, skeletal face.

Peter stumbled away from it. He was on one knee, the third Taleless a hand's width from him. He swung wildly with his sword, and it found its mark. But in its dying flails, the creature grabbed the blade and pulled it toward itself. Peter sprawled forward on the ground, his sword ripped out of his hands. One Taleless was destroyed, but the first had recovered from Peter's kick and was lurching toward him. Peter threw his dagger straight into the hooded opening, and the thing flew back with the force of it.

That left the unhooded one, which was now stalking Peter. Its red blade was out, and it crept forward, an evil shine in its unnatural black eyes. Peter scrambled for his own weapon, but the Taleless used the tip of its blade to flip Peter's sword up and then caught it in one swift motion. The Taleless held one blade in each bony hand now, and it moved inexorably on. Peter's heart turned to ice. He crawled backward, fumbling along the ground for a stone, for a stick, for anything to fend off the approaching threat.

The red blade was coming closer. Peter knew there was only a moment left. And then something slammed into the creature's side, knocking a chunk of rotting flesh off. The Taleless crumpled forward, and a small form darted toward it, striking the Taleless hard on the head with a stick. Peter's foe crumpled to the ground in a heap.

Peter let out a shaky breath. He was safe. The next second, someone was upon him. Someone light, scrabbling toward him, pinching his arms. Tickling him.

"How's our brother the Hero now?" Rufus asked.

He had both arms around Peter's neck, giving him a giant bear hug.

Bastian shoved Rufus aside. "Bet you were glad to see us, huh, Peter?"

Peter sat up. "What in the world are you two doing here?"

"Hmmmm," sniffed Bastian. "How's that for a thank-you?"

"Thank you," Peter said with a laugh. "Really. Thank you. But"—he sprang to his feet—"this is a battle. We've got to get you somewhere safe."

"*Nowhere* is safe. Not while the Enemy's trying to take over Story," Rufus said. "At least that's what Trix said when she brought us here—"

"Some leprechauns came to Bramble Cottage after you left—" Bastian interrupted.

"And Trix had to come find the Resistance." Rufus shot Bastian a dirty look.

"And we said we wanted to fight the Enemy, even if we are only kids—"

"We left the babies with the really old grandmas," Rufus said, as though it was something they did every day. "And the rest of us came straight here. Just in time, too, it seems."

Peter punched his brother in the arm. "No way."

"Yes way," Rufus and Bastian said, pummeling him right back.

"Well, look at you," Peter said. "My brothers. Heroes."

Chapter 33

The Muses stormed into the ballroom, filling the crumbling hall with dazzling light. Virtus had his bow out, three raven-black arrows fitted into the notch at the center. He let them loose, and they arched over Una to pierce three wild beasts. Every place they hit burst into flame.

One wall was gone, and Una could see all the way out to the drawbridge. Everywhere, characters were fighting. The courtyard had exploded into a tangled mass of battles that spilled across the drawbridge onto the hillside beyond. It was hard to tell who was winning, but Una felt a flicker of hope.

Clementia held a golden trident in one hand and in the other, a wooden shield. She leaped over one of the tables toward the battle raging outside. The sweep of her trident took out two Taleless before they even knew what had happened.

Alethia was already among them, two short swords flashing through the air as she cut her way toward Duessa.

The Enemy was writing something in black flame, the Silver Quill etching burning script onto the Scroll of Fire. Una crouched in the ballroom's doorway. Her father finished with a flourish, and the stones from the castle wall behind him shot toward Kai.

Kai didn't have a Quill. "Stop." He spoke in a low voice, and the stones crumbled before his face, falling into a pile of gravel at his feet. "Oh, Fidelus," he said. "You think you can best me in a battle of words?"

The heat of the Enemy's spell was suffocating. A blaze of black lightning pierced the air like a twisted sword of tainted fire. Kai blocked it with a wave of his hand.

Fidelus was ready. He scratched a command on the Scroll, and the earth under their feet shook. Every word he wrote was happening in Story.

Smoking craters dotted the ballroom floor where Fidelus's missiles had found their marks. Duessa's red cloak fluttered throughout their midst, and her flaming fireballs ricocheted off the remains of the wall. Una rubbed her eyes. It was ridiculous, she knew, but for a minute, Una thought she saw Snow Wotton fighting her way past a pair of Taleless. When Una looked back, Snow was gone.

The ballroom's ceiling was nearly obliterated, and the blinding battle shattered the night sky. Her father must have written something about the wind, for a great gust was swirling into the room, picking up the skeletal furniture and hurling it toward the King.

Una couldn't hear the word he said, but Kai spoke, and the furniture began dancing instead, an eerie tune whistling through the hollow bones.

Una's father gave a loud cry. He took the Quill and slashed his arm a second time. The floor around him glowed with a strange light. Whatever he was conjuring was burning red, pulsing with the same blood color as Duessa's cloak. Her father stood holding the Quill aloft, his black figure bathed in the red light.

This is it. Una felt her mouth go dry. Her father was going to kill Kai.

Una darted a horrified glance over at the King. He stood grinning at Fidelus, and she wondered if he knew what was about to happen.

The air around her father grew dark. The wind
shifted uneasily, and the floor began to shake. The
Enemy raised one arm, as though he were pulling up
the weight of the world, and a thin bar of liquid silver
rose with him.

"Quicksilver, Fidelus?" Kai asked, as Fidelus reached
back toward the line of silver. "You really are such an
interesting subplot." He picked up his royal scepter and
twirled it over one shoulder like an umbrella. "But you
must know quicksilver consumes everything it comes
into contact with. It will consume all of Story if you
use it like this."

"All of *your* Story," Fidelus said, summoning the
quicksilver with a swirl of his hand. "I will write my
own."

"It is over, Fidelus," Kai said in a gentle voice. "This
will not bring the End you desire."

The air around Una's father was taut with the pulsing quicksilver. And then the sky went opaque, the
clouds around the Enemy swirling into a thick black
inferno. Lightning struck near Una and echoed with a
hollow rumble.

"The End I desire," Fidelus cried, "is yours!" The

unholy wind buffeted Una, and she pressed close to the wall. Fidelus raised his arm, the quicksilver like a sword of lightning held high in the air. The stones from the castle floor tore from their places and were caught up in the maelstrom. The swirling vortex whirled around him, and he wove it into a tight funnel.

Kai remained unmoved, watching Fidelus work from his perch on the balcony railing. "You have the Elements to write a grand Tale," Kai said with a sad smile. "But you will not rewrite Story." He thumped his staff on the wooden floor, and his form flickered, grew taller, and then morphed into a towering warrior-king, crowned with white fire and readied for battle. "My name is Story, and I cannot be unwritten."

This time, there was no blinding rainbow of color. Kai made no move to deflect the wave of blackness headed straight toward him. Instead, he opened his arms wide. His body wavered slightly with the impact as the all-consuming quicksilver rushed into him. Just when Una expected him to crumble under the force of the spell, he reached forward and drew the poison of the liquid lightning into himself.

"Nooo!" the Enemy cried out. The storm whipped

against Una's skin, her hair a cloudy mass around her eyes. The darkness deepened, until all the sky was blotted out. Then, when it seemed impossible Kai could withstand any more, there was a violent explosion, and the whole world tore apart.

Chapter 34

 s Snow leaped out of a crumbling window, the castle rumbled behind her as though it were ripping open. Thick columns of black smoke swirled in the air above the remains of the ballroom. In front of her, a fiery white web of magic met blinding red. Then a column of green. But Snow didn't have time to consider what other magical battle was happening around her. Her own fight was upon her.

"Stand with me," Horace said, as a pair of Taleless rushed toward them.

Snow stood back-to-back with Horace, her branding iron making a fatal boundary for any who came near. The witch in front of her crumbled with a soft crunch. Snow couldn't see Horace, but she felt his movements, heard the howl of the Taleless who met his perilous fists.

The characters were fighting valiantly. Across the way, Snow could see fairies flitting above their foes, aiming fiery arrows at their heads. Dazzling volleys of spells halted many of the half-dead before they even reached the lines of battle. But Snow's side was out-numbered. The sheer volume of the Enemy's forces gave him the advantage. And his minions were deter-mined. Like the Taleless at the Ranch, their current flesh was rotting away, and Snow had no doubt that they had been promised the bodies of those they killed.

"I think it was a stupid idea to stay," Horace grum-bled, and Snow could hear the soggy sound of his fist striking Taleless flesh. "We could've been halfway home by now."

"Just shut up and be a Hero, Horace," Snow said as she heaved her branding iron at a snarling beast.

She couldn't see the fairies anymore. She and Hor-ace were an island in the midst of walking horrors. The wave of foes kept coming. Many fell, but more slipped out of the ever-present cracks in the castle walls. Snow swung hard at a grasping mummy, and it evaporated into a cloud of dust. It was the same as it had been at the

Ranch. Once their temporary bodies were destroyed, the Taleless disintegrated, gone forever. But no matter how many Snow defeated, more came at her.

"I think I'd rather be a live Villain than a dead Hero," Horace muttered from behind her.

Snow's heart sank. Horace was right. They were outnumbered. There was no way they could survive this. A crumbling Taleless had got past the deadly range of her weapon. She punched it hard in the jaw, and it crumbled back, but five more rushed in to fill its place. She swung her iron, and two were gone. They were surrounded. Snow felt Horace's free hand fumbling backward for hers.

"Do you see my mother?" Snow gasped, squeezing Horace's hand hard. The Witch nearest her was reaching out toward Snow with decaying fingers, her eyes crazed with hunger. Then Horace was at her side, backhanding the Witch. Snow scanned the shifting mob for her mother. The End was coming. And Snow wanted to see her one last time.

"There," Horace said. "By the drawbridge."

A flash of yellow light, and Snow spotted her.

Her mother stood looking down over the battle-field like some savage leader. She didn't see the Red

Enchantress coming out of the gatehouse doorway behind her. She couldn't have known that Duessa aimed a bolt of red fire straight toward her back.

"Mother!" Snow screamed.

Her mother looked up, her gaze meeting Snow's, and then the blow struck her. The force blew her mother forward, and it seemed to Snow that time stopped as her mother hovered in the air and then crumpled to the ground in a heap.

"No!" Snow ripped the word from her throat. Her iron swung wildly, whipping paths through the remaining half-dead. Horace was at her side, cutting and scything a wide road forward, and the next moment, she was there. Her mother's eyes were closed, and she lay peacefully on her back. She might have been sleeping.

"Mother?" Snow whispered, leaning low over her body. Snow felt wetness on her cheeks and knew she was crying.

"What a pity. I forgot it had a daughter." Duessa's low laugh was full of mockery.

Snow froze. The Enchantress was right behind her.

Snow inched one hand down, so that her fingers closed around the iron rod. And then, she flung her body around, ripping the weapon through the air. It caught Duessa hard across her arm with a satisfying crunch. Snow stumbled, the momentum of the blow throwing her off-balance.

The Enchantress did not cry out. She let her wounded arm dangle and advanced toward Snow. "The little snake has some venom," she said with a cruel smile. "Let's see if we can knock it out of you." Snow flipped over onto her back just in time to see Duessa aim one arm at her face. As the blast of red light shot straight at her, Snow rolled to one side, and the spell hit her shoulder. Liquid fire seared through her, and Snow screamed in pain.

"You will regret that." Snow's mother was there, standing between her and the Red Enchantress, sword out and aflame with silver fire.

"You were the Warlock's Apprentice all along," Duessa hissed. "I should have killed you when I had the chance." Duessa was fast. A flaming streak crossed the air, but Snow's mother blocked it smoothly. Red light flashed with white, and the two enchantresses teetered on the edge of the drawbridge. Snow's shoulder was on fire, the heat of Duessa's spell ripping through the muscle and down to the bone.

Snow managed to get up on all fours. She heard her mother cry out. She was losing ground, the red flames overtaking the silver. Her face looked hollow with the strain of it. Snow saw her iron weapon lying where she had dropped it. If she could just get a bit closer. She crawled forward, the pain exploding with each movement. And then her fingers were on it. Duessa's back was to Snow. The red cloak swished nearer, as its owner was consumed with the duel. Snow pulled herself within reach. She gripped the handle of the rod, biting down hard through the pain, and swiped the air with all her remaining strength.

Duessa screamed in agony, and Snow saw a flash of red fabric as she hovered on the edge of the moat, and then fell out of sight. The world was swimming before Snow's eyes. A man's voice was ringing from somewhere behind her, but it didn't make sense. "My name is Story," he cried. "And I cannot be unwritten." Snow wondered if she was dying. She was witnessing things that couldn't really be happening. She saw her mother aim a stream of silver fire down after Duessa. And then there was a flood of children, cheering and waving wooden swords as they scrambled over the drawbridge and up toward the castle. And Indy, supporting the old man they had first released from prison. And then there were beautiful warriors, appearing out of nowhere and moving to and fro among the wounded. A tall black woman, with the most beautiful golden eyes Snow had ever seen, leaned toward her. She laid a cool hand on Snow's shoulder and drew out the poison of the Red Enchantress's spell.

"You're going to be all right, child," the goddess said. "What is your name?"

"I'm Snow," she managed through dry lips. "Snow Thornhill."

Chapter 35

When Una opened her eyes, a hazy gray smoke hid the night sky. Broken stone lay all around her, and her ears pounded with the echo of the explosion. She remembered seeing Kai's silhouette framed by the fiery black inferno and then all the quicksilver racing into him.

Una sat up and cried out from the pain. Her ankle was twisted under her at an odd angle. A figure appeared out of the fog, coming toward her. "Kai?" she called out.

But it was a gravelly voice that answered. "Who's there?"

The Enemy. How had he survived the blast? Una scooted backward. The smoke would soon be gone. He would find her.

Huge pieces of the destroyed tower lay everywhere, silent witnesses of the great battle. Una pushed herself up, limping forward on her one good foot. She had to put more distance between herself and her father. Had to see if Kai had survived. Una stumbled over something, landed on her bad ankle, and toppled to the floor with a moan. Her hand struck something wet and sticky.

Please don't let it be blood, she thought as she peered at the thick liquid. It wasn't blood. Her hand was covered in Ink.

"Duessa? Is that you?" Her father was coming closer.

Someone across the way moaned. Elton maybe. Una inched forward on her belly. Kai's words came crashing back into Una's mind. *You write the Tale*, he had said. And with a flash of clarity, she knew what she needed to do.

Una fumbled around on the stone floor. The puddle of Ink was there, lying next to the goblet. But what about the Quill? It was hard to see anything. Even the ground was covered with a fine layer of soot. She felt around in the debris. Her hands struck something sharp. The silver color of the Quill glistened under the ashes.

Una could see her father clearly now, his face covered with the grisly remains of his dark magic, the whites of his eyes peering out into the dust.

The Scroll. Where is the Scroll? Her hands pawed fruitlessly through the rubble. She stopped trying to be quiet, pushing aside broken china and the remains of a table. And then she saw it. The faintest glow of fire, a smoldering roll of embers nearly hidden under the throne.

Una snatched up the fiery Scroll. It was cool to her touch, and she spread it out on the floor next to the pooled Ink. And then Una realized that she had no idea what to write. Not the Story the Enemy wanted, of course. It would have to be a Tale that would bind him up and keep him away from Story forever. *You write the Tale.* Una dipped the Quill in the Ink.

The Enemy was kicking aside broken stone. The crunch of his steps was coming closer.

Una twisted the Quill in her fingers. Perhaps it was her Muse blood, or maybe it was because she had read so many books in her old world, but Una knew in that moment how it would be. This would be the Tale of Fidelus, not the Tale of the Enemy. He would not be a Villain. He would not have power to hurt anyone. His would be a very ordinary Tale.

She spread the paper out flat with one hand and began to write: *Fidelus*—

"Elton!" Fidelus shouted. "Elton, is that you?"

The Tale Master moaned, and Fidelus darted toward him. "Who is writing my Tale?" Una heard the sound of her father slapping Elton hard across the face, and then, "Una!"

Una gripped the Quill tighter. It was hard to write quickly. She had to dip the point every few letters. When the Ink spilled, it had sunk into the stone, and she had to scratch at the surface to get enough to form the letters: *often told himse*—

"Una!" The Enemy hissed her name like it was a dirty word. "Stop."

Una didn't look up. He had seen her now. It was only a matter of time. "I'm writing your Tale," she said. "Isn't that what you had planned? A great Tale that would change all of Story?" She could feel something happening. She wasn't just writing the words. She was giving them life. The paper felt hot beneath her fingers, as though it were alive. Tiny particles of light drifted up from the words, spreading from the page toward her father. "Though I prefer something different. How about: The Tale of Fidelus Fairchild?"

"Don't do this." His face twisted into anger . . . and was that fear? Una could see the gash along his arm, where the Ink-blood had spilled out. She scratched at the stone with the Quill, but the Ink was gone.

"It won't work, anyway." Her father was very close now. "There is no Muse to bind the Tale."

And then Una saw it: the empty shell of the goblet upturned on the paving stones, a spot of Ink puddled in the center. She sank the Quill into it and kept writing: —*If that he was invisible.* The first sentence was complete. The shaft of blue light had grown, arching across the air to her father. It hovered for a moment, as though it were unwilling to touch him, before it sank into his chest. She knew the moment he felt it. A bittersweet victory. He had forgotten that his Muse blood also ran through her veins.

"Oh, but, Father," Una said, "*I* will bind it for you."

His face twisted into fury then, as he realized the meaning of her words. But it was too late. The binding was already upon him. The Tale had begun.

"No one will write my Tale," he said, frozen where he stood with a crazed look on his face, "but me."

Una didn't respond, but she kept writing, the words flowing quickly out of the silver Quill, nearly as fast as she could write. She stripped him of his magic powers. With a stroke of her Quill, his immortality was gone. Next came the setting of an ordinary house in an ordinary town. An ordinary job. With each word, her father's strength waned, until he was left in a crumpled heap on the floor.

"A quiet Tale," a voice said from behind Una. "Very good choice, Una."

"Kai!" Una exclaimed, and jumped to her feet. She wouldn't have known him but for his voice. The King of Story was walking through the remains of the ballroom, coming toward her in his royal clothes. Kai moved past her and bent low toward the broken figure on the floor. Fidelus didn't even lift his head.

"The Tale of Fidelus Fairchild," Kai said, "will be sealed by the King. And there will be no escape this time."

Kai came over to Una and took the Scroll in both hands. There was no flash of light. No extraordinary spell. Just a gentle breeze, followed by the quiet rustle of paper. And then Fidelus was gone.

"What happened?" Una asked.

"You wrote the Tale, Una," he said, and he sounded like the Kai she knew.

"Yeah, but what did you just do? It's like he disappeared or something."

"His Tale cannot be undone now. He is in it forever, to make the best he can of his ordinary life." Kai smiled at her. "Well done."

"Well done!" Una stared at him. "Look at this place." Below them, the desolate landscape smoldered with the remains of the battle. "Everything is ruined. Why didn't you come back sooner?"

"Una," Kai said, looking at her very fondly. "I never left."

She shook her head. "But you let Fidelus . . . you just let him . . . be . . . this whole time. Duessa, too. Couldn't you have bound him up in a Tale right from the beginning? Or used the Elements to unwrite him so that he never would have done all this?"

"Unwrite evil, and you'll unwrite goodness right along with it. The best Tales have to have both." Kai picked up the Silver Quill and ran the feather along his finger. "Better to strengthen the good than to rid the world of evil. Which is why I Wrote you In to Story."

"*You* Wrote me In!" Una knew it was true as soon as she said it. "But how could you have known—?"

"That you were the Enemy's daughter?" Kai smiled at her. "I know all my characters, Una. You all belong to me. I am Story."

"That's what you said to Fidelus, too. When he tried to kill you." She looked up at Kai. "But the quicksilver didn't even harm you, did it?"

"I have no End, Una, no matter how much Fidelus might have wished it."

Elton moaned and rolled over onto his back. Kai frowned at him. "Mortimer Elton. The boy who was Written In. A tragic Tale."

"You know his Tale?" Una asked.

"I know every word of every Tale," Kai said. He was looking at Elton sadly. "Even if I wish they turned out differently. Perhaps especially those."

Una watched the Tale Master. He was nearly awake. She thought of the way he had hurt her in the exam. How he had betrayed many others in Story. "What should we do with him?"

"Must we do anything?" Kai asked, running the feather over his chin. When he saw that this answer didn't satisfy Una, he said, "What would you suggest,

Una? Kill him? Lock him up for ever and ever? You know his beginning, what he once was and what made him the man he is today."

Una thought of the boy who had been Written In. She wished his Tale would have turned out differently, too. "But if we let him go, won't he just keep doing bad things?"

"Perhaps." Kai shrugged. "But keeping bad things away will not fill the world with more good. Busy yourself with filling the world with goodness, Una, and you will find it a much better Story."

Una started to walk away, but she couldn't just leave Elton there. Maybe demanding justice wasn't the answer, but there might be something else she could do. With Kai's help, could she finally send that lost little boy back home? "Do you think a Tale like his can have a happy ending?" she asked.

"I hope so," Kai said, as he handed her a blank piece of paper. "What did you have in mind?"

Chapter 36

Snow leaned against her mother. The salve the Muses had rubbed on her wounds tingled as she and her mother watched the joyful reunions from under the shelter of a tree. After the battle, Indy had brought the freed prisoners to meet the others. Characters who had been locked up in Duessa's castle found family members they hadn't seen in ages. Some of the very old ones had been imprisoned since the days following the Unbinding. A stick-thin old woman half carried the old man Snow had rescued.

"I've got you now, Da," she said as they limped along.

"No place I'd rather be than with my Trix," the old man said, tears streaming down his face.

Some characters sat in little groups eating the healing

soup the Muses were serving. Others were following the legendary immortals around with worshipful eyes, hanging on their every word. A few still looked up toward the castle wall that had exploded with black flame some time before.

Snow's mother cleared her throat. "You did well, Snow," she said.

There it was: the formal mask back in place. But then her mother leaned in and gave her a hug. "I'm so proud of you."

Snow hid her smile. The whole thing was still awkward. But she didn't care. That's how her mother was. "Thanks," Snow said. "Mother." And if Snow was truly honest, she was pretty awkward herself. Just like her mother.

They sat in silence for a few moments until her mother nudged her gently in the elbow. "Do you know why I finally came back after thirteen years?" she asked.

Snow watched two boys swipe at each other with short swords. "Why?" she asked in a low voice.

"I watched my friend die," her mother said. "A common cold took the great Warlock Amaranth." She let out a sad little laugh. "Not the end you'd imagine for a brilliant man, but there he was. And I was the only one with him. No one who loved him. No family or friends. Just his apprentice." She cleared her throat. "And in that moment, I knew. It didn't matter who your father had been. It didn't matter what he had done to me. I couldn't leave you alone anymore. You are my daughter." She laid her arm lightly across Snow's shoulders. "And I love you."

Peter sat with his back against a tree trunk. Indy was next to him, sharpening his dagger with a stone. A little ways away, someone had lit a fire, and the cats crowded around it.

"Would you like some soup?" the Muse who had come up to their campfire asked.

Peter's mouth went dry. She was lovely, and her long red hair flowed in the wind. Her eyes were as gray as the sea.

"Well, would you?" Indy jabbed an elbow into Peter's ribs.

"Um . . . yes." Peter finally found his voice. "Thanks." The Muses were all over the place, some bending down and pouring a silvery liquid on the wounded, others handing out steaming mugs of soup.

Peter didn't know where they had gotten the food, and he didn't care. It was delicious.

The animals were restless now that the battle was over. Sam was sitting on the back of the unicorn, next to the Siamese, who was cleaning Sam's fur.

"Quite the cat, isn't he?" Indy asked Peter.

"He's a fierce one." Peter nodded. "You didn't do so bad yourself," he added. "Rescuing all those prisoners."

Indy didn't say anything, but he gave Peter a nod, like he would to another man, and Peter knew that from that moment on, he could count Indy as a friend.

A tall Muse stood at the edge of the clearing, a sheaf of arrows strapped over his back, and he carried a plate of something green and leafy. It looked different, but even from where Peter sat, he could smell the mint.

"The King has sent fresh leaves from his tree," the Muse said in a low voice. "For the healing of Story."

Peter held the sprig in his hands for a moment before eating it. The coldness of a mountain stream filled his mouth, and a strange tingling began in his fingers and toes and then filled up his whole body. Peter felt as though he could run up to the castle walls and back again.

Dawn was breaking, and the worst of the battle felt

like a distant memory. Little reunions sprang up all over the place. Peter watched a woman with familiar clothes embrace a soot-covered man. When they pulled apart, he realized he knew who they were and leaped to his feet.

His mother wrapped one arm around him, and his father swallowed them both up in a bear hug.

"Good job, Peter." One lens in his father's glasses was missing, and his mother's face was covered with dirt.

Peter stepped aside as his mother was ambushed by Rufus and Bastian. "My boys! What in the world are you doing here?"

"Some leprechauns came to Fairy Village after you left." Bastian rubbed a filthy sleeve across his even filthier glasses. "They had a message for the Resistance."

"One was only this high!" Bastian pointed to the top of his boot.

"And Trix was going to come alone." Rufus's hair was sticking up all over his head. "But we wanted to help save Story—" Rufus pulled out his practice sword. "It was so cool. Just like we were knights and stuff."

"And then we went through the Enchanted Forest—"

"And there was this huge battle—"

"And Trix found her dad, did you know?"

"And I fought a beast, Peter, I really did!"

But Peter wasn't listening anymore. A small figure was making her way out of the ruined castle. A girl with a long black braid. *It can't be* . . . and then Peter knew it was.

"I want to hear all about it, really I do," Peter told his brothers. "But give me a minute." He sped over to the drawbridge. Indy and Snow must have seen her at the same time, for the next moment they were by his side. There, limping across the empty drawbridge and onto the battlefield, was Una Fairchild.

Una sat near the crackling campfire. Alethia had brought her a mug of something hot that tasted like berries and smelled of wild roses. With every sip, she felt the aching in her muscles disappear. The Enemy and his lies were gone, defeated forever. Story would rebuild itself, and the characters were stronger for what they had endured. Already Duessa's hold on the land was waning, the power of her enchantments fading with her memory. Una was sad for her parents, and something inside still hurt when she thought of the family they could have been. But the end of that part of her Tale had come, whether she was ready for it or not, and, as she saw the faces of her friends, she knew she had a different kind of family now. The kind that would last.

What was it Kai had said about filling the world with goodness? That it would make a fine Tale? She looked around at all her friends. Peter, who had clapped her on the back and called her a true Hero when he heard what had happened in the ballroom. Snow, sitting next to her mother, for once looking relaxed and happy. Indy, leaning lazily up against the trunk of a tree with two cats curled near his feet. Horace, lying flat on the ground and snoring softly. And Sam, sprawled delightfully across her own lap, purring loudly. She gave a great sigh of contentment. She couldn't have written a better ending herself.

ACKNOWLEDGMENTS

*L*aura Langlie, you'll never know how often I've marveled at my good fortune in having you as an agent. Thank you for your unfailing encouragement, for your belief in this project, and for all your hard work.

Erica Sussman, I cannot express how much I feel that these books are such a product of your creative investment as well as mine! Without your dedication, enthusiasm, and efforts, these stories would be the poorer. Thank you.

Tyler Infinger, Alison Klapthor, and the many others at HarperCollins who make the magic happen and transform a fat stack of printed pages into the lovely book readers hold in their hands, I so appreciate your hard work that has sent this story out into the Readers' World!

Brandon Dorman, your skill and imagination have brought these stories to life. Thank you for your fabulous illustrations!

All the bloggers, reviewers, librarians, teachers, and early readers of *Storybound* and *Story's End*, thank you for doing what you do, for sharing your love of reading with the world, and for making space for debut authors.

The Apocalypsies & Harbingers, how glad I am we've shared this journey together! Thank you for your companionship, moral support, encouragement, and friendship.

My lovely friends and family who have been so gracious and interested in my writing journey, your cheerleading and support have meant the world to me.

Mom, Dad, Ben, Jon, Kim, and Casey, your ongoing love, enthusiasm, and help have made the thought of writing a reality for me. Thank you for loving me well and for sharing life with me.

Aaron and my boys, thank you for our family. I'm so glad to be yours. I love you.

(